# *She was*

# *the sort of woman with whom he usually had affairs.*

Not at all the sort of woman he would normally have chosen to go to bed with him. He needed a sophisticated, rather jaded, jet-setting traveler, but tonight he found himself strangely intrigued by a woman who should have been home in the States, baking cookies. Precisely the wrong sort of woman, Jase told himself once more as he took a sip of rum.

Then again, she was in precisely the wrong sort of place tonight.

# STEPHANIE JAMES

is a pseudonym for bestselling, award-winning author **Jayne Ann Krentz**. Under various pseudonyms—including Jayne Castle and Amanda Quick—Ms. Krentz has over 22 million copies of her books in print. Her fans admire her versatility as she switches between historical, contemporary and futuristic romances. She attributes a "lifelong addiction to romantic daydreaming" as the chief influence on her writing. With her husband, Frank, she currently resides in the Pacific Northwest.

JAYNE ANN KRENTZ
WRITING AS

# Stephanie James

# SERPENT IN PARADISE

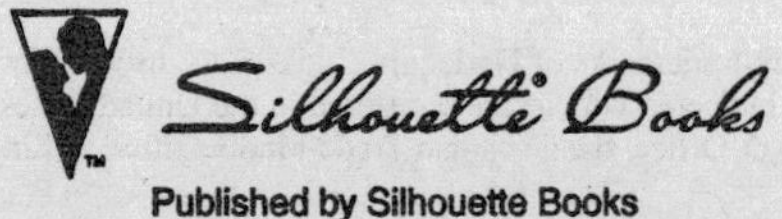


Published by Silhouette Books
America's Publisher of Contemporary Romance

ISBN 0-373-80675-2

SERPENT IN PARADISE



This edition published by arrangement with Harlequin Books S.A.



**Printed in U.S.A.**

***Available Titles From***
***STEPHANIE JAMES***

A PASSIONATE BUSINESS
DANGEROUS MAGIC
CORPORATE AFFAIR
STORMY CHALLENGE
VELVET TOUCH
LOVER IN PURSUIT
RENAISSANCE MAN
RECKLESS PASSION
PRICE OF SURRENDER
AFFAIR OF HONOR
GAMEMASTER
RAVEN'S PREY
SERPENT IN PARADISE
BATTLE PRIZE
BODY GUARD
GAMBLER'S WOMAN

***And coming soon...***

TO TAME THE HUNTER
THE SILVER SNARE
FABULOUS BEAST
NIGHT OF THE MAGICIAN
NIGHTWALKER
THE DEVIL TO PAY
WIZARD
GOLDEN GODDESS
CAUTIOUS LOVER
GREEN FIRE
SECOND WIFE
THE CHALLONER BRIDE

For my editor, Alicia, who understands about a writer's oversensitivity and delicate ego…
and who makes the books better anyway

# One

She was not at all the sort of woman with whom he wanted to have an affair.

Jase Lassiter lounged quietly in the shadowy depths of the huge curving rattan chair and watched her through slightly narrowed eyes. She was seated on the other side of the tavern's open-air terrace, near the railing. Partially obscured by the overarching back of her chair, she watched every man who came into the bar with a strange, tense expectancy that faded in moments when he failed to approach her table.

She's waiting for someone, Lassiter thought, a man. He was vaguely aware of an unaccountable unease at the thought. Any man? Or one special man? Here on Saint Clair she must be several thousand miles from home, and she looked it. Out of place, he told himself. A tourist whose South Pacific vacation was not living up to the promises in the travel agency brochure? Or a woman who had arranged to meet a lover on a clandestine vacation in the tropics?

That last possibility seemed to fit the circumstances. It would explain the tense expectancy in her as she surveyed each new arrival at The Serpent. It would explain why she had come alone to a bar frequented mainly by locals and a scattering of knowledgeable tourists, who were just beginning to discover Saint Clair. It explained a lot of things about her.

So why didn't he like the explanation?

Jase's mouth twisted wryly as he reached for the rum in front of him. The sardonic grimace was almost out of character for him. Any unnecessary gesture or movement was out of character. There was a certain waiting quality about Jase Lassiter—a vast stillness in him that seemed to come from his depths.

There was nothing quiet or calm about the woman who had emerged out of the warm tropical night to choose a secluded seat in his bar. She was tense, nervous, restless and very vulnerable.

Not at all the sort of female he would normally choose to go to bed with him. So why couldn't he take his eyes off her?

Perhaps he'd been on Saint Clair a little too long. A nagging sense of deterioration nibbled at the edges of his consciousness, and he ruthlessly shoved it aside. It wasn't that he'd been in the tropics too long, Jase decided grimly; he'd simply been too long without a woman. He took another swallow of the rum.

But she wasn't the right sort! He needed a sophisticated, rather jaded jet-setting traveler who would view a few nights in his bed as an interesting, faintly amusing souvenir of her trip. Much more fun to discuss when she got back home than a collection of sea shells. The sort of tourist who found Saint Clair usually fit into the right category. The island was far enough off the beaten path to discourage the average middle-class tourist for whom a South Seas vacation was a once-in-a-lifetime experience. Instead, in addition to the occasional US Navy ship, a collection of expatriates and the usual flotsam and jetsam that wound up in such South Seas ports, Saint Clair tended to attract a small group of world-weary tourists looking for Eden.

The visitors usually didn't stay long, but while they were there, a few could be counted upon to search out The Serpent, a flourishing oasis in the somewhat scruffy paradise of Saint Clair. And among those who turned up in the nightclub, Jase could sometimes find what he needed.

But not tonight. Tonight he found himself strangely intrigued by a woman who should have been safely home in the States, supervising a couple of kids and a devoted husband. Precisely the wrong sort of woman, Jase told himself once more as he took another sip of the rum. Then, again, she was in precisely the wrong sort of place.

Where was the man for whom she was so obviously waiting? In spite of himself he found his eyes following her quick, expectant gaze as she watched the entrance. What would he be like, this man she had come so far to meet? What would it be like to be the man who could satisfy that sense of anticipation in her, the one who could soothe that vulnerable, high-strung temperament?

"I'm a fool," Jase muttered a little savagely to himself as he got to his feet and reached down to collect the glass of rum he had been drinking. This was what came from doing without a woman too long, he decided laconically as he moved slowly across the room toward the table occupied by the lady tourist. Doing without for too long made a man do foolish things—like introduce himself to the kind of female who would undoubtedly tell him to go straight to hell.

On the other hand, he thought wryly, she was on his territory and she had managed to pique a sense of curiosity he would have sworn was quite dead. For having been guilty of intriguing him, she deserved the consequences of figuring out how to deal with him when he approached her. It might be interesting to see how she managed that.

It was going to be amusing to see if that look of expectancy came into her eyes as he came close; even more amusing to see how long it lasted. Jase watched what he could see of her profile as he made his way toward her table. She wasn't aware of him, her whole attention focused on the entrance to the bar.

Again the question sizzled through his brain. Was she waiting for a special man? Or just any man? If the latter was the case, why not him? Perhaps she was, after all, merely a fast-lane tourist looking for some tropical action. If she was only searching for a little adventure, perhaps he could persuade her to let him try to provide whatever it was she sought. *God knows, I need something myself;* he thought, and then experienced a flicker of self-disgust. Was he actually starting to feel sorry for himself? Ridiculous. There was a cure for what ailed a man at times like this. He wondered if the woman across the room would be willing to provide it.

She didn't see him until he was almost upon the little table. When her peripheral vision belatedly registered the man's presence, Amy Shannon reacted with a flinch of startled surprise, and as anyone who knew her could have predicted, disaster ensued.

The nearly full wineglass that had been resting near her right hand toppled over as her fingers bumped into it. The burgundy that The Serpent served as its house wine ran in a small wave across the surface of the polished wooden table and cascaded over the far edge.

Amy watched the entire process with fatalistic acceptance.

"I'm sorry," the man drawled softly in a voice as dark and rich as good sherry. "I didn't mean to startle you."

"Then you shouldn't sneak up on people," Amy retorted, more as a matter of form than anything else. Automatically she began dabbing rather uselessly at the spilled wine with the tiny napkin that had accompanied the glass.

The man standing beside her didn't move. He watched her hopeless flurry of effort and then said blandly, "I'll have that taken care of for you." He nodded toward the thin young man with the trim beard who worked behind the bar.

"You'd better be careful or you'll get wine all over your

slacks,'' Amy noted irritably. She eyed the khaki trousers as if it was only a matter of time before they became involved in the disaster.

The stranger ignored the potential peril, however, merely standing politely aside so that the bartender could mop up the evidence of Amy's awkwardness.

''Don't worry about it,'' the bartender said sympathetically. ''Have another glass on the house.''

''Thank you, Ray,'' Amy said, humbly grateful. She had met him a little earlier, when he'd first served her. She'd asked him who had done the hauntingly lovely paintings of Saint Clair that hung on The Serpent's walls. Ray Mathews had shyly confessed that he was the painter responsible. ''Strictly an amateur,'' he'd assured her hastily. He cleaned up and then retreated behind the bar.

By the time the mess had been cleared and a new glass of burgundy had appeared on her table, Amy realized she now had company. The quiet stranger had somehow invited himself to join her.

She blinked in confusion as he lowered himself into the rattan chair across from her. Then in a rush of delayed realization it occurred to her that this might be the man she was searching for. ''Who are you?'' she demanded bluntly.

''Him. I hope.''

Over the unsteady flame of the candle on the table Amy looked fully into his face for the first time. She found herself gazing into the most unusual pair of eyes she had ever seen. *Turquoise,* she thought with a measure of wonder. *He's got eyes the color of turquoise. And just as hard and unreadable as any gemstone.* ''What are you talking about?''

A flicker of wry amusement lit his face as he leaned back in the oversize chair. ''I hope I'm him,'' he explained softly. ''The man you're so obviously waiting for.''

Amy swallowed in astonishment. Was this Dirk Haley? In hasty assessment she ran her gaze quickly over his features, trying to mesh the reality of the man with her own inner preconception.

The color of his eyes was surely the only beautiful thing about him, she thought uneasily. The rest could only be described in terms of *not: not* beautiful, *not* handsome, *not* gentle, *not* fully civilized. He was probably somewhere in his mid-thirties, Amy decided. But she would have been willing to bet that he had already learned more about the dark side of life than most of her acquaintances would know by the time they were in their eighties.

His hair, the shade of deep mahogany, was cut in a casual style and combed roughly back from the hard planes of his face. The nose was a bluntly carved hunk of granite that went well with the equally aggressive jawline. The mouth looked as if it could be either savage or sensuous, and Amy shivered a little at the dichotomy. She didn't think she would want to be the focal point of either emotion from him.

Surprisingly, there was little about the stranger to suggest he had succumbed to the seedy, entrapping pull of the tropics. The rum hadn't yet extracted its vengeance, Amy guessed. Either that or somehow he had defied the odds and learned to control it instead of vice versa. But surely it would be only a matter of time before he wound up with that dissipated, weary look she associated with expatriates living in the South Seas.

Still, the body beneath the khaki shirt and slacks looked hard and strong, she realized. There was a sense of quiet power in him that made itself felt. Amy didn't care for the feeling.

Her personal preferences didn't matter, however. She was there on business.

"You're all wrong, you know," the man was saying conversationally as he scanned her with cool consideration.

"I am?" Amy frowned, not understanding.

"Ummm. You ought to be cool and sophisticated. A little world-weary and jaded, perhaps. Ideally you should be beautiful and blasé enough to carry this off properly."

Amy looked at him through narrowed eyes. "You may take your complaints to another department. I'm only here to get some answers, not an assessment of my person and character!"

"I wasn't complaining, he said gently. "I find your person and character rather intriguing, as a matter of fact."

Amy shook her head once in silent denial of the statement. She knew full well what he saw when he looked at her. It was a little hard to imagine why he should find her interesting. Then it hit her. "I gather I'm something of a novelty?" she hazarded dryly.

"Let's just say you appear a little out of place here in The Serpent. Out of place of Saint Clair, come to that."

She waited while he finished a deliberate perusal of her tense figure. Amy didn't appreciate the laconic scrutiny, but she thought she understood the motivation behind it. She probably did appear a little out of place here on this remote island. Her kind of tourist usually stopped in Hawaii. But then, she wasn't really a tourist.

His turquoise eyes wandered over her spice-colored hair. The tawny strands were anchored in a loose knot on top of her head. Amy had fastened the long length in that fashion as a defense against the warmth and humidity of the evening.

The style emphasized her wide, candid eyes, whose color hovered somewhere between gray and green. Amy staunchly refused to let her gaze waver from his face as he took in the effect of her firm, straight nose, cheekbones that were less than classic and a reasonably well-defined throatline. Her overall appearance was one of attractive wholesomeness, as far as Amy was concerned. She spent a lot of time and energy trying to disguise the wholesome aspects and play up the attractive part. Unfortunately it was difficult to do under the best of circumstances. In the heat and sultry atmosphere of Saint Clair she hadn't even bothered with her normal makeup. Her expressive mouth twisted slightly at the thought, and amusement shone in her gray-green eyes. What had Dirk Haley been expecting?

Her body, too, lacked the sophistication she would have preferred. It had neither sleek, elfin slenderness nor sensuous voluptuousness. Instead the breasts were nicely rounded but small, and the hips were a little too well rounded for Amy's satisfaction. Still, it was a strong, healthy body and, having reached the mature age of twenty-eight, Amy had decided to stop worrying about her figure.

She was dressed in a white cotton dress that just skimmed her body, leaving throat and arms bare. It had been too hot to wear pantyhose, so she had slipped into a pair of low white sandals before heading for The Serpent. Her only jewelry was a tiny gold chain around her neck.

"All wrong," Jase repeated almost wistfully.

"Look," Amy began a little grimly, "I'm not sure what you were expecting, but I hardly think it matters. Are you going to introduce yourself?"

"So straightforward," he sighed. "Aren't you even going to flirt a little?"

She stared at him, astounded. "Why should I do that?"

"Because I know how to handle that approach. I'm not too sure how to deal with the more businesslike, direct style," he explained.

"Well, that's the only approach you're going to get from me," she told him heatedly. "Introduce yourself!"

"Jase Lassiter," he returned obediently, inclining his head with grave politeness.

She drew in her breath. "Very well, Mr. *Lassiter*...." If that was the name he wanted to use, it was all right with her.

"Do we have to be *that* businesslike about it? Couldn't you at least call me Jase?"

"Jase." She repeated the name stonily, her brows lowering into a line. "Now can we proceed to business?"

"Is this the way it's done back in the States these days? No flirting? No delicate innuendos? No attempt at romance?" He shook his head in mock regret.

"I am not in a joking mood!" she hissed, her fingers clenching the stem of her wineglass. "Would you kindly skip the wisecracks, Mr. Haley—or Mr. Lassiter, or whatever it is you want to call yourself—and get to business?"

Jase regarded her thoughtfully. "Haley?" he finally asked simply.

Amy froze. "Aren't you... I mean, you're not Dirk Haley?" she whispered carefully.

"In a word, no. I haven't the foggiest notion of who Dirk Haley is. But I'm more than willing to take his place. I think." His hard mouth curved faintly as he watched her widening eyes. Then, with a smooth, controlled swiftness that surprised Amy, he reached out and removed the tottering wineglass from her too-tense grip. "The burgundy isn't the best, but it's a shame to waste any more of it this evening," he remarked calmly, setting the glass down safely out of her reach.

Amy's appalled glance went to the glass and back to his face. "If you're not Haley, then who the hell are you? Why did you come over to my table?"

"I've told you, I'm Jase Lassiter," he said quietly. "I own this place."

"Oh." Amy stared at him, unable to think of anything else to say.

"I know. Sometimes that's about all I can find to say about it too. Oh." He lifted one strong hand in a negligent, dismissing gesture, and something close to humor was evident in his turquoise eyes. "But it's a living. Are you going to tell me who you are?"

Amy considered the question closely for a moment and then decided there was probably no harm in revealing her name. He might even be able to help her find the man she was supposed to be meeting. "Amy Shannon."

"Amy Shannon." He tried the name out cautiously, testing it. "Where are you from, Amy Shannon?"

"San Francisco."

"Two kids and a husband, right? Does the husband know how far beyond Hawaii you came on this little vacation jaunt?" Jase asked, his tone suddenly much too cold.

Amy's eyes hardened as she sat back in her chair, chin lifting. "No husband, no vacation and most definitely no kids! Also, I think, no more questions. Unless you can help me find the person I'm supposed to be meeting tonight, Mr. Lassiter, I would appreciate it if you would remove yourself from the vicinity of my table."

He nodded, as if agreeing with her. "I should leave. I shouldn't have come over here in the first place."

"Very true!"

"Then again, perhaps we're looking at this backward. Perhaps you're the one who shouldn't be here. I am, after all, in my own territory. You're the one who appears to have wandered into the wrong place."

"I'm here on business, Mr. Lassiter!" Amy felt her inner tension building. This whole mess had been bad enough until now, but at least there hadn't been any major problems yet. Everything had gone according to plan. Jase Lassiter, however, was not part of the plan.

"You've just said you're here to meet a man. Whoever it was has had the poor manners to miss the rendezvous. Why not let me stand in for him?"

"That's utterly ridiculous!" Amy got out tightly. "Will you please leave?"

Instead of responding immediately, Jase took a long swallow of rum. Amy had the oddest sensation that he was gathering his nerve for the next statement. "I'm told," he finally said very softly, very deliberately, "that I make a nice souvenir."

"What in the world are you talking about?" she breathed, startled.

"Much more interesting than assorted shells and coconut candy." He half smiled.

"Are you suggesting I take you home with me?" she snapped waspishly, not liking her own reaction to the self-disparagement she thought she sensed in his words. What was the matter with her? She had the strangest impulse to offer a measure of kindness to this hard-bitten stranger. It was ludicrous under the circumstances.

"Oh, no, I wouldn't expect you to go that far," he assured her seriously. "I was thinking more in terms of an experience. You know, something to chat about when you get home."

"I see. Something along the lines of 'What I Did on My Vacation'?" Amy muttered furiously. "Forget it. I haven't come all this way just to have an affair with some sleazy expatriate who runs a South Seas Bar!"

"Put that way it does sound a little tacky, doesn't it?" he sighed. But he made no move to get out of his chair.

"*Very* tacky."

"Are you sure there aren't any kids or a trusting husband back in San Francisco?" he asked again.

"Of course I'm sure!" Rather vengefully Amy reached for her glass of burgundy and took a large sip. Then, feeling goaded, she asked, "Why? Would it matter?"

"It might," he admitted.

"You amaze me," she retorted dryly.

"You don't expect sleazy proprietors of South Pacific bars to have any ethics?" he drawled. For the first time there was a hint of steel buried somewhere in the sherry-rich voice.

Some instinct in Amy recognized the warning for what it was. Jase Lassiter was willing to be pushed a bit but there were limits. "I only meant that I'm amazed it would bother you to have a brief affair with a married woman. After all, I doubt you ever see any of your tourist acquaintances again after they leave the island."

He looked at her very steadily over the rim of his glass. "If there was just a husband or a boyfriend involved, I might sacrifice a few of my ethical standards. Especially if the woman in question was making a distinct effort to sacrifice a few of her own standards. But, strange as it may seem, I draw the line when there's a whole family involved. If you've got kids as well as a husband, Amy Shannon, you're safe from my sexual invitations."

Amy couldn't help it. She began to giggle. The giggle turned into a chuckle and the chuckle into a full-throated laugh.

"It's that funny?" Jase inquired curiously.

"I'm sorry," Amy managed, making an effort to bring her flash of humor under control. "But not even to save myself from a shabby vacation fling would I make up a bunch of kids waiting at home!" She forced back the last of the dying laughter and let it fade into a genuine smile.

Jase stared at her mouth as if temporarily fascinated by the smile. Then he lifted his eyes to meet hers. "You don't like kids?"

Amy shook her head, still mildly amused. "Not every woman is, by definition, maternal in nature. What about you, Jase? Did you leave a wife and a bunch of kids back in the States when you decided to follow the sun?"

"The wife left me. And there were no kids." There was a crispness about the way he spoke that told her the topic was closed.

Amy lifted one shoulder in an attempt to show that she didn't particularly care to pursue such a personal discussion anyway. Silently, though, she found herself wondering about the life Jase Lassiter had left behind when he'd made his way to the South Pacific. Was his the usual tale of a man who could no longer handle responsibility and had chosen to escape to a world where people didn't ask a lot of questions or put too much pressure on each other? Or was there some personal tragedy involved?

"So," Jase was saying deliberately, "now that we have established that neither of us is betraying a spouse or a family, is there any reason why I can't seduce you?"

"One major reason that I can think of," Amy retorted, "is that I'm not interested."

"But you've already said you're here to meet a man."

"On business."

"Curiouser and curiouser. Tell me about this 'business.'"

"No."

"Don't I have a right to know something about it?" he demanded persuasively. "After all, you're trying to arrange it here in my bar."

"It wasn't my idea. I was told to wait here," Amy explained stiffly.

"To meet whom?"

"Someone named Dirk Haley," she exploded, annoyed.

"Who's Haley?"

"I thought people out here respected each other's privacy!" she snapped.

"A myth. People are people. We're as curious about each other as people are back in the States," Jase murmured. "And I am getting extremely curious about you in particular."

"Because I look so out of place," she finished for him with a groan. "Look, you've said yourself that I'm all wrong," she began forcefully.

He leaned forward with an abrupt movement that made her jerk backward. She realized that she hadn't expected restless or unnecessary actions from this man. When he did move, it would be with purpose, and that could be dangerous. Uneasily she eyed his set, unyielding features.

"You're all wrong," he told her ruthlessly, "because there is something rather soft and vulnerable about you. You're all wrong because you face a man with a straightforward expression instead of cool calculation. You're all wrong because you look as if you ought to be wearing some man's ring instead of traipsing off to the South Pacific to carry out an illicit rendezvous. You're all wrong because there is something rather endearing and rather sexy about you that makes me want to stay when I should leave. And you're all wrong because I find myself too damned interested in finding out who you're meeting and why you're meeting him in my bar. Is he married, Amy? Is this Dirk Haley some married businessman on his way back from a trip to the Orient who had you fly out here to meet him for a few stolen days?"

"No!" She glared at him, shocked. "I've never even met Haley in person. And while you draw the line at dating a woman with a family, I draw the line at dating a man who is married! I realize that living out here probably isn't conducive to developing an objective view of human nature, so allow me to tell you that your assessment of me is rather far off the mark. Now, if you don't mind..."

"What's your assessment of me?" he interrupted calmly.

That threw her for an instant. "I beg your pardon?"

"You heard me."

Amy shook her head. "You're not going to just give up and go away, are you?"

"I belong here," he reminded her equably. "You're the outsider. You're the one who should give up and go away if you don't like the atmosphere."

"You're probably right," she surprised herself by agreeing unhappily. "But I've come too far now to just give up and go home."

"So tell me what you think of me," he ordered roughly, sinking back into the shadowy depths of the chair.

Perhaps it was the combined effects of jet lag and the tension she was under. Perhaps it was because she was feeling taunted, a little goaded. Or perhaps she was simply feeling a bit reckless so far from home. The tropical night, the bar that could have come from the pages of an adventure novel, the baffling man sitting across from her—they all went together to form a slightly unreal scene. Whatever the reason, Amy stared into Jase Lassiter's beautiful turquoise eyes and told him what she thought of him.

"I think you are a rather dangerous man," she said starkly.

His long lashes lowered slightly, but not before she had seen the flash of surprise deep in his eyes. There was a taut silence before Jase said quietly, "I thought I was a rather seedy, expatriate proprietor of an island bar. Annoying, perhaps, but not dangerous."

"Did you?" Amy looked away from him, already regretting her words. "Well, you probably know yourself far better than I do."

"That's debatable. But I do know what I want tonight. Will you come home with me this evening, Amy Shannon?"

Her head snapped around sharply. He hadn't moved. He simply lounged there in his dangerously quiet way and watched her. "No," she whispered. "No, I won't go home with you. I don't even know you!"

"You know me better than you appear to know this Dirk Haley you're supposed to be meeting," Jase pointed out with whimsical logic.

"It's not the same thing at all!"

"You think he'll make a better souvenir than I will?"

"Stop talking about being a souvenir, for heaven's sake!" she blazed, suddenly angry and not quite sure why. She only knew she didn't like to hear him deride himself in that way. It wasn't accurate, anyway. Going to bed with this man would never be as casual as collecting a souvenir! She knew that much with a certainty that went very deep. "Do you have a lot of success with that particular line?" she went on gruffly.

"Sometimes," he drawled.

"How often does the woman involved realize that you're really the one collecting the souvenirs?" Amy asked scathingly.

For the first time that night he grinned at her, a devastating, charming, purely masculine grin that made her stare for an instant. She had been right, she thought dazedly. This man really was rather dangerous.

"In general," he told her thoughtfully, "I don't think the woman involved cares a whole hell of a lot what I get out of it. Would you?"

"Care what you got out of it? Not particularly," Amy declared with a false heartiness. "But I have no intention of being used. And I'm not in the market for souvenirs of any kind. So why don't you run along now and find yourself the right sort of tourist?" she added sweetly.

"That's very unkind. Don't you feel a little sorry for me?" he asked blandly.

"No. Would you rather I did?" she asked mildly. It was true. She didn't feel sorry for him. One didn't pity a man who radiated that quiet, contained inner strength. But something about him was drawing her, and she couldn't quite figure out the attraction. Which only made him all the more dangerous, Amy decided grimly.

"No," Jase said reflectively. "I don't think I want you feeling sorry for me. I think that if I can get you into my bed, I'd like the satisfaction of knowing you were there for some reason other than pity."

"Don't worry about it. I'm not going to wind up in your bed."

He nodded obligingly as if accepting her words without buying the argument itself. "How long are you going to wait for your mystery man tonight?"

Amy shrugged and glanced toward the door. "Not much longer. I'm very tired. I haven't had a chance to recover from the flight yet. As soon as I landed I checked into the guest house, had dinner and then came directly here."

"And if he doesn't show up?"

"Then I come back tomorrow night. The message said..."

"What message?" Jase interrupted coolly.

"Never mind. It's a private matter." Determinedly, Amy got to her feet. "But it is getting late and I think I've waited long enough this evening. If you'll excuse me, I'll be on my way." She put money down on the table for the two glasses of wine.

"I'll see you back to the guest house," Jase said formally, covering her hand on the table with his own. "And the drinks are on the house." He folded the bills back into her palm.

Amy moved nervously. "There's no need to see me back to my room," she began quickly. She tried to jerk her hand out from under his. Unexpectedly he released her fingers.

The momentum of her own effort propelled the edge of her hand against the half-full wineglass.

"Oh, no!" But she'd been through this too many times before, and there was no real shock in her words, only a kind of dismayed resignation. The wineglass seemed to topple over in slow motion, the burgundy inside sloshing toward the edge in anticipation.

Then, miraculously, strong male fingers closed around the bowl of the glass, righting it and stabilizing it before disaster could strike. Amy sucked in her breath. "You're very quick, aren't you?" she breathed a little weakly.

Jase's mouth went up at one corner as he let go of the glass and stepped around the table to join her. "Are you always this, er, klutzy?"

"When I get nervous I get a bit awkward," she confessed, wondering how she was going to get rid of him now. He was already taking her arm to guide her toward the door.

"Do I make you nervous?" he inquired politely.

"Yes!"

"Look at it this way," he advised, stepping out into the balmy night and forcing her gently along with a firm grip on her arm. "I'm a known quantity. Much safer to have me walking you back to your guest house than to be risking the walk alone."

Amy gasped. "Is this a dangerous area of town?" she asked, peering around at the nearly empty street. The quayside buildings appeared suddenly gloomy and slightly menacing in the tropical moonlight. Out on the water a few small sailing boats bobbed at anchor.

"You're not in Waikiki, lady!" he growled.

Amy frowned. "You don't have to sound impatient with me. Nobody asked you to see me back to my room tonight!"

"Speaking of which, where are you staying?" he countered neatly.

"The Marina Inn. Know it?"

"Sure. The guy who owns it is a friend of mine. You should be safe enough there."

"Terrific," she muttered caustically, aware of the firm grip of his hand. Jase set the pace, keeping her easily at his side. She had the distinct impression that if he had wished, he could have scooped her up under one arm and still proceeded at a strong, even pace. Now that she was beside him, she realized that he was tall and solidly built. Amy felt a little dwarfed by the size and strength of him. Her own five feet four inches appeared rather insignificant next to this sort of masculine power.

"Relax," he said quietly, and she knew he had sensed her sudden wave of nervousness. "I'm not going to hurt you."

"No?"

"No. It's been a long time since I politely escorted a woman home in the moonlight," he remarked quietly. "The souvenir hunters usually walk *me* home!"

Amy laughed. "I think you've been spoiled, running a bar here at the edge of the world."

He slid a glance down at her smiling profile. "Possibly. But I haven't forgotten all the quaint customs of civilization."

"Such as?" she challenged, and then caught her breath as he halted alongside the concrete railing that divided the harbor from the shore. When her gaze swung up to collide with his, she knew she had wandered into very dangerous territory.

"Such as the practice of stealing a kiss in the moonlight on the way home," he told her huskily.

Then, before she fully realized what was happening, he leaned back against the sun-warmed concrete of the barricade. Bracing himself, his feet planted widely apart, Jase pulled her into the heated strength of his body.

# *Two*

"No," he whispered as her fingers splayed against his chest. "Please. Don't fight me. It's just a kiss."

During the first few seconds of the embrace, Amy had been more concerned with maintaining her balance than struggling. She dug her nails into the khaki fabric of his shirt in an instinctive effort to right herself. Then her head came up sharply, the beginning of an angry protest shaping her expressive mouth.

In the next instant the words were blocked in her throat as he covered her lips with his own. Amy was suddenly conscious of a variety of sensations, sensations that should have been secondary to the main problem of freeing herself but that somehow predominated in that moment.

She could taste the essence of rum mixed in with the warmth of his mouth. His hands gripped her forearms, not hurting her but holding her still for the embrace, and the feel of his strong fingers was something she didn't think she would ever forget. And then there was the indelible impression his body was making on hers as he held her off balance and gently forced her to lean against him.

Amy was vividly aware of each hard plane and contour of him. Her breasts were crushed against the smoothly muscled chest. Her hips were arched into the hardening line of his lower body, and she felt caged between the strong thighs.

"You feel good," he grated against her lips. "So good. Soft. Warm. Very female." His hands slid up to her shoulders and around to the nape of her neck.

"You...you said I was all wrong," she managed, trying for the cool, blasé facade that could carry a woman through this sort of situation. She sensed a certain masculine aggression in him, but the sensual threat really wasn't worrying her. Not yet. Which made no sense. After all, Amy told herself, she barely knew the man, and what she did know of him should have made her very wary indeed.

"I was the one who was wrong." He nibbled at the corner of her lips, tasting her. "Amy, come home with me tonight. I'll make it good for you. And I need you so."

"You need a woman," she stressed, deliberately telling herself it was the truth, "any woman. Or think you do. I don't intend to make up for the recent shortage of female tourists on Saint Clair!"

His powerful hands tightened on her at the words, slipping down the length of her back and molding her body more tightly to his. "Perhaps I can make you need me a little," he muttered with a new level of intensity. His mouth covered hers once more, forcing apart her lips. His tongue sought the warmth within as his hands curved around her buttocks.

Amy caught her breath as the sensual assault registered on her nerves. When his invading tongue met hers, forcing a response, she tried to break the contact and couldn't. The only option was to fight back, and somehow the battle only seemed to enhance the deep sensuality of the kiss. Her nails dug into his shirt, finding the muscled shoulder beneath, and Jase groaned. But it was a groan of male hunger, not protest.

It wasn't until Amy began to recognize the signs of her own response that she finally panicked. That was where the real danger lay, and she was woman enough to know it.

"Stop it, Jase. Please!" The muttered words were an order, not a plea, as she managed to free her mouth.

"Why should I stop now when we're both enjoying it?" he inquired gently, lifting one hand to toy with a tendril of spice-colored hair that had fallen loose. With his other hand he kept her lower body pressed close to his own.

"Because I want to go back to the inn. Because you're supposed to be walking me home, not seducing me, and because I said to stop it. All reasons enough," she snapped. When she met his eyes in the moonlight, though, she almost forgot what she was saying. The gleaming desire in his moon-silvered turquoise gaze sent a strange chill down her spine. It left her feeling weak and breathless and all the other stupid things that could get a woman into so much trouble.

"Are you afraid of me?" he asked musingly.

"No, I am not. But I am getting a little annoyed with you!"

The fingers that had been playing with her hair dropped lightly to her shoulder and then, with a casualness that startled Amy, to the curve of her breast. "I can feel your nipple," he breathed in husky wonder. "Hard already. My God, you're a responsive little thing, aren't you?"

"Let me go!" She glared up at him, trying to ignore the touch of his hand.

Abruptly she was free. Jase watched through half-closed eyes as Amy found her balance and pulled away from him. "You see?" he said. "I'm harmless. You have nothing to fear from me."

"You can't imagine how relieved I am to hear that," she grumbled waspishly, making a show of arranging her hair. "Now, if you'll excuse me, I'll be on my way."

He smiled slightly. "I intend to finish walking you back to your room." He took her arm and resumed his task of escorting her along the quay. Neither of them said another word until they stood in the tiny, slightly shabby lobby of the Marina Inn. The sleepy desk clerk nodded familiarly at Jase and then went back to the girlie magazine he had been reading.

"I'll see you tomorrow," Jase said quietly as Amy prepared to make her way up the little staircase.

"Will you?" She tried to sound totally uninterested.

He shook his head in faint amusement. "You try so hard to be a tough little lady, don't you? But I can see straight through to the softness."

"You missed your calling, then, didn't you? You ought to have studied for a career in psychology instead of aiming to run a dockside bar on some forgotten island in the Pacific!" Without waiting for a response, Amy raced up the staircase and disappeared down the hall to her room.

Jase watched her flee and then turned to find the grizzled old man behind the desk grinning at him. "What's the matter, Jase? Couldn't interest her in a souvenir of the island?"

"I don't think she finds me very picturesque," Jase murmured, moving purposefully over to the desk to gaze down at the centerfold spread out across the clerk's lap. "You ought to be careful of those girlie magazines, Sam. Too many centerfolds will make you go blind, you know."

"I'll take my chances," Sam closed the magazine regretfully and tossed it on the desk. "Where'd you run into our little tourist?"

"She wandered into The Serpent a couple of hours ago. I'm surprised you didn't warn her off the place, Sam."

"I did. Could tell by looking at her it wasn't her kind of place. Too many rowdy sailors. But then, Saint Clair isn't exactly her kind of island either."

"True." Jase gazed thoughtfully at the ceiling for a moment. "Ever hear of a man called Dirk Haley?"

"Haley?" Sam shook his head with certainty. "Nope. Can't recollect anyone by that name."

"No reservations for anyone under that name?"

"Don't think so. Lemme see." Sam flipped through the few names in his booking file. "No one by the name of Haley."

"If you should hear anything about him, will you let me know?" Jase persisted.

"Sure. But why? What's your interest in Haley?"

"She's interested in him," Jase said simply.

"And therefore you're interested in him?"

"Sam, you missed your calling. You should have studied for psychology instead of aiming to run the desk of a sleazy little inn on some forgotten island in the Pacific."

Sam considered that. "Do shrinks get to read girlie magazines while on duty?"

"No. They're aware of the fact that it might make them go blind," Jase explained.

"In that case I think I'll stick with my chosen profession," Sam decided, and picked up the magazine again.

Jase walked back toward The Serpent with a strange feeling of new energy. He ought to be feeling frustrated, he told himself as he headed toward the bar. Frustrated and angry and annoyed at one particularly uncooperative little tourist with spice-colored hair and honest eyes. Or else he ought to be disgusted with himself for wasting his time on a woman he knew wasn't the right sort.

But he didn't feel any of those things. In fact, Jase decided with wry amazement, he was feeling a curious sense of anticipation. That kiss tonight had been oddly satisfying in its own way, even though it had left him hungry for more. The feel of her body on his had made him long for a warm bed and her willing agreement to share it with him, but the kiss would hold him for tonight.

And he would be seeing her tomorrow.

That was where the sense of anticipation came in, he thought. He was looking forward to seeing her tomorrow, even though he hadn't gotten what he wanted and needed tonight. Jase wasn't used to thinking about tomorrow.

He was on the veranda of The Serpent when another thought struck him: How would he be viewing the prospect of seeing Amy Shannon tomorrow if he *had* managed to talk her into bed tonight?

Some instinct told him that he would be feeling something a hell of a lot stronger than mere anticipation. His fist closed a little violently around the bamboo railing. He didn't want to consider the ramifications of that. The last thing on earth he could afford to do was to find himself feeling possessive about a woman like Amy Shannon.

But the irony of living at the end of the world was that a man sometimes found himself thinking about the last things on earth.

"Damn!"

"Something wrong, boss?" The bartender arched an eyebrow as Jase slid onto a stool and hooked a foot over the brass rung. Ray finished drying a glass and slid it into the overhead rack with one hand while reaching for a bottle of rum with the other. Without being asked, he set up Jase's drink. "You strike out with the lady tourist?"

"No, I dragged her down onto the beach and made mad, passionate love to her in the sand. Just like in a movie." Jase reached for the glass in front of him.

"You don't look very sandy," the younger man noted with a grin.

"I'm neat by nature," Jase growled. "Ray, do we know anyone named Dirk Haley?"

Ray Mathews went through the incredible mental file of names and faces acquired by an active bartender and then shook his head slowly. "Doesn't ring any bells. Should it?"

"The lady is looking for him," Jase explained with a frown as he downed a swallow of the rum.

"Ah."

"What the hell's that mean, 'Ah'?"

Ray shrugged, refusing to be intimidated by the glittering turquoise eyes of the man who was his boss. From long experience he knew when Jase Lassiter was dangerous and when he was not. "It means 'Ah'! Now I know why you're interested in this Haley character—because the lady is interested in him."

"You know, you and Sam over at the Marina Inn both seem to have missed your calling," Jase muttered. "Should have been shrinks, what with your amazing ability to see through to the inner motivations of folks like me."

"I didn't miss my calling. All good bartenders are pretty fair psychologists. We just don't make as much money as our colleagues who happen to have formal degrees."

"Get a degree to hang up on the wall behind the booze cabinet and I'll raise your salary at least a dollar a week."

"Geez, boss. A buck-a-week raise isn't even going to be enough to pay off the guy I'll have to hire to forge the degree!" Ray complained.

"Yeah, well, that's the way it goes when you choose to practice your profession on some damn forgotten island in the Pacific. Upward mobility is limited."

Ray leaned both elbows on the polished surface of the bar and eyed his boss. "The lady tourist got to you, didn't she? How'd that happen?"

"Beats me." Jase stared down at his drink. "How many of these have I had tonight, Ray?"

Ray followed his gaze to the glass of rum. "I wasn't counting. Want I should start?"

Jase's mouth tightened. "No. But maybe I should start paying closer attention. We've both seen what too much of this stuff can do to a man out here."

"You're a long way from that stage," Ray murmured.

"That's probably what all the others said en route to 'that stage,'" Jase decided, staring broodingly at his unfinished rum.

"Hell, that little tourist really did get to you, didn't she?" Ray observed with a low whistle. "Don't worry, boss. She'll be gone in a few days. Tourists never stay long on Saint Clair. Especially the nice ones. She liked my paintings, you know."

"So that makes her one of the nice ones, doesn't it?" Jase chuckled dryly. He pushed aside his drink and got to his feet. "Keep your eyes open for anything on that Haley guy I mentioned, okay?"

"Sure." Ray nodded and went back to polishing glassware.

Jase decided to do something he hadn't done in a long time: He decided to go to bed before two in the morning. It made a nice change.

Amy had also gone to bed before two in the morning, but she didn't get to sleep until nearly three. She found herself tossing and turning between the old worn sheets provided by the Marina Inn management. The rattle of the ancient window air conditioner eventually proved more obnoxious than the heat of the night, so she slid out of bed, her two-hundred-dollar French nightgown trailing gracefully behind her, and shut off the offending contraption.

Standing at the open window for a moment before going back to bed, Amy leaned against the sill and stared down at the night-shrouded harbor. The lights of The Serpent and a few of the other local bars near the wharf were the chief evidence of life at this hour. There was a Navy ship in the bay, and occasionally a gaggle of seamen weaved their way along the dockside below her.

How had a man like Jase Lassiter wound up in a place like this? For some reason Amy found herself filled with a deep and abiding curiosity on the subject. There was a fundamental strength in him that didn't seem to fit into a sleazy South Seas harbor town. On the other hand, she reminded herself grimly, perhaps it took that kind of strength to survive in this sort of atmosphere. She wondered about the wife who had left him. Not many women would be foolish enough to set up permanent housekeeping on Saint Clair.

The unknown wife had probably had good reason for divorcing Jase Lassiter.

With a small sigh Amy turned away from the window and went back to bed. She had other matters to worry about on Saint Clair. The history and future prospects of one Jase Lassiter were the least of her concerns.

Still, when she finally did drift off to sleep that night, it was to dream of turquoise eyes that gleamed with controlled hunger and of a man's mouth that sought both to dominate and persuade. Somehow, in the realm of the dream, the hunger seemed more than simple male desire, and the dominance and persuasion combined into a plea that made no sense at all to Amy.

The morning sun managed to dazzle Saint Clair with a tropical brilliance that hid a little of the weathered, seamy side of the harbor. It really was a lovely island, Amy decided as she dressed for breakfast. But who would want to spend his whole life here? Men who couldn't handle real responsibility?

She brushed her hair into a coil and clipped it high on her head. The easy-fitting, softly pleated white trousers and matching wrap shirt were the best she could do by way of dealing with the oncoming heat and humidity of the day. She belted the outfit with a sash of black and slipped on black-and-white canvas shoes before going downstairs to the small cafe attached to the inn.

The place was filled with a colorful variety of locals and a handful of seasoned tourists. Amy took a corner table and ordered coffee. When she saw the way a few of the local fishermen were wolfing down the cook's fried eggs, she decided to risk some herself.

From where she was sitting she could see the entrance to the cafe, but Amy was too busy examining the huge platter of greasy eggs and toast that had just been delivered to her table to notice the exact moment when Jase Lassiter entered the room. The first warning she had, in fact, was the ripple of familiar greetings that went through the room. By the time she glanced up, he was nearly at her table.

"Good morning, Amy." Jase favored her with a polite, hopeful smile as he slid into the booth across from her. "Don't look so surprised. I told you I'd be around in the morning, didn't I? I thought you might like to go swimming."

He was wearing khaki trousers and a matching shirt again. The sleeves of the shirt were rolled up on his forearms, revealing a sinewy length of arm that was sprinkled with mahogany-colored hairs. In the crisp morning light the heavy pelt of red-brown hair on his head gleamed damply from a shower. The turquoise eyes were vivid and penetrating as he studied her cautious expression. He looked, she decided with a feeling of confused astonishment, a little younger than he had the day before.

"That's very kind of you," Amy began carefully, "but I'm afraid I..."

"Good. When you finish breakfast we can take off for this nice little cove I know on the other side of the island. Are you going to eat all that toast?"

"Er, no. No, I'm not," she admitted, surveying the huge stack in front of her. "Help yourself," she invited politely. She couldn't think of anything else to say. "But about your invitation to go swimming, I think I'd better decline. The man I'm supposed to meet may show up this afternoon. He may have been delayed last night."

"No problem," Jase said coolly, munching toast. "I told Ray to keep an eye out for strangers. If the guy shows, he'll be told you're here on the island." Jase waited.

Amy saw the prepared expression in his turquoise eyes and stifled a groan. She knew without being told that he would counter whatever excuse she thought up. What did it matter? she added silently. She had actually been instructed to meet her contact during the evening hours. There was no real reason to think that Dirk Haley would show up during the day and expect to find her. Why not accept Jase's invitation? "All right," she surrendered with a small smile. "Thank you."

Jase appeared amused by the play of expression across her face as she came to the final conclusion. "Don't fret. I'm really quite harmless."

Amy's brows beetled into a frown. "Why do I keep getting this nagging feeling that your self-assessment may not be entirely accurate?"

"You're not a very trusting sort, are you?"

Amy thought about that. "No," she said finally, "I'm afraid I'm not."

"Finish your breakfast and we'll be on our way." Jase reached for another slice of toast, smoothly terminating the discussion.

Twenty minutes later Amy found herself in an open Jeep racing along a narrow island road. On one side the surf crashed with a picturesqueness that could have qualified the scene for Hawaii. On the other, tall palms lined the winding pavement. The island was virtually uninhabited outside the small port town, and there was not a house in sight.

But it wasn't the scenery that kept drawing Amy's cautious, speculative glances; it was the profile of the man beside her. Her first thought on seeing Jase that morning had been that he looked younger than he had the night before. Now, with the wind ruffling his mahogany hair and his hand resting with casual expertise on the wheel of the Jeep, she realized that he didn't exactly look younger, he just looked happier. There was an almost carefree enthusiasm in the way he drove, and the hard lines of his face seemed more relaxed.

"Still worrying about being kidnapped?" He slid her a taunting glance as he slowed the Jeep and pulled off to the side of the road.

"Should I be?"

He grinned briefly as he switched off the engine and reached into the back seat for a bag. "Maybe. I *have* been living away from civilization for a while."

Amy arched one brow as she climbed out of the Jeep and collected the small beach bag she had carefully packed before leaving the inn. "If you try anything that underhanded, I'll report you to the Better Business Bureau of Saint Clair."

He slammed the door of the Jeep with a laugh. "You'd have to find it first! Even if there were such an entity on Saint Clair, I have a feeling that reporting my ill-bred behavior would only enhance the reputation of The Serpent. People love a place with atmosphere."

"Something tells me you don't have to work very hard to provide it," Amy grumbled good-naturedly as they made their way into the secluded cove Jase had selected. "The Serpent just reeks of atmosphere!"

"Yeah. Especially when there's a Navy ship in the harbor," Jase agreed with great feeling. "Managing a bar can be a real challenge sometimes."

"You seem to be doing all right at the task." Amy kept her tone carefully neutral.

"I take it you don't altogether approve of my chosen career?"

"It's really none of my business, is it?" she countered, unrolling her blanket on the sand. She kept her gaze studiously focused on the striped beach blanket.

"What sort of work do you do, Amy Shannon?" he asked in a too-casual drawl.

"I run a couple of boutiques in San Francisco," she told him very carelessly.

"Women's clothing?"

"Ummm." She pretended to study the little gem of a cove, admiring the small stretch of sandy beach and the gently lapping waves. With any luck he wouldn't press the issue. Most people didn't. It was ridiculous to be embarrassed about the matter, but it was a bit hard to explain.

"What kind of clothing?" As he watched her face, Jase slowly began to unbutton his shirt. "Sportswear?"

There it was. The question she had hoped to avoid. "Lingerie,'' she mumbled, industriously unfastening her jeans to reveal the sleek white swimsuit underneath.

"Lingerie. Fancy ladies' underwear?'' She could hear the smile in his words. It was a reaction she'd seen before when she described her business.

"*Designer* lingerie. French and Italian and New York designers. Very expensive stuff. Also very beautiful,'' she stressed as she peeled off her shirt.

"Wait a second. You're telling me you sell sexy underwear?'' he demanded, turquoise eyes brimming with laughter. "You're in a business like that and you have the nerve to criticize *my* profession?''

"It's hardly the same thing,'' she sniffed, flinging off the last of her clothing and heading determinedly for the water's edge.

But he was laughing delightedly behind her as she dove into the light surf. Amy wondered how often he laughed out loud like that. It was a surprisingly pleasant sound, full of rich, masculine amusement. It made her want to smile.

He caught up with her a moment later, his body moving through the warm water with a lithe grace that told her how he kept himself in such strong, sleek shape.

Amy was swimming easily, no particular direction in mind, when she felt Jase's hand on her waist. The strong fingers closed gently, snagging her neatly in the water and pulling her upright to face him.

She stood breast-high in the lapping water and looked up at him inquiringly. He handed her a face mask and a snorkel that he had brought with him into the sea. "Thought you might like to come with me and look at some fish,'' he invited. "There are some beauties around here.''

The remainder of the afternoon was a moment out of time for Amy. Together with Jase she explored the fascinating and brilliantly beautiful underwater world of the small cove. They sunned themselves on the sand between swims and munched sandwiches Jase had brought along.

But far more fascinating than the aquatic life he was showing her was Jase, himself. As the afternoon progressed, he seemed to grow increasingly relaxed and easy-going. By the time they climbed back into the Jeep to return to town, Amy was almost able to forget that the man she was with was a man who made his living running a bar on a distant island in the Pacific. This Jase Lassiter was a man she could like—a man who, if he lived in San Francisco, she would be willing to date.

"What are you thinking?" he asked, shifting gears in the Jeep.

"I was wondering how you ended up here on Saint Clair," she told him honestly.

At once she wished she'd kept her mouth shut. A great deal of the easy, lighthearted enthusiasm went out of his face in an instant. "It's a long story. One I'm sure you'd find uninspiring."

"Meaning you don't want to tell me?" she pressed gently.

"Do you want to tell me what you're doing on Saint Clair?" he tossed back. "I'll swap tales if you like."

"No, thanks." It was her turn to revert to a more distant attitude. "My story is a little complicated."

"Meaning it's none of my business, right?" he clarified grimly.

"Yes." She spoke very firmly.

"Then we appear to be at an impasse," Jase noted politely. "I suggest we find another topic."

"Before we manage to ruin the day?" she quipped with a flippancy she wasn't really feeling.

"Exactly. Are you going to come over to The Serpent tonight?"

"Unless the man I'm waiting for finds me before this evening, yes."

Jase gave her a laconic smile. "You can sit with me and get the inside story on how to run a sleazy Pacific island bar."

Amy didn't respond to that, knowing he was deliberately goading her and also knowing that she probably had no real choice in the matter of how she spent the evening in The Serpent. There, she was in his territory. If he chose to spend the evening with her, there wasn't much she could do about it. And from what she had seen of the clientele the previous night, having the owner of the club as an escort probably wasn't a bad idea.

"Thank you for the invitation," she said demurely.

"It wasn't precisely an invitation," Jase growled.

"I'm aware of that. I was trying to pretend you meant it as such."

"Because it makes it easier for you to acquiesce?" The perceptive glance he gave her held a baiting quality now, and Amy knew she was being punished a little for her refusal to explain her presence on his island.

"Jase, I'm aware that in The Serpent you give the orders," she said quietly.

He relented, the corner of his mouth crooking upward. "Not a very large kingdom, but I am in charge of it."

"Do you enjoy ruling it?" she flung back, suddenly very interested in the answer. Did he truly like being who he was, where he was?

"I get by." It was clearly all he intended to say about the subject.

"I'll bet." Amy decided she wasn't nearly so willing to let the subject die. Not before she'd made a point. "You're living out every male's private fantasy. I'm sure you get by very well."

He frowned. "Every male's fantasy? Saint Clair? You've got to be joking!"

"Hardly." She waved a negligent hand at the lush tropical surroundings. "Here you are running a successful bar in paradise. A life of adventure on a tropical island. Miles from the nearest lawn mower, screaming infants and nagging wife. What man wouldn't give his soul to trade places with you? The perfect life-style. No responsibilities. Just sit back, drink a little rum, or maybe a lot of rum, and wait for a passing female tourist to pick you up for a night of uncommitted, free-spirited sex. Of course any man would envy you!"

"We can't always have what we want in life," Jase ground out brutally. Clearly she had hit a nerve. Amy decided to obey her instincts and back off that conversational topic at once. Besides, she realized she didn't want to hear him expound on the virtues of such an irresponsible life.

That evening she found herself grateful for Jase's presence at the small table she occupied. From the outset it was obvious that several of the seamen off the Navy ship in the harbor had found their way into The Serpent. The place was packed with a rowdy, enthusiastic crowd of men, and it would have been awkward indeed to be a lone female sitting at a table.

"Picturesque, isn't it?" Jase demanded wickedly above the din of raucous male laughter.

"You spend a lot of your evenings like this?" Amy flicked a disparaging glance around at the lively crowd.

"Evenings like this are good for business," Jase pointed out politely, but the turquoise eyes gleamed sardonically.

"Aren't you worried that there may be a fight or something?"

"Boys will be boys. We can deal with it if it happens."

"It happens a lot?" she asked worriedly, feeling more than a little uneasy at the thought.

"No, not a lot. The Serpent has a reputation: That sort of thing isn't tolerated."

"Which means *you* have a reputation for not tolerating brawls?" she corrected.

"The glassware is hard to replace," he drawled. "Takes months to get a new shipment in from the States. No, I don't encourage brawling."

Amy shuddered. "I should hope not!" Then curiosity prompted her to pry further. "How long have you been running the place, Jase?"

"I started out as a bartender working for the previous owner about ten years ago. I bought The Serpent from him when he decided he'd had enough of island living and wanted to go back to the States."

"How old was he when he reached that monumental decision?"

"In his sixties. George had a couple of kids he hadn't seen in years. Found out he had grandchildren and realized he wanted to meet them."

"I wonder what kind of reception he got from the children he'd ignored for so many years," Amy muttered wryly.

Jase gave her a level glance. "I don't know. Haven't heard from him since he left. Maybe his kids decided to be charitable."

"Maybe. I'm not sure I would be."

"You sound like you've got some firsthand experience," Jase observed dryly.

"My father left my sister and me to be raised alone by my mother when I was six," she told him bluntly. "He couldn't handle the responsibility of a family. It's been my observation that a lot of men feel the same way."

"You sound very sure of that," he clipped out.

"Just take a look at the statistics. The number of women left to raise kids alone is pretty damn high. I wouldn't be surprised if you're catering to a few of the runaway fathers right here in this room!"

"Now wait a minute, Amy. You're not going to get away with blaming me for every runaway father who ever decided to head for the South Pacific!"

"I'm not blaming you, but you've got to admit that places like this certainly perpetuate the image of a pleasant, irresponsible, macho life-style that is very alluring to most men," she began earnestly.

Her lecture was interrupted by the sound of shattering glass. Startled, she swung around, aware that Jase was already on his feet.

"What in the world is happening?" she breathed. Across the room four seamen were wading into each other, fists flying. With the frightening speed of an erupting volcano, a full-scale brawl was blossoming.

"This is what we call atmosphere," Jase explained laconically. Then he was gone, forging a path through the ring of cheering, yelling spectators.

Amy was appalled by the savagery of the fighting. The male of the species could be so very dangerous and seemed to have so little control over his own violent instincts, she thought. A few minutes earlier the bar had been filled with laughter. Now the sickening thud of fist striking flesh ricocheted around the room.

She watched, unable to tear her gaze away, as Jase arrived at the center of the small hurricane. The four fighting men seemed unaware of his presence, although everyone else in the room was waiting expectantly.

"All right, Ray, let's cool these folks down a bit," Jase said calmly.

"Right, boss." Ray ducked down behind the bar for a moment.

The level of expectancy in the crowd went up a few more notches. Amy could sense it. It was as if a lot of the watchers knew what was going to happen next and looked forward to it.

When Ray appeared again, he was holding a small garden hose in his hand. A stream of water poured forth, showering the four fighters. A cheer went up as the brawling men staggered apart in astonishment.

Before they could figure out exactly what was happening, Jase was between them, his expression placid as the water was turned off by Ray.

"Gentlemen," he said in a smooth voice that brooked no argument, "we don't allow that kind of thing around here. If you want to exercise your inalienable right to fight, you'll have to continue outside. I'm sure the shore patrol will be happy to referee. Now, I'd certainly appreciate it if you would kindly take your leave."

The words were softly spoken, but the four dripping men paid heed. The mild threat of calling the ship's own police apparently did not go unnoticed either.

But Amy knew it wasn't the garden hose or the soft-spoken command that had the effect of sending the four grumbling men toward the door. It was Jase himself. The easy, self-confident power was very much in evidence. Tall, assured and casual, arrogantly in command of the room and the situation, he dealt with the four brawlers. There was no doubt that the remaining inhabitants of the bar were satisfied with the performance. Clearly they had got what they expected.

And then, just as it seemed everything was under control, one of the four men who had been banished turned away from the door, an expression of frustrated rage on his features. Plainly the crowd's derisive laughter was too much for his already bruised ego.

A knife flashed in his hand as he launched himself at Jase.

"Think you're so smart, you bastard? Let's see you handle this!"

What happened next nearly paralyzed Amy with shock. She went cold, literally frozen to the spot, as the enraged man leaped toward Jase, the knife already arcing through the air.

Jase's response was unbelievably fast. His arm came up, blocking the attacker's forearm. The knife went flying uselessly across the damp floor. Thrown off balance by the parrying blow, the seaman slipped in a puddle of water and went down flat on his back.

Before he could even raise his head, there was cold steel lying along his throat. It had appeared in Jase's hand as if my magic.

"Maybe I didn't make myself clear," Jase growled in a voice that matched the blade he was holding to the other man's throat. "Here at The Serpent, we don't encourage any sort of roughhousing."

For what must have seemed an excruciatingly long moment to his victim, he continued to let the sailor feel the edge of the blade. No one in the room moved. Then Jase stepped back, handing the knife over to Ray, who calmly replaced it within easy reach.

"Get him out of here," Jase ordered quietly, nodding at the other three men who had been involved in the fight. "And if the four of you manage to stay out of The Serpent, I will refrain from notifying your superior officer. Show up here again and you're going to find yourselves explaining everything to him. Take your choice."

Not surprisingly the four men staggered out the door. A collective sigh went through the room—one of satisfaction.

But Amy didn't feel the relief and satisfaction that everyone else in the bar seemed to be experiencing. She continued to stand where she was, staring with undisguised horror and disgust at the man who had handled the whole mess as if he did such things routinely.

For as long as she lived, Amy knew she would remember the sight of Jase's deadly blade lying along a man's throat. She'd never been so close to genuine violence in her life, and the sight of it effectively destroyed the beginnings of the cautious, friendly relationship that had started to grow that afternoon in the cove.

How could she have ignored, even temporarily, the reality of this rough island world? How could she have failed to realize that, in a place like this, Jase Lassiter wouldn't command respect simply by running a successful business and being a pillar of the community! Out here a man held his own with violence if necessary. It was part of the male fantasy.

Except that it wasn't fantasy. It was far too real.

Shocked and furiously angry with herself at the knowledge that she had felt any kind of attraction at all for such

theft down at the wharf and that's about the extent of our problems."

"And once in a while someone accidentally gets his throat cut?"

"Only accidentally," Jase drawled, refusing to rise to the bait. "But I'll stake The Serpent on the guess that whoever did this isn't a local or even off the Navy ship."

Amy said nothing as she absorbed the implications of the scene in front of her. She realized she was trembling, and the heavy weight of Jase's arm was suddenly and unexpectedly welcome. Of course whoever had done this wasn't a local. Dirk Haley was trying to go back on the bargain.

Nervously she tried to step out from under Jase's arm, aware of a need to establish some distance between herself and this man. She seemed to be surrounded by violent males this evening.

He turned his head as she made the small bid for freedom. "It's okay, honey," he soothed. "I'll take care of everything."

"That's quite all right, thank you. I've seen how you take care of things!" The feeling of masculine possessiveness that she sensed in the weight of his arm around her shoulders made her uneasy. And Amy didn't care for the gleam in his turquoise eyes. The last thing she needed right now was to have Jase Lassiter start claiming rights to her. She had never released such rights to any man and she certainly didn't intend to start now with the proprietor of a South Pacific bar who settled barroom brawls with the aid of a knife.

"Don't be afraid of me, Amy," he whispered. "Please."

"I'm not afraid of you!" she lied. "I'm just feeling rather tense at the moment. Don't you think I have cause?" She didn't like her own reaction to the hard pleading in him. Why on earth did she have to find herself lapsing into these stupid moments of softness toward Jase Lassiter? This wasn't the first time today it had happened!

He nodded in response to her caustic question. "I think you have cause." Then he pulled his arm away from her shoulders and stepped into the room, glancing around curiously. "Care to tell me what that cause is?" he added very casually.

"No!" Amy stopped herself, stricken by how much she had revealed with the impulsive answer. "I mean, it's obvious what the cause is! I've just watched five grown men try to beat each other up and stab one another, then I arrive back at my room to find someone's been having fun with my possessions. Surely that's cause enough?"

He lifted one shoulder in silent dismissal as he prowled toward the bed. Amy stifled a groan as he came to a halt and stood staring down at the two-hundred-dollar French nightgown, which had been snatched out of a drawer along with several other items of expensive intimate apparel.

Without a word Jase reached down and buried his hand in the exquisitely soft fabric of the nightgown. He seemed quite fascinated by the champagne-colored garment.

"Nice," he murmured, letting it go with obvious reluctance. "Very nice. Sophisticated and soft."

"Thank you," she replied stiffly. "It's one of my best-selling models!"

"I can see why. I'd like to see you in it sometime."

"Don't hold your breath."

"You are in a fractious mood tonight, aren't you? What was he after, Amy?"

She blinked, rapidly trying to marshal her defenses. "Who? The man who did this? How should I know? Money, I suppose. Or jewelry."

He sighed. "Amy, my brains haven't been completely disintegrated by the tropical sun. Don't expect me to buy that. I've told you we don't have this kind of crime around here. You arrive on my island to meet a man none of us know. You won't discuss your 'business.' You spend two nights in a waterfront bar, waiting for a mysterious contact. On the second night your room is broken into and searched.

Don't give me that bull about not knowing something about what's going on!"

"I don't have to make explanations to you, Jase," she tried to say with quiet emphasis.

"No, I suppose you don't. Want to make them to Fred Cowper instead?"

Amy's eyes narrowed. "Who's Fred Cowper?"

"He passes for the local law. An ex-cop from New York who probably left a wife and five kids behind when he departed for the South Pacific. When something like this comes up, he represents the government's interests."

Amy shifted uneasily. "Jase, I don't want to do any explaining to this Mr. Cowper. What could I tell him? It's obviously the work of vandals. Or a petty thief."

He favored her with a pitying glance, as if she weren't very bright. In truth, Amy decided sadly, she wasn't feeling very bright at the moment. "Take your pick, Amy, honey," he said bluntly. "Either you tell me what's going on or you explain all this to Cowper."

She stared at him balefully, aware he meant every word of his threat. "You have no right to give me orders like that," she said resentfully, knowing it was a useless protest.

"Who's going to stop me?" he asked curiously.

"Damn it! Just because you're accustomed to taking the law into your own hands, don't think you can get away with using that approach on me! I don't intend to be bullied!"

He watched her tense features for a long moment as if trying to make up his mind about how to deal with her. Then Jase slowly walked across the room to stand in front of her. He kept his voice low, almost placating, but every line of his body was hard and determined.

"Amy, it's pretty damn clear you've got some problems. I know I'm not your idea of a knight in shining armor, but this is my island and I know it, as well as the people on it. Like it or not, I'm probably the best-qualified help you can get at the moment. I know that, even if you don't choose to recognize it. Yes, I'm going to bully you into accepting my help. I sure as hell am not going to leave you alone to handle whoever did this!''

Amy sucked in her breath, aware she wasn't going to talk her way out of the mess but feeling she had to make one more try. ''Jase, this is a private matter....''

''Then we'll discuss it in more private surroundings. Let's get your things packed and get out of here.''

''What?'' she exclaimed as he turned back into the room and reached for her suitcase, which had been left lying open on the floor. ''Jase, I'm not going anywhere with you.''

''Yes, you are. You're coming home with me. Now, do you want to do your own packing or do you want me to do it for you?'' He was already lifting the champagne-colored nightgown in his hand. The silky stuff flowed across the rough khaki that covered his arm.

''Jase, please!'' Panicked, Amy heard the pleading desperation that had crept into her voice.

He dropped the nightgown into the suitcase without a word and went on to the next garment that lay wantonly across the bed, an ivory-toned lace bra embroidered with tiny flowers. Amy winced at the sight of the delicate garment against his tanned hand.

''All right, all right,'' she said through gritted teeth, dashing forward to rescue the antique-rose-colored bikini underpants that were next in line to be packed. ''I'll do it. Just give me a few minutes, will you?''

Jase nodded in grim satisfaction. ''I'll wait for you downstairs.''

She glanced up with renewed worry. ''You won't tell Sam what happened?''

''Not yet. Not until I know the whole story myself,'' he promised. He turned away and walked out of the room.

Amy sank down onto the bed, the bikini underpants in her lap. What a mess. What in the world should she do now? Or did she really have much choice? Jase meant what he said; he would call in the local law and leave her to explain everything if she didn't do as he wanted.

But was she any better off going home with Jase Lassiter? Hardly! It had all seemed straightforward when she made the arrangement with Dirk Haley. Why was he reneging now? All she wanted from him in exchange for the mask was the truth about what had happened to Ty Murdock. She and her sister deserved that much, at least.

Damn Haley and damn Murdock. Maybe she ought to throw Lassiter into the heap too! Men were probably universally damnable. With a frustrated motion of her hand, she tossed the panties into the suitcase and reached for the next item.

She would let Jase take her home. But if he thought he was going to wind up with a bed partner as well as a few explanations, he could think again!

It occurred to her a few minutes later as she stuffed the last of her things into the suitcase that although she was angry at Jase, she didn't actually fear him, at least not on a personal level. If she did, she wouldn't have let herself be forced into packing up and going with him.

If she handled him adroitly, she might still be able to salvage the situation. And perhaps he was right. Perhaps he could be of some help to her. As she went out the door of the room, suitcase in hand, another stray thought assaulted her unsettled mind.

She no longer knew how dangerous Dirk Haley might be. Perhaps she had bitten off far more than she could chew when she'd arranged their deal. If that was so, then the protection of a man who knew how to deal with knife-wielding brawlers might be rather welcome.

Fortified with that thought, Amy came slowly down the stairs with her suitcase to find Jase waiting patiently at the bottom. He took the case from her hand and nodded at Sam, who merely grinned cheerfully and went back to his newest girlie magazine.

"I can imagine what Sam must be thinking," Amy complained in a low mutter as she obediently walked beside her new host.

"Don't worry about Sam. After forty years out here he's seen it all."

"Really?" she demanded scathingly. "That's a great comfort. How many women has he seen you drag out of the Marina Inn to take home?"

Jase favored her with an unexpectedly wicked grin. "Talk about two-edged questions! That's like asking me if I've stopped beating my wife!"

"Did you?"

"Did I what? Beat my ex-wife? What do you think?"

Amy hugged herself with her arms, not looking at him. "No," she mumbled, feeling ridiculous. "I don't think you did."

"Should I take that as a compliment?" he asked dryly.

"Take it any way you want."

"You're right, you know," he went on smoothly. "I didn't beat her. Which is not to say I'm incapable of beating a woman, given sufficient provocation," he added deliberately.

"Is that a threat?"

"Take it any way you want."

She flinched inwardly as he tossed her own words back at her. "Let's get something clear between us, Jase. I'm going home with you tonight because you give me no alternative. I don't want anyone else knowing my business on Saint Clair, and you threatened to make it public knowledge by forcing me to talk to this Fred Cowper person. So I'm going to give you the explanations you seem to want, but that's all. I am not going to share your bed. I realize there's a shortage of tourists on Saint Clair, but you'll just have to wait for the next batch if you're looking for a bedmate. Understood?"

"You know, you have all the makings of a first-class shrew," he observed. "If some man doesn't take you in hand soon, you're going to become rather unmanageable."

"I'm not in a mood for your chauvinistic jokes. Just tell me that you understand and accept the terms under which I'm agreeing to accompany you tonight."

"Seeing that I set the terms myself, I guess I understand them," he retorted.

"Jase, you're twisting my words!"

"Relax, Amy. You'll be safe enough under my roof," he said with sudden seriousness. "And I won't have to lie awake wondering if whoever searched your room tonight is planning on coming back to confront you in person."

Amy swallowed. "Yes, that thought did occur to me too."

"Sensible," he approved. "Better the devil you know than the one you don't, hmm?"

"I hardly know you," she whispered morosely.

"But you trust me more than whoever it is you're on Saint Clair to see, don't you? Given what you think of me, that sure doesn't say too much for him, does it? How the hell did you get involved with this Dirk Haley, anyway?"

"I'm not *involved* with him. At least not personally. I have a...a business arrangement with him," Amy said, picking each word carefully. "I've never even met the man. I've only corresponded with him once or twice."

"Don't make me drag it out of you," Jase groaned. "Just tell me in short, simple sentences about this 'business' arrangement. What was it your unknown visitor was searching for tonight?"

"A mask. A carved wooden mask from Africa," she told him starkly.

Jase slanted her a sidelong glance. "How large is this mask?"

"Not very. It will fit inside my purse. Which is where it was tonight when whoever it was came looking for it," Amy concluded with some satisfaction. "I haven't let it out of my sight since I left San Francisco. It's the only thing I've got with which to bargain."

"What's so special about this wooden mask?" Jase inquired levelly.

"To tell you the truth, I don't know. I had it evaluated by a dealer in San Francisco who specializes in such things and was told it does have some value as a collectible, but not a great deal. I only know that Haley seems to want it very badly."

"Where did you get it?"

Amy shut her eyes briefly. "My sister's ex-husband sent it to her shortly after her son was born."

"What happened to this ex-husband?"

"That's what I want Dirk Haley to tell me."

There was a long moment of silence while Jase digested that bit of information. Then: "What was the ex-husband's name?"

She didn't like the soft way he asked that question. But what was the harm in answering? She'd told him so much already. "Ty Murdock."

"Okay, so give me the punch line," Jase demanded. "What was your sister's ex-husband to you? Why are you the one on Saint Clair, looking for answers about him, instead of his ex-wife?"

"Look, the personal side of this matter is entirely irrelevant to the problem." Amy lifted her chin in defiance.

"The hell it is," he shot back, apparently totally unawed by her aloof rebuke. "I'd say it had everything to do with the problem!" As he spoke, they turned down a badly paved street a couple of blocks from where the lights of The Serpent gleamed on the water.

"Where are we going?" Amy peered into the gloom. Saint Clair didn't boast anything as advanced as streetlighting. All she could see were a few quiet houses of indeterminate age and structure. Everything quickly became weathered and well used-looking here in the tropics, Amy decided. Including people.

"I told you. My home. Don't panic, I'm not leading you off into the palms in order to ravish you."

"I wish I could be certain of that," she shot back furiously.

"You can be absolutely positive of that," he stated. "When I ravish you, it's going to be in a nice comfortable bed, not on top of a bunch of spiky palm fronds on the hard ground. I'm not as young as I once was," he added darkly by way of explanation.

"I'm not in the mood for your lousy jokes! Don't tease me, Jase. I've had a hard night!"

He came to an abrupt halt—so abrupt that Amy, who was concentrating fiercely on deciding whether or not she had jumped from the frying pan into the fire, managed to collide with him.

"Damn you!" she gasped, her voice muffled against the fabric of his shirt as she clutched madly at his sleeves for support. In spite of the unexpectedness of it, her impact had virtually no effect on him. Jase stood rock steady as she pushed herself away, seeking her balance again.

"As charmingly klutzy as you are," he said calmly, "you'll probably fall into my bed of your own accord when the time comes." He set the suitcase on the ground beside his right foot and reached out to touch her face with the tips of his rough fingers. She could barely see his face in the overwhelming darkness of the island night, but Amy was suddenly so vividly aware of him that she could hardly breathe. "I wasn't teasing you, honey," he went on with grave gentleness. "I wasn't making jokes. I want you. Sooner or later I think I'm going to have to take you to bed."

"You...you said I was all wrong," she reminded him desperately. "And you were right. Furthermore, it works both ways, Jase. You're all wrong for me too!"

"I know," he agreed almost wistfully. "But it's all your fault for being here. You shouldn't have come wandering through paradise unless you were prepared to meet up with a serpent." His hand fell away, and at the loss of his touch she felt oddly bereft. "Come on, Amy. We're almost home."

"Home" proved to be a two-story rustic house that overlooked the harbor. It had been built early in the century, Jase explained absently as he switched on lights, and had been the home of a retired sea captain. Later, during World War II, the US military had commandeered it for a while as officers' quarters. After the war it had been through a variety of owners until Jase had bought it eight years earlier.

"It's lovely, Jase."

He watched her take in the hardwood floors, the high, beamed ceilings and the arching, open windows that stretched from floor to ceiling. "You sound surprised," he said with suspicious blandness. "Where did you think I lived? Over The Serpent?"

"Well, frankly, yes. Or in one of the small houses nearby. You seem to spend most of your time at your bar, so I assumed you probably weren't much interested in having a home like this."

He walked over to a liquor cabinet and lifted a bottle of rum. "You tend to make a lot of assumptions about men, don't you?"

She swung around, abandoning an examination of a tapa wall hanging, and glared at him. "Meaning?" she challenged.

His mouth crooked as he poured their drinks. "Never mind. We've got too many other topics on the table tonight. We'd better get through them first. Tell me the rest of the story, Amy."

She knew what he wanted, and her resistance suddenly seemed to be very low. Here in the pleasant, airy protection of his home it was too easy to let down the barriers, too easy to unburden herself of the depressing story. Jase had offered aid and comfort, and Amy found herself in need of both.

Perhaps it was because she was so far from home. Perhaps it was because she had just been through an extremely unpleasant experience. Or perhaps it was because she was beginning to realize she might have taken on more than she could handle in trying to deal with Dirk Haley on her own. Whatever the reasons, Amy found herself sinking down onto the padded wicker sofa and finishing the tale of how she'd wound up on Saint Clair.

"I met Ty Murdock a little over two years ago," she began.

"I knew it," Jase interrupted heavily. "I knew you were doing more than just running an errand for your sister! You were involved with him!"

"If you want to hear the rest of this, you had better shut up!"

"Were you in love with him?" Jase asked coolly, dropping into the seat across from her.

"Sort of," she muttered grudgingly.

"'Sort of'!" he exclaimed. "What kind of an answer is that?"

"Well, I suppose I loved him as much as a woman can love a man she doesn't fully trust," she explained with an honesty that astonished her. It was the truth, she realized.

Jase exercised his patience. "Tell me. Everything."

Amy lifted one shoulder in a small shrug. "Ty Murdock was an exciting, dashing, glamorous man. He had some mysterious job with the government and he played the polished, sophisticated James Bond role with a nice understatement. It worked very well. Women loved it. And the best part was that it was for real. He was stationed in San Francisco when I first met him. I don't really know what attracted him to me. For my part, he made an interesting, charming escort. But from the first night I met him at the home of some friends, I knew I would never be able to trust him."

"Why not?"

How could she explain it? Her wariness was so much a part of her now. "I don't tend to trust men in general, I guess. I don't think they always know what they want. At any rate I sensed that Ty was restless, searching for an excitement that I knew instinctively I could never provide. I liked him, and Lord knows he was exciting to be with, but some part of me knew that he would never be able to stay very long with any one woman. Eventually I realized that there was no point in the relationship. I would only get hurt if I kept seeing him, and he was starting to ask for more than I wanted to give."

"Meaning you wouldn't sleep with him?" Jase drawled, one brow lifting.

Amy watched him for a moment through narrowed eyes. "As soon as he felt me withdrawing emotionally from the relationship, all of Ty's hunting instincts were aroused. Typical masculine attitude," she explained carelessly. "Men always want what they can't have. Before I knew what was going on, he was suddenly talking marriage. It was a ridiculous idea. A man like him had no business getting married, and I told him so."

"I'll bet he really appreciated that," Jase growled.

Amy winced, remembering the scene. "He, uh, took it as a personal affront. In fact he got furious. The last time we quarreled he had been drinking. He said he would force me into bed, get me pregnant and then see if I would refuse his offer of marriage. I told him I would never sleep with a man I couldn't trust and that the very last thing on earth I wanted was his child." Amy sighed. "I was very angry myself. I didn't like being threatened."

Jase eyed her broodingly. "You told him you wouldn't give him a child? Lady, you're lucky you came out of that little scene without a black eye or worse. In fact, all things considered, you're lucky he didn't carry out his threat!"

"Oh, he tried," she tossed back stonily, stifling a shudder at the memory.

In spite of his own laconic warning, Jase's fingers tightened visibly around his glass. "He raped you?"

"No. Fortunately our quarrel was interrupted by the arrival of some friends. I was never so grateful to see anyone in my life as I was the Harrisons that night,'' she concluded in a whisper. After a moment she went on with the story. ''Ty left in a rage, but I thought it was all over. The next thing I knew, he started seeing my sister. Two months later she was pregnant.''

Jase groaned. ''He got his revenge on you by using her.''

''Yes. What really made it so bad was that she loved him. Really loved him. She had all along. And he knew it. When I turned him down, he went straight to her arms, looking to salve his ego, I suppose.''

''And she loved him enough to take the risk of having his child,'' Jase concluded softly.

Amy nodded, her throat very tight. ''For a while they seemed relatively happy, much to my surprise. Melissa is very beautiful and very sweet. It would be hard not to love her. If any woman could have changed Ty, settled him down, it would have been her. He married her and I was keeping my fingers crossed, hoping it might work out.''

''But it didn't?''

''Toward the end of the pregnancy there was so much tension between them, Melissa said you could have cut it with a knife. I didn't see much of either of them during that time. I knew things were deteriorating, and I just couldn't bear to see my sister so unhappy. When she was in her seventh month, Ty started seeing other women. It wasn't a surprise. He had cheated on me even during the short time we had been dating. That was one of the reasons I knew I couldn't trust him. Then one night I got a phone call from her. She was in labor and Ty was nowhere around. I wound up taking her to the hospital. I was the one who waited to find out if it would be a boy or a girl. I was the one who brought her flowers afterward and I was the one who drove her home from the hospital two days later. Ty had spent the weekend in Carmel with a girl friend. I could have killed him for what he did to Melissa.'' Desperately Amy blinked back the shimmer of tears, turning her head to glance out over the dark harbor so that Jase wouldn't see them.

"Tell me the rest, Amy," Jase said softly.

"There's not much more. Ty told Melissa that he really didn't care to remain married, that he wasn't cut out to play father and he was going to do her a favor and get out of her life. He applied for a transfer to an overseas post and shortly after that he filed for divorce. For a while he sent a little child-support money and an occasional trinket. The mask was one of those trinkets. My sister kept the gifts, saying they were her son's legacy from his father. Then, a few months ago, the small trickle of communication between Ty and my sister dried up completely. She's decided he's probably dead. His job, we always understood, was a dangerous one, so I suppose it's a possibility. But for his son's sake she wants to know for sure what happened to his father. When the request for the mask came from Dirk Haley, we decided there might be a possibility of learning the truth about Ty's fate."

Jase frowned. "Haley contacted her out of the clear blue sky?"

"He sent her a cable, claiming to be an old friend of Ty's, and told her that Ty had said he could have the mask. We held a family counsel and decided that we needed to know if the mask was more valuable than we had thought. If so, it should be preserved for Craig's future."

"Craig is Melissa's child?"

Amy nodded. "In any event Melissa and I thought that this Dirk Haley might be able to tell us what had happened to Ty. The government has been no help at all. They won't even claim him on their payroll, much less tell her anything about his fate."

"So you and Melissa decided to use the mask as leverage to get information out of Haley about it and Murdock." Jase shook his head in disgust. "A pair of idiots."

"That's what Adam said," Amy muttered tightly.

"Who's Adam?" he asked sharply.

"Adam Trembach is a very wonderful, responsible, mature man who has fallen in love with my sister," Amy explained with a glimmer of a smile. "He's also very protective of her. He wasn't about to have her go running off to the South Seas to find out what had happened to her ex-husband!"

"I can't blame him for that," Jase said with feeling. "So you and Melissa decided you should come instead?"

"Someone had to find out what was so important about that mask. Maybe it's worth a fortune. If so, that fortune belongs to little Craig. In any event, someday he's going to start asking questions about his father, and Melissa needs to know the answers for his sake."

"So here you are on Saint Clair, looking for those answers." Jase looked at her as though he was having second thoughts about her intelligence. "Do you know anything about this Haley character, other than the fact that he claims to be an old buddy of Murdock's?"

"Not really," Amy admitted uneasily. "When Melissa responded to his cable, saying she was willing to discuss the matter of the mask with him, he sent her a follow-up cable telling her to come here this week and he would contact her."

"He probably picked Saint Clair because he doesn't feel vulnerable here. We don't have much in the way of governmental formalities," Jase decided. "If he wants that mask for something other than legitimate reasons, Saint Clair would make a fairly safe contact point for him. He can slip in and slip back off the island fairly easily. Not like Hawaii."

"He's less vulnerable here, while I'm more so," Amy noted wryly, hiding a shudder.

"Not anymore." Jase got to his feet. "The odds are a bit more even now."

"Because you're on my side?" she whispered.

"What's the matter, Amy? Afraid that having a rum-soaked sleazy expatriate tavern owner on your side isn't going to be much help?" he taunted softly.

"Don't give me that routine! It certainly doesn't make you sound any less dangerous, you know. I've seen the way the locals treat you, and I saw you send four brawling sailors on their way this evening. I'm fully aware that out here in a *man's* world you don't gain that kind of respect by being too rum-soaked!"

"How about sleazy?" he pressed with a flash of amusement.

"I'll let you have sleazy," she agreed too sweetly. "Which room is going to be mine, Jase? I think it's time I went to bed."

"Alone?"

"Definitely," she retorted, moving to collect her suitcase. "Don't get the idea that I might be willing to repay you for your help by warming your bed. If you choose to get yourself involved in this mess, it's not because I asked for your help!"

"Have you ever asked any man for help, Amy Shannon?" he demanded softly.

"No," she stated proudly, "I haven't."

He hesitated a moment, as if he wanted to say something else. Then he smiled. "Second room at the top of the stairs."

Amy grabbed her bag and hurried toward whatever sanctuary awaited at the top of the staircase.

# Four

An hour later Amy finally abandoned her efforts to sleep and tossed back the sheet. Soundlessly her bare feet found the hardwood floor, and the French nightgown drifted around her ankles as she padded across to the open arched window.

The second room at the top of the stairs was clean and pleasantly furnished with bamboo and wicker, but there was a strange emptiness about it. It was as if no one had inhabited the room for a very long time.

Which was entirely understandable, Amy decided wryly as she stood staring out to sea. Jase's souvenir-hunting houseguests undoubtedly slept in the master bedroom along with the master!

She pushed that annoying image aside, gripping the edge of the window lightly. Below her the Navy ship still rocked gently, and a few men came and went in the darkness. But they were quite a distance away from her. Jase's home was removed from the working docks of the waterfront, unlike The Serpent. Had he needed to have a place where he could get away from his demanding business, even for a short period of time? Was he ever lonely? Did he miss the wife who had left him?

No, he was probably far too satisfied living out the classic male fantasy, Amy told herself firmly. She mustn't romanticize such a man, not even for a moment.

Yet, she trusted him. It was incredible, given everything she knew about him. What in the world was the matter with her? Here she was in his home, more or less agreeing to accept his help. What was it about Jase Lassiter that made her so incautious? It wasn't like her at all.

Restlessly she stepped through the open window and out onto the veranda. A night breeze drifting in off the ocean caught the silky fabric of her nightgown, and she found herself remembering how the material had looked draped over Jase's tanned fist. Sensuous. Exciting. The picture in her mind wouldn't be banished. It stirred uneasy, dangerous sensations that she knew better than to cultivate.

The veranda stretched completely around the house. Amy glanced to one side, looking for lights in some of the other rooms that opened onto it. All was in darkness. Was Jase in bed? Or had he stayed downstairs to contemplate his glass of rum? She found herself wondering which bedroom was his.

Leaning forward, Amy rested her elbows on the railing, her spice-colored hair tumbling around her shoulders.

"You shouldn't have come to Saint Clair, Amy. You're in the wrong place at the wrong time."

Amy froze at the soft drawl of his voice in the darkness behind her. Then, with a feeling that she was somehow about to face her fate, she turned slowly to find him standing in the shadows of the entrance to the room beside hers. So close. Dear Lord! She hadn't realized he would be using the room next to hers.

For a long moment they met each other's eyes in the shadows. Amy could feel the heavy tension in the air between them and knew that she was now facing a far more dangerous situation than she had faced when she'd gone back to her room to find it ransacked. She couldn't even move.

"The wrong place at the wrong time," Jase repeated huskily, coming slowly toward her. He was still dressed in the khakis he'd had on earlier, the shirt open at the throat and the sleeves rolled up on his forearms. The dark mahogany of his hair was almost black in the dim light, but his brilliant turquoise eyes glittered with masculine decision. There was hard promise in every line of his body.

"Is it, Jase?" she got out as he came to a halt a couple of feet away from her. "Is it really the wrong place and the wrong time?"

He went to stand beside her at the railing, leaning back against it, sipping the rum. Then he set the glass down beside him and nodded. His eyes never left her face. "For you it is."

"But not for you?" she whispered. A shiver went through her as she waited for the unbearable tension to burst. All she had to do was turn around and walk back into her room and close the window. Why couldn't she move?

"Out here a man learns to make things right. Even if it's only for a night or two. And especially when he wants a woman as badly as I want you."

Amy couldn't look away from his steady, gleaming gaze now. She felt completely trapped, mesmerized by forces she didn't even want to try to understand. "Do you…" She stopped and licked her lips nervously. "…do you really want me that badly? Or would any woman…?"

She never got a chance to finish the question. In her anxiety her right hand swept jerkily to the side and caught the edge of his rum glass, which was sitting on the railing.

Jase put out his hand almost casually and caught the glass in midair. Only a few drops spilled. He set it on the railing again, a strange smile playing around the edge of his mouth as he watched her stricken expression.

"Yes, I want you that badly, and no, not just any woman would do. Not tonight. Do I really make you so nervous?" He glanced briefly at the salvaged glass.

"You make me very nervous," she confessed throatily.

"We're equal then. Because you are playing havoc with my nervous system too!"

Jase's mouth came down on hers with an unconcealed, almost desperate hunger.

The impact of that male hunger was beyond anything Amy had ever experienced or ever expected from a man. Last night when Jase had kissed her, there had been a deliberate seductive quality, a tasting, teasing, testing quality. He had been trying to lure her and tempt her to come home with him.

Tonight she was in his home, and the trap had closed shut around her. Tonight Jase was going to take by storm the feminine prey he had lured into reach. Amy had known, deep in the core of her body, what his intentions were the moment she heard his voice behind her on the veranda. She couldn't run then and she couldn't raise her defenses now.

"Amy...!" Jase broke the contact for a split second to groan her name against her mouth, and then he was pressing her back against the rail, letting his body lean heavily into hers while he forced her lips apart with his own.

Amy gasped as he invaded her mouth, her senses reeling. She was dimly aware of the hard line of the rail against the small of her back. The weight of his aroused body took away her breath and at the same time fed her passion.

As his tongue surged between her teeth, seeking the moist warmth beyond, Jase slid his left foot between her legs, prying them apart just as his mouth had pried apart her lips. The champagne-colored silk of the French nightgown was whipped lightly around his khaki trousers by the midnight breeze.

"Jase, oh, Jase, *please,*" Amy breathed achingly. "I don't...this isn't...oh, *Jase!*"

He caught her face between his rough, urgent palms,

holding her still as he rained a scorching line of kisses across her cheek and down her throat. "Hush, sweetheart. It's too late. It was probably too late the minute you walked into The Serpent."

She sensed the unyielding truth of his words, her body shivering with reaction. Somehow it was all too overwhelming, too vast, too ordained, to even think of resisting. Amy was being swept up into the vortex of passion Jase was unleashing, and she couldn't get her bearings long enough to find reality.

The large, strong hands cradling her face moved lower, slipping down to trace the curve of her shoulder. Jase was trembling with the hot rush of desire pouring through his body. She could feel the unmistakable need in him, and a very primitive part of her thrilled to it.

"Put your arms around me," he grated against the vulnerable point just below her ear. "Hold me, for God's sake, Amy. I need you tonight!"

With an incredulous sigh of surrender, Amy reacted to the husky command. Her fingertips, which had been splayed half protestingly against his chest, lifted to curl into the thickness of his mahogany hair. How could she deny this man? He drew a fierce, totally feminine response from her that brooked no rational attempt at explanation. In that moment Amy found she couldn't even think coherently. All she wanted to do was obey the passionate, timeless call of the senses. She wanted to give herself completely to Jase Lassiter.

Jase felt the totality of her surrender in every fiber of his being. He wanted to shout his savage exultation, and it came out as a hoarse groan. "Amy, Amy, I want you so." He slid his hands down to cover her breasts, enthralled with the silky feel of the fabric beneath his fingers. Through it he felt the budding thrust of her nipples, and the heady pleasure waving through him rose to an even higher level. *She wanted him.*

He tugged at the bodice of the beautiful nightgown, and

she lowered her arms so that he could pull the shoulder straps down. Jase raised his head, gazing down into her face as he lowered the elegant gown to her waist. Amy's head was thrown back, her eyes closed in dreamy supplication. She was caught up in the magic of the moment as thoroughly as he was.

He had brought her to this point, Jase told himself, glorying in the knowledge. She hadn't wanted this, hadn't wanted to give herself to him, but he had managed to find the primitive core of her and now she would be his.

Jase pulled her against his shoulder as he touched the small, full curve of her breast with trembling fingers.

"Oh, Jase, Jase, I'm aching," she whispered at his throat.

"Not any more than I am," he vowed hoarsely. "God, you feel so good. Take off my shirt for me, sweetheart. I want to feel you against me!"

Shakily Amy's fingers dropped to the buttons of his khaki shirt. Jase uttered a deep, husky laugh as he felt the uncoordinated movements of her hand. She was unable now to stand alone, he realized, thoroughly aroused by her helplessness. She needed to lean on him. She needed him to hold her.

"Easy, honey," he crooned as she fumbled in obvious frustration with his clothing."I'll take care of it. I'll take care of everything."

He shrugged out of the shirt, ripping the last button off as he did so, and dropped it heedlessly to the veranda floor. Then he brought her toward him with a slow, savoring movement. Amy opened her eyes as her hardened nipples brushed the crisp hair of his chest, and Jase looked down into the endless depths of the gray-green pools.

"Like the sea in a storm," he muttered. "A man could drown and not even care."

Then her softness was crushed against the wall of his chest, and Jase thought he would lose what control he had left. The deepening level of her surrender was far more intoxicating than the finest rum. It sent him to a high he had never known, made him feel both aggressively dominant and exquisitely tender. The urge to possess a woman had never been stronger, never more consuming.

"I have to have you, Amy." For some reason he wanted to explain the level of his own passion to her. "My blood is burning for you tonight. I would go out of my mind if I didn't take you tonight."

He barely heard her reply. "Yes, Jase. I know. I know."

Unable to wait any longer, he swung her up into his arms. The champagne gown flowed down over his arms. From the waist up she was naked, and in the shadows she looked and felt like a captive Sabine.

"And, God help me, I feel like a conqueror," he muttered thickly, carrying her through the open windows of his bedroom. Carefully he lowered her onto the turned-back bed. Amy lay looking up at him through her lashes, her lips moist and slightly parted, her breasts inviting. He read the desire in her face and shook his head once in amazed disbelief at the knowledge that she was giving herself to him so completely.

Slowly he sank down onto the edge of the bed, his eyes never leaving hers. "I'm going to make you mine," he managed heavily. "Do you understand? Tonight you're going to belong to me."

"Why do you keep trying to warn me about your intentions?" she asked softly, her fingertips drifting upward to his chest, where they grasped hungrily at the short, curling hairs. "I know what they are." Her smile was infinitely seductive.

"Maybe I'm trying to give you a chance to run," he admitted roughly.

"I couldn't run," she replied simply.

"And even if you tried, I wouldn't be able to let you go," he sighed, reaching out to stroke his hand across her breast and down to the small curve of her stomach. Then he leaned closer and slipped his fingers beneath the nightgown, pushing it down over her hips until it formed a silky pool at the foot of the bed.

For a long moment he sat drinking in the sight of her body, entranced with the signs of her arousal. When her legs shifted languorously, he put out a hand and threaded his fingers through the thicket of hair at the apex of her thighs. His pulse pounded violently as he touched her intimately. When it came time to take her completely, he thought dazedly, he was going to literally explode. Never had his own sense of control been so dangerously lacking.

Almost violently he surged to his feet beside the bed and yanked at the fastening of his trousers. As he stepped impatiently out of them, Jase glanced up to find her staring, wide-eyed, at his thoroughly aroused body.

"You're very beautiful," she whispered in wonder.

"No, you're the beautiful one." He came down beside her, reaching to pull her against the hard, waiting length of him. "Soft and warm and womanly. God, Amy...!"

Shaping the curve of her rounded thigh, Jase luxuriated in the silk of her skin. Deliberately he forced his knee between hers, opening the center of her passion to his touch. There he found the damp heat of her and thought he really would go out of his mind.

"Honey, I know I should wait a little longer, give you a little more time, but I don't think I can!" he groaned, burying his face against her breasts while he teased the core of her with his hand. "I need you too desperately this first time."

"Oh, Jase, I've never felt like this," she confided, twisting her arms around his neck. "Don't wait. I want you so!"

Unable to resist any longer and knowing he had to have her or go crazy, Jase pushed her onto her back and lowered himself onto her soft, inviting body. She reached up, urging him to her. He felt the touch of her palms on his back, and when she parted her legs and lifted her hips, he knew the throbbing excitement of being wanted.

He came down against her in a passionate rush, his hands

gripping her shoulders as he thrust himself heavily into her moist, clinging warmth. She gasped as her body absorbed the unrelenting impact of his, and he covered her mouth with his own while he forged deeply into her.

Then he was losing himself in that which he had sought to conquer. With Amy's every response Jase fell further into the luscious trap. He knew in some distant corner of his mind that he was seeking to bind this woman to him totally. In that same corner of his brain a small voice whispered the impossibility of doing any such thing.

But the need to make her his was far more primitive and far more urgent than any amount of rational thought. Jase knew that even if it was hopeless, he had to try to achieve the impossible. He had to try to chain her to him.

Exquisitely soft sounds emanated from far back in Amy's throat now as the spiraling tension carried them both to higher and higher planes. Jase knew the sting of her nails on his back and growled a fierce response. He surged again and again into her, sliding one hand beneath her hips to lock her body more tightly to his. He felt fevered, his passion heating his whole body. Soon he would explode, just as he had known he would.

"Amy, Amy," he cried out hoarsely as the most delightful tremor rippled through her. He could feel the spasmodic shivering deep inside her body, and as she called his name aloud, Jase knew a fierce, masculine triumph that was beyond anything he had ever experienced.

He drove into her one last time as the world seemed to come apart around him in small, shimmering fragments. Then he was clutching her tightly as they both fell through passion's gate.

It was a long time before Jase could rouse himself enough to even lift his head, and when he did so, he found Amy lying quietly beneath him, her eyes closed and an expression of total relaxation on her face. He smiled to himself in tenderness and satisfaction, reluctantly shifting his body to one side and tucking her against him.

Had he exhausted her so thoroughly? It was only fair. She had certainly done the same to him. He hadn't felt so at ease with himself and the world for longer than he could remember. In the morning, he promised himself as he drifted off into a deep sleep, he would tease her a bit about falling asleep on him. And after he'd teased her a little, he would make love to her again. Only this time it would be slow and voluptuous. Now that he'd made his claim, he could afford to relax and enjoy what he had taken.

It was Amy who awoke first, coming out of a thick, sensuous slumber to find the tropical dawn filtering into the room. For a long moment she lay still, aware of the possessive weight of Jase's arm across her breasts. She was curled tightly into his body, spoon fashion, and one of his ankles rested heavily against her own as if he would chain her in case she tried to slip away in the night.

The night. Amy drew a long breath, remembering the passion of the night. Reality returned with a savage jerk.

"Oh, my God!" The words were a bare whisper on her lips, but they fairly screamed inside her head. What had she done? She must have been out of her mind!

Out of her mind. Yes, she'd gone a little crazy in the heat of the island night. Crazy enough to surrender to a man she hardly knew, a stranger she would never see again when she left Saint Clair.

A man who would not care about the emotional risk she had taken—or the physical one. Men rarely seemed to care about the ultimate risk they took such pleasure in letting a woman run. It was a woman's responsibility to protect herself.

And she hadn't even thought about protecting herself. Good Lord, what had come over her? She'd always been so incredibly cautious, so circumspect and wary. Her extremely limited sexual experience had taken place years earlier, shortly after graduation from college, and even caught up in what she had assumed was the throes of passion, she'd had more than enough presence of mind to take precautions. There had been no man in her life for so long now that for ages she hadn't had to worry about getting pregnant.

After twenty-eight years of being careful, she'd gone crazy. And it had happened with a man she knew almost nothing about, a man whose need of her had stripped her of rational thought and normal caution.

"Oh, my God," Amy breathed, shaken. Her palm went instinctively to her stomach. She might even now be pregnant. What on earth would she do?

Cautiously she edged out from under the restraint of Jase's arm and leg, inching across the sheets to the edge of the bed. There she sat up and nervously glanced around for her nightgown.

"Going somewhere?" Jase's lazy tone held all the satisfaction in the world. When his palm wrapped around her waist, Amy panicked and leaped to her feet. "Amy?"

She couldn't look at him, but she sensed the quizzical way he watched as she frantically searched for her nightgown. She felt ridiculous, bouncing around the room naked.

"Amy, what the hell's the matter with you? Come back to bed," Jase ordered coaxingly. "We have things to talk about, you and I."

"Later," she gasped, seizing the crumpled nightgown and slipping it hastily over her head. "We can talk over breakfast."

She whirled and fled through the open window, darting along the veranda to her own room. God, she felt stupid. She couldn't seem to think straight. Everything in her brain seemed to be churning with self-admonishment and incipient panic.

"Amy, settle down and tell me what's wrong."

Clutching to her breast the shirt she had just dragged out of the suitcase, Amy spun around to find Jase standing naked in the window. He regarded her with wary determination, as if he didn't know what had gotten into her but sure as hell intended to resolve the matter.

"It's all right, Jase," she said, trying to inject calm into her words. "I...I just want to get dressed. I'll meet you downstairs in a little while."

"Honey," he soothed, starting forward cautiously, "you're staring at me as if you were a rabbit facing a wolf." He stopped when she instinctively backed away a step. "Surely after last night you know I'm only a man," he added gently.

"I *know* you're a man," she wailed. "That's the whole problem."

"Care to explain that one?" he invited with a touch of dryness.

She drew a deep breath and forced herself to calm down. "Never mind. I know it's my fault. It's always the woman's fault, isn't it? My only excuse is that I just wasn't thinking last night." She stared at him, her incomprehension plain in her widened eyes. "I honestly don't know what came over me. It's never... I've never been like that before...." She clutched more tightly at the shirt in her hands. Damn it, she was going to be cool about this if it killed her. "I'll be fine," she concluded starkly.

He arched one eyebrow. "Will you?"

"Yes, yes, of course I will."

"You sound like you're having a hard time convincing yourself of that."

"Well, you won't have to worry about it one way or the other, will you?" she snapped back angrily.

He eyed her broodingly for a moment and then ran his fingers distractedly through his tousled hair. "Do I get an explanation for all this or are we going to play Twenty Questions for the remainder of the morning? I warn you, I haven't got a lot of patience with games of any kind."

She stiffened. "I've told you, it's not your problem."

"That's a ridiculous statement under the circumstances. I'd say it definitely is my problem!" He reached out and snagged her wrist. She flinched and dropped the shirt into a heap on the floor. "Well, at least it wasn't another glass full of wine or rum,'' he noted, glancing down at the awkwardly released shirt as he sank down on the edge of the bed and yanked her into his lap. ''Now, tell me exactly what's going on here, Amy Shannon. There are other things I'd rather be doing right now than chasing you around the house, demanding explanations!''

She reclined tensely across his naked thighs, tremblingly aware of every inch of him. It was incredible, she thought in amazement. She was in a panic about the consequences of last night's passion, and he had only to put his arms around her again to make her start thinking of taking the same risks once more!

''Please let me go, Jase,'' she said with forced steadiness.

''Not until you tell me why you're running around in hysterics this morning. Was my lovemaking so bad? Are you afraid of having to submit to my clumsy efforts again?'' He stroked the side of her cheek with the edge of his thumb, turquoise eyes gleaming with amused exasperation.

''You know damn well there was nothing clumsy about your...your bedroom technique,'' she told him tersely. ''I'm the only clumsy one around here. And knowing me, I'm probably just klutzy enough to get myself pregnant, even though I only went to bed with you one time!''

His thumb stopped its sensuous movement at the side of her face as Jase stared at her. ''That's what this imitation of a chicken with its head cut off is all about? You're afraid I've gotten you pregnant?''

''Not a very attractive description of my behavior, but yes, that's why I'm feeling nervous this morning,'' she gritted. ''As I said, it's hardly your problem. I don't know what came over me last night. I've always been so careful! I haven't even been that...that close to a man for so long that I...''

''Amy,'' he stated, his sherry-rich voice more inflexible and harsh than she had ever heard it, ''you're not pregnant.''

She tried to smile bravely. "No, probably not. I realize I'm undoubtedly worked up over nothing. It's just that I won't know for almost three weeks, and you can't know how awful the waiting is for a woman! And besides, I can be so very *clumsy* at times," she ended on a miserable note.

"Believe me," he growled heavily, "you're not pregnant!"

"I appreciate the positive thinking," she retorted dryly, growing angry.

"Damn to hell, woman, it's not a case of positive thinking! If you want to know the truth, I'd give my soul to get you pregnant!"

Amy froze in astonishment. "What are you saying?"

"That I can't think of anything more intensely satisfying this morning than the idea of your carrying my child!"

"Of all the cruel, chauvinistic, macho things to say!" she gasped in outrage. "How dare you admit such a thing! You'd send me back to San Francisco to raise your child on my own? Knowing you'll never see me again? My God, Jase. How many other tourists have you sent home carrying a little extra souvenir of Saint Clair? Do you take pride in it? Are there notches on your bedpost for all the little bastard children you may have fathered?"

The sudden, violent tightening of his body was her first indication that she'd gone much too far. But it was too late to run. When his strong fingers went to her throat in menace, Amy went very, very still.

"Do you really believe I'm that kind of man?" The question was a harsh, grating whisper.

Amy shut her eyes, collapsing against his chest. "No, no, of course I don't think you're that kind of man. I'm sorry, Jase. I'm all strung up this morning. I'm sure that in most cases you're a responsible adult. We...we both got carried away last night."

He gave her a short little shake. "Amy, shut up and listen to me. I'm going to tell you something I haven't had to tell anyone in ten years. Amy, I know for a fact that you're not pregnant because a doctor told me over ten years ago that I couldn't father children."

"What?" Her head snapped up from where it had been resting on his shoulder, and she stared into his hard eyes.

"You want the clinical details?" he rasped. "It's called a low sperm count. You want to know how I found out? When my ex-wife and I tried to have a baby and couldn't, we went for examinations. I turned out to be the one at fault. That's why my wife left me, Amy. She wanted children and I couldn't give them to her. She didn't want to adopt; she wanted her own. So she left to marry another man."

"Oh, Jase," she cried softly, suddenly wanting to soothe away the raw look of self-disgust from his taut features. "Jase, I didn't realize...."

"Naturally you didn't realize," he bit out savagely. "And I don't make a habit of announcing it to the world. It's not something of which a man is particularly proud!"

She began to relax in his arms, all her instincts urging her to comfort him. "You haven't had to soothe other panicked lady tourists?" she asked gently.

"The issue hasn't arisen with any of the others. I told you once, they were different from you. They always seemed to come prepared for a little island adventuring. Who was I to tell them their preparations were unnecessary with me?" he growled.

"Jase," Amy murmured with sudden perception, "is that how you wound up here on Saint Clair? When your wife left, did you just start drifting?"

His mouth tightened. "You have to admit that I haven't got much to offer a woman who wants to marry and have a family. I was only in my mid-twenties when Sara left me. I think I had some wild idea of filling my life with adventure, since I couldn't fill it taking care of a family. So I quit my job and decided to see the world. I finally landed in Saint clair and realized I didn't want to go on traveling aimlessly. That life palls very quickly—at least for me it did. I took a job here and one thing led to another. There never seemed to be anything to go back to the States for, so I stayed. I don't think I *could* go back now."

Amy turned her head into her bare shoulder. "I can't pretend I'm not terribly relieved, Jase," she said in a small voice. "The last thing I want to risk is having children. I've seen far too many women, my mother and sister included, left to manage on their own. My mother was never able to remarry because she never found a man who wanted to take on two daughters. I've always had a sense of guilt about that, I suppose. My mother was very intelligent and attractive when she was in her thirties, raising us. If my sister and I hadn't been there, I know she would have found happiness with another man after my father left. I told myself very early in life that I would never take the risk of ending up like my mother, lonely and bearing all the responsibility of raising children alone. I decided that men often think they want children, but it's just another macho fantasy for them. When reality hits, they're as likely as not to walk away from the added problems and responsibilities."

"Amy, that's not a fair assessment..." Jase began levelly.

"I know, I know. There are exceptions to every rule. I'm sure there are some perfectly excellent fathers in the world, but I personally haven't seen many. Look at what Ty Murdock did to my sister. Over half the women who work for me in my boutiques are divorced and raising kids by themselves. Don't get me wrong. I have great admiration for them and for my mother and sister. They're all very brave women. One can't help but admire that kind of inner strength. But I'm not going to end up like them, Jase," she concluded finally.

"So until last night you've never taken any risks, is that it?" he queried in a neutral tone.

She laughed shakily, closing her eyes as she rested her head on his shoulder. "For someone with a lifetime of clumsiness behind her, I guess I was very lucky the one time I got klutzy in bed, wasn't I?"

His hands tensed on her, and she wondered what he was thinking. "From your point of view I suppose you were. Don't expect me to be as relieved as you, though, honey. I meant what I said earlier: If I thought there was any possibility that you might have gotten pregnant last night, I'd be very, very pleased this morning! But the whole issue is, unfortunately, academic."

"Hardly!" she snapped, annoyed with his blunt admission. "It's not the least bit academic to me! It makes one hell of a lot of difference!"

"Meaning you'll come willingly to my bed now?" he asked smoothly.

She flushed, the color rushing up her throat to her cheeks. "Jase, we have to talk about that," she began very earnestly. "That's...that's another issue entirely. Last night we rushed things; *you* rushed things," she corrected righteously. "We hardly know each other and we should never have gotten carried away like that. I still don't know what came over me," she added uneasily, "but I definitely did not come to Saint Clair for an island fling!"

"You're overlooking one salient fact, honey," he drawled, letting her slide off his lap as he got to his feet.

"What's that?" she demanded, frowning up at him.

"Here on Saint Clair you've found the one perfect lover for you—the one who can't get you pregnant! I want to make sure you take full advantage of him."

Jase turned on his bare heel and left the room in long, angry strides, leaving Amy staring after him, her mouth open in amazed indignation.

# Five

"Don't you think it's about time I got to see this infamous mask?" Jase asked half an hour later over morning coffee.

Amy looked up from stirring some canned milk into her own mug of the dark, steaming brew. She had been lucky to find any milk at all. Jase's kitchen was a sadly barren place. What food he had was all in tins, many of them suspiciously old in Amy's opinion. Some couldn't be identified at all because the labels had peeled off in the relentless humidity. Fresh food was virtually nonexistent except for a carton of eggs and a loaf of bread, which was showing signs of mold. Jase had apologized briefly and explained that he ate most of his meals at the cafe where she had eaten the previous morning. Knowing what she did of the cafe's food, Amy had decided that the man was definitely not eating properly, but she was smart enough to keep her observation to herself. Jase's mood had been decidedly uncertain since the scene in her bedroom that morning.

"There's not much to see," she said in response to his

question. "You're welcome to take a look at it if you like. It's just a rather weathered old wooden mask. The gallery dealer who evaluated it for me said it was fairly recent and not a particularly good example of that art form."

"But this Haley character seems to want it rather badly?"

Amy nodded, her hands wrapped tightly around the mug. "If it weren't for the fact that the stupid mask represents the only legacy little Craig is ever likely to see from his father, it would undoubtedly have been tossed out with the trash."

"Your sister wanted to hang on to it for sentimental reasons?"

Amy's mouth curved wryly. "Don't ask me why. Ty Murdock was definitely not a man a woman should get sentimental about! But there was Craig to think of, and Melissa knows that someday she'll have to tell him something about the man who was his father. I think she's going to tell the boy his father was killed in a far corner of the globe and shortly before his death had sent the mask to his son. She'll let Craig think his daddy was intending to come home. She wants to give Craig a romanticized image of the whole thing—let him think his father was some sort of romantic adventurer who loved his son and meant to come home to him as soon as possible. Melissa thought the mask would be a nice keepsake of the fantasy she intended to spin."

"You don't approve?"

Amy shook her head. "No, I don't. What's the point of romanticizing a man like Ty Murdock? Adam Trembach will be Craig's *real* father. Still, I'm realistic enough to know that someday Craig will be curious about Ty. Melissa will have to tell him something."

"You like this Adam Trembach?" Jase asked curiously.

"Very much. He's a real rarity among the male of the species: a boy who actually grew up to be a man in every sense of the word. So many don't."

"You don't have much of an opinion of my sex, do you?"

"I've told you why I don't trust men. They tend to get caught up in their fantasies and they can cause so much pain while they're living out the illusion."

"And when it comes to having children?"

"You want proof of how irresponsibly men can behave toward their own children?" she challenged. "Then take a look at the number of Amerasian children who were casually abandoned by their fathers when the military shipped the men who had been stationed in Southest Asia back to the States."

"Amy," Jase began carefully, "I'm not saying for a moment that I approve of that sort of irresponsibility, but men have been leaving children behind on every battleground since the dawn of time. It's not right, but it's a fact of life."

She drew a long breath. "This is a pointless argument. Come and I'll show you the mask." Doggedly she got to her feet and headed for the stairs.

"Damn it, Amy" —Jase swung around as she went by his chair, catching hold of her wrist and forcing her to a halt— "I am not condoning that kind of irresponsibility, regardless of the circumstances, but you can't judge all men on the actions of a few."

"A few! More like a majority!"

"You're right. This probably is a pointless argument," he muttered. "Why the hell should I take it on my shoulders to defend the entire male sex? And on an issue that is moot in my case anyway!"

She heard the frustration and controlled anger in his voice, and something in her relented. "I know I shouldn't tar all men with the same brush, Jase. It's just that back in the States family life seems to have gotten a little precarious, to put it mildly. I know there are some exceptions. Men like Adam Trembach."

"But because of your mother's situation and your sister's mess, you've had a front-row view of the changing role of the family in modern society, hmmm? Maybe I haven't missed so much by avoiding civilization during the past decade,'' he suggested with a conciliatory smile.

She stared at him in silence, a part of her longing to point out that wasting one's life on an island in the Pacific was hardly a viable alternative to civlization, but she, too, was tired of the argument. ''I'll be right back with the mask.'' She hastened up the stairs.

It really was a rather ugly thing. Carved out of a nondescript wood, the mask was about the size of Jase's palm. It had once been painted, but the garish coating had long since chipped away from the surface. The maniacally grinning features were a caricature of human ones, probably representing some minor devil.

''Not a very prepossessing work of art, is it?'' Jase commented dryly, examining the thing carefully.

''No. I can't imagine why Haley wants it so badly. But I'm certainly going to find out.''

''Well, I think the first thing to do is hide this.'' Jase tossed the old wooden carving idly into the air and caught it.

''Hide it?''

''I don't like the idea of your carrying it around in your handbag. If Haley comes looking for it again, I'd rather he didn't have the satisfaction of finding it.''

That made sense. ''Where shall we put it?'' Amy asked with interest.

He thought a moment and then started down the hall to the far end of the house. ''I think I know just the place. The old sea captain who built this house had a library with some interesting built-in features.''

''Like what?'' Amy demanded, following in his path.

''Like a bookshelf with a false back. I'll show you.'' Striding into a sparsely furnished room that contained a surprisingly large book collection, Jase walked across the sisal matting on the floor and tugged at a seemingly solid bookcase shelf. Amy watched in pleased astonishment as two shelves full of books swung open on hinges to reveal an empty shelf built into the wall.

"A very clever sea captain!" she said. "You'd never know the opening was there. I wonder what he used to keep in that space."

"One of the most interesting collections of Victorian erotica I've ever seen," Jase told her dryly, placing the mask on the empty shelf of the wall and swinging the bookcase shut.

"Dirty books! Jase, you're kidding!" For the first time that morning real humor filled Amy's gray-green eyes.

"This island is a little isolated, Amy, in case you haven't noticed," he reminded her politely. "A man sometimes has to use his imagination. Just ask Sam."

She thought of Sam and his girlie magazines and grinned. "I get the point. What did you do with the erotica, Jase?"

"Read it, naturally," he drawled. "And then gave it to Ray, who in turn made a tidy profit selling it to sailors."

"Men and their fantasies," she groaned.

"Are you trying to imply that women don't fantasize?" he challenged.

She lifted her chin and moved regally toward the door. "You're not going to draw me into an argument like that!"

"Coward," he taunted gently behind her.

She ignored him. "What are you going to do today?" she asked, deliberately changing the topic as they headed back toward the kitchen. It occurred to her that she knew little or nothing about his daily routine.

"I'll be doing down to The Serpent after lunch to check in with Ray and make sure everything's in order. There's some paperwork to do. You can come with me."

"No, thanks," she said quickly. "I'll have to spend the night in the place, waiting for Haley to show up again. I'd just as soon do something else this afternoon."

"Amy, I don't think you quite understood. I wasn't exactly issuing an invitation. I don't want you wandering off by yourself today. Neither of us knows what Haley's up to, and I'm not taking any chances. You'll stay with me today. I'll try to get through the business at The Serpent as quickly as I can and then we'll go swimming or something,'' he added placatingly as she turned toward him with rebellious eyes.

Amy took a firm grip on her nerve: It took some nerve to stand up to this man, she realized wryly. ''It's you who doesn't understand, Jase,'' she said carefully. ''I appreciate your interest in my...my problem, but this is my business and I'll handle it. I don't want to be tied down all day long. I'm sure there's no real danger to me personally in all this, but I'll be careful regardless. I thought I'd do some shopping this afternoon while you're taking care of business.''

''*Shopping!* On Saint Clair? You're in for a disappointment. Neiman-Marcus hasn't opened a store here yet. Amy, don't be ridiculous. Other than a few tourist items down at Harry's store near the wharf, we don't have any genuine shopping.''

''You have a food store, don't you?'' she charged gruffly, not meeting his eyes.

That took him back a bit. ''A food store? Well, yes, I guess you could say we have a grocery shop. What the hell do you want with a food store?'' He was staring at her, clearly perplexed.

''If you must know, I was going to do some shopping for dinner!''

''Dinner! You're going to make dinner?''

''You should watch your exposure to the island sun, Jase. I think it's affecting your brain. You're repeating every word I say,'' she told him in a chilly tone.

''Amy,'' he asked with exaggerated patience, ''why do you want to go shopping for dinner? We can eat at the cafe. I told you I eat most of my meals there.''

''That's obvious from the condition of this kitchen!'' she blazed, her own patience fizzling completely. ''When was the last time you had a decent meal, Jase Lassiter? A balanced, well-made, home-cooked meal?''

He stared at her. ''Home-cooked?''

''Yes, damn it! Cooked at home in a kitchen. Made from scratch. A meal that has been cooked by other means than a deep-fat fryer?''

''Beats the hell out of me.'' He eyed her with an unreadable gaze. ''Probably ten or fifteen years.''

''That's terrible, Jase!'' She was truly appalled and it showed.

He shrugged. ''I hate to cook.''

''Well, I don't,'' she declared forcefully. ''And I'm tired of that cafe food. I'm going shopping for dinner and that's final.''

Suddenly, devastatingly, he grinned. ''You look like an outraged housewife.''

''More like an outraged tourist,'' she retorted.

''Who am I to alienate the few tourists we do get here on Saint Clair?'' he asked rhetorically. ''Okay, if it means so much to you, I'll let you go grocery shopping this afternoon. You should be safe enough if you stay on the main street in front of the harbor and don't wander beyond that. Our sole claim to a grocery store on Saint Clair is located about a block and a half from my bar. You can shop while I'm talking to Ray. But you're not to go any farther.''

''Jase, you have no right to give me orders!''

The amusement that had lightened his features for a moment faded into cold determination. ''Lady, you're on my island, staying in my home, and you just spent the night in my bed. That set of facts gives me all the right I need. Now, if I hear one more word of argument out of you on the matter, I will probably do something extremely chauvinistic like paddle your sweet rear until you can't sit down.'' He took a menacing, gliding step forward, his hands on his hips, dark brows in a solid line. ''Do I make myself understood?''

''Quite!'' she agreed with fine hauteur as she told herself

she wasn't allowing him to intimidate her. She was merely choosing not to lower herself to his methods. "It's also quite clear that your manners, if indeed you ever had any, have deteriorated to almost nothing here in the South Pacific!" Amy spun around on her heel and stalked out of the room.

"I don't need you to tell me I'm out of touch with civilization," he grunted as she disappeared down the hall. Jase wasn't certain if she heard him or not.

Two hours later he saw her safely through the front door of the small grocery store at the end of the wharf and then, after watching rather wistfully as she moved out of sight down a row of canned goods, Jase swung around and started back toward The Serpent.

"Rights," he muttered a little violently to himself as he strode along the dock with his long, economical stride. Didn't she realize she had given him a whole fistful of rights the night before?

Halfway down the street he paused in front of Fred Cowper's office window. Whether Amy liked the idea or not, Cowper should be told about what had happened, Jase decided grimly. Unfortunately there was a very familiar sign hanging on the door: Gone Fishing. As Usual. Jase sighed, wondering if the government man would be back by the following day. He'd check in the morning. Perhaps Cowper would know something about Dirk Haley.

Striding off once more, he studied the sea's horizon with an implacable expression, thinking of Amy in his bed. Never had a woman given herself so completely, engulfed him so totally, as she had last night. God! What an experience! From the beginning everything about her had aroused not only his physical hunger but also his long-dormant protective instincts. And after possessing her so thoroughly last night, he had some rights, damn it!

If only he could make her love him, give her a child. It was one way of tying down a woman like Amy. Jase turned away from the docks and stepped into the comparative shade of The Serpent. Getting Amy pregnant was a physical impossibility, nothing short of a fantasy. And wouldn't she be furious if he told her how strong that fantasy was in his head? She sure as hell didn't think much of male fantasies.

She was safe enough, he thought. In two years of trying, he hadn't been able to give Sara the child they had both wanted so badly. In the end his ex-wife has almost hated him, had hated the act of physical surrender that they both knew to be futile. The divorce had been a blessing for both. His mouth tightened grimly.

"Somehow," Ray drawled mildly from behind the bar, "I'd thought you'd be in a better mood today."

"Did you?" Jase retorted in his most repressive voice as he slid onto a stool. "Goes to show, I suppose, that employees shouldn't try to second-guess the boss. Let me see last night's receipts."

"Ouch! Does this mean you're no longer open to a little razzing on the subject of the lady tourist?"

Jase gave the younger man a savage glance. "The subject is closed. It now comes under the heading of personal business."

Ray grinned irrepressibly. "Call it anything you want. By now most of the island knows you took her home last night."

Jase's oath was short, violent and resigned. Saint Clair was too small and he was too well known to keep even the smallest personal activity totally private. As far as he was concerned, it didn't particularly matter. He didn't give a damn who knew he'd made Amy his. In fact, underneath the mild disgust he felt about the casual gossip, there was a certain satisfaction in knowing that everyone knew she was now off limits. But he could guess that Amy wouldn't be too pleased if she found out the relationship was public knowledge.

"Where'd you leave Miss Shannon this morning. Tied up to the bedpost?" Ray went on conversationally, wiping glasses. The bar was virtually empty at this hour, with only one lone drinker sitting across the room, nursing a beer.

"Any more cracks like that and I'll throttle you with your seltzer tubing," Jase growled, and then silently wished there *were* some way of tying Amy to his bed. "She's at Maggie's store."

"Maggie's! What's she doing there?"

"Shopping for groceries," Jase returned with a trace of smugness.

"What the hell's she going to do with groceries?" Ray demanded, startled.

"Cook my dinner tonight. What else?" The trace of smugness became blatant satisfaction as Jase allowed himself to contemplate that thought fully.

Ray whistled in soft amazement. "You lucky bastard. What the hell did you ever do to deserve that?" He leaned forward, elbows on the bar, dark eyes intent. "Listen, boss, if I put back that five bucks I borrowed from the till last week, do you think you could get her to set an extra place at the table tonight? I haven't had anything except Hank's greasy French fries and hamburgers for so long, I've forgotten what a home-cooked meal tastes like!"

"If you were in my place, Ray, would you be that generous?"

"Nope," Ray admitted immediately. "I'd keep Amy and the home-cooked meal all to myself."

"I'm glad you understand," Jase murmured smoothly. "Tell you what. I'll give you first crack at the next lady tourist who walks in here."

"Hah! Fat lot of good that'll do me. You know damn well The Serpent doesn't attract the domesticated sort. We always get the type who are looking for some variation on Humphrey Bogart in *Casablanca.* They want excitement and adventure. They don't want to go home with a man and cook his dinner!" Ray complained.

Jase got to his feet, picking up the box of receipts Ray had given him. "If it's a home-and-hearth sort of female you're looking for, Ray, you know you're not likely to find her out here. Go back to Kansas City."

"I'm desperate, but not that desperate. The light's better for painting here."

Jase smiled crookedly and started to turn away. Then he hesitated. "Anyone unusual come in after I left last night?"

"You mean anyone who looked like he might be waiting for Amy? No. Just the usual assortment of sailors and cargo runners. Everyone got drunk, spent a lot of money and went back to their boats."

"Okay. I'll be in my office if anyone wants me." Jase seated himself at the large table in the booth at the back of the room that served as The Serpent's office. From there he could look out over the railing and see most of the quay. When Amy started home with her sack of groceries, he'd be able to spot her. That realization brought a small smile to his lips. He delved into the stack of receipts with more enthusiasm than usual.

While Jase pondered the bar totals, Amy pondered the assortment of odd-looking vegetables that lay in the small chilling bin at the rear of Saint Clair's version of a supermarket. They were fresh-looking, but she didn't recognize most of them. Brow furrowed as she studied the array, she didn't hear the approach of the proprietress until the comfortably large woman in the flowing, flower-printed dress spoke directly behind her.

"Need a little help, honey?" the elderly woman inquired cheerfully. She spoke with a curiously pleasant mixture of Texas drawl and island lilt.

Amy smiled gratefully. "I'm looking for something to go into a salad. But I don't recognize these greens."

The woman, whom Amy assumed must be the Maggie whom Jase had mentioned when he'd left her at the front door, grinned broadly. Amy estimated she was probably in her sixties. The shining black hair, swept back in a tight bun, was liberally streaked with gray. She had flawless golden skin and large, intelligent dark eyes that reflected a limitless sense of humor about life. In her youth, Amy knew, Maggie had been a beauty. She was still a handsome woman.

"A salad, hmm? Well, you'll need some of this." She reached into the bin and scooped up a lettucelike vegetable. "And some of these good local radishes. Best radishes in the whole world, my husband always said."

"Those are radishes?" Amy asked dubiously, eyeing the plump white objects.

"Yup. Let's see. How about some of these peppers?" She stacked something vaguely resembling a green pepper into Amy's small basket. "Don't worry, this stuff's all local-grown by some friends of mine. They have gardens in their backyards, and when they get in more than they can eat, they sell it to me. Good stuff," she assured Amy cheerfully. "Now, what else you going to need?"

"Er, perhaps some fresh fish?" Amy suggested hesitantly, grateful for the help.

"Fresh fish is one thing we've always got. Come on over to the counter and take your pick. Got some beauties in this morning from another friend of mine."

"They've still got their heads on!" Amy exclaimed in dismay as she surveyed the array of whole fish lying on rapidly melting ice.

"Well, 'course they do. That's how you can tell they're fresh. See those nice shiny eyes? Good, fresh fish. Take your pick. How many you going to be feeding?"

"Uh, there will be two of us," Amy submitted carefully.

"I *knew* it!" Maggie exclaimed in tones of the greatest satisfaction. "You're Jase's woman, aren't you? The one he took home last night. You really going to fix him dinner tonight?"

Amy stared at her, astounded. "I am definitely not his 'woman.' I have no idea where you got that idea. And as for fixing him dinner tonight, I'm beginning to have a few second thoughts!"

"Hey, don't go gettin' upset now, Amy," Maggie

soothed gently. "That's your name, isn't it? Amy? Thought so. That's the way I'd heard it earlier this morning. Look, why don't you set those vegetables back in the bin for a while and have a beer with me? I could do with a break, and you're lookin' a little peaked yourself." She swept the basket out of Amy's hands and put it back in the chill bin. Then Maggie opened a nearby locker and triumphantly removed a six-pack of beer.

"Actually," Amy said, eyeing the six-pack with increasing interest, "that sounds like a good idea. It's getting quite warm, isn't it?"

"Always warm on Saint Clair," Maggie confided, popping the tops on two of the cans and handing her guest one. She took a long swallow and sighed in appreciation. "Traded the ship's cook a hell of a lot of fish for a couple of cases of beer. He wanted some fresh fish for the officers' mess."

"The cook on the Navy ship that's in the harbor?" Amy asked, sipping tentatively at her beer.

"Yup. Got a regular supply line going with cooks on various ships that dock in Saint Clair. My husband taught me how to set up supply lines, you know."

"No, I didn't. That's fascinating. Was he with the military?"

"Yup. He was here for 'bout a year during World War Two. After the war he came back to stay and we ran this store. Died two years ago and I sure miss him," Maggie went on, shaking her head.

"You met him while he was stationed here?" Amy took another sip of beer. It really tasted quite good in the heat.

"Love at first sight. My parents said he'd never come back after the war. Said he'd go home to Texas and marry a girl with his own sort of background. But I figured he was worth the risk. I loved him."

"I...I can see why your parents must have been a little worried, though," Amy ventured thoughtfully. "I mean, it certainly was a risk to let yourself fall in love with someone you might never see again."

"Women are good at that," Maggie said simply.

"Takings risks?"

"Sure. Sometimes we luck out and sometimes we don't. But the whole human race benefits when we take a risk and win."

"It does?"

"The way I figure it, a home with a lot of love and laughter is the most civilizing force at work in the world. Leave it to the men and there wouldn't be any homes. They don't know much about making a home. Takes a woman to teach 'em."

"What do you do when you get hold of a man who is, uh, uneducable?" Amy asked dryly.

"Sometimes a woman wins and sometimes she loses." Maggie downed some more of her beer and reached for another. She gave Amy a wise glance over the rim.

"And if a woman takes a risk and guesses wrong? If she winds up with a couple of kids and no man to be a proper father?"

"Most women can handle it. Like I said, we're the risk-takers. Do you think there's a single man alive in the whole world who'd take the risk of getting pregnant if the good Lord had made such a thing possible? Hell, no!"

That idea struck Amy as very insightful. "You may have a point. I never thought of it quite that way." She took another swallow of the beer.

"When my man Steve returned after the war, he had a two-year-old son waitin' for him," Maggie chuckled.

"Oh."

"I'd had a few doubts during those two years, but no regrets. I figured any way I looked at it, the risk had been worth it. I'd been in love. That's the only part a woman ought to be sure of, first."

"That she's in love?"

"Right. Now, just how did you plan to cook that fish?"

"Any way but fried." Amy made a face, remembering how everything at the local cafe seemed to come out fried. "Poaching is a good way to handle most fish," she added. "What do you think?"

"I think any way you fix that damn fish will be good for Jase. A little home cookin' and a little home lovin' are what that man's been needin' since the day he arrived on Saint Clair. And I think you're just the woman to give him both."

Amy felt the flush creep up to her cheeks. "I wish you wouldn't assume quite so much about my relationship with Jase," she managed formally.

Maggie heaved herself to her feet, eyes full of understanding laughter. "Honey, I know a sister soul when I see one! Now, come over here and I'll get you some good local herbs that will make that fish come alive."

"Not an entirely pleasant image," Amy grumbled, thinking of the bright eyes of the fish she was going to buy.

She emerged from Maggie's shop twenty minutes later with the fish carefully wrapped in butcher paper and a bag full of fresh vegetables and herbs. The sack of groceries was stuffed so full that it took both hands to carry it in front of her. The strange lettuce, along with the leaves of the radishes and the paper-swathed head of the fish, was sticking up in front of her face. She could barely see where she was going.

And it was for that very reason that she didn't get a good look at the tall, rangy, blond-haired man who was striding rapidly toward her along the busy quay. He didn't hesitate as he came abreast of her, and his hand moved quickly, dropping a crumpled wad of paper into her already overstuffed sack.

"Hey, I'm not a walking garbage bin!" Amy snapped huffily. The man didn't even turn around to apologize. "Turkey," she muttered vehemently, and continued on her way to The Serpent. The manners of some of these backwater island inhabitants were appalling. Then she remembered the hazards of crossing a San Francisco street in front of a taxi and decided that rudeness was pretty universal.

A moment later she carefully climbed the steps to The Serpent. The lazy overhead fans seemed to make some small difference in the temperature, and she was grateful for it. She had barely reached the entrance when the sack of groceries was scooped out of her hands.

"Thanks," she told a grinning Ray. "I think that fish Maggie sold me must weigh ten pounds!"

Ray looked down into the sack. "I'm drooling already. Tell me how you're going to cook the fish. I want to torture myself, and then tell me what you're going to serve with it. I can fantasize about that later on this evening."

Amy frowned and then broke into light laughter. "I give up. The whole island seems to know about my plans for dinner tonight!"

"Envy—sheer, unadulterated envy," Ray told her, setting the sack down on the bar.

"Listen, there's more than enough fish for three," Amy began easily, intending to extend an invitation.

"No, there's not," Jase interjected flatly, emerging from the booth where he had been working. "There's only enough for two, and even if there were enough for three, Ray has to work this evening."

"Oh, I see." Amy gave the unfortunate Ray an apologetic glance. Then she caught sight of the new painting hanging behind the bar. " A new one, Ray? It's beautiful," she said enthusiastically. "A tropical fantasy, hmmm?"

"It looks like a fantasy," Ray agreed, pleased by her interest, "but it really does exist. It's a grotto-like area at the other end of the island. Jase would probably love to show it to you sometime," he added slyly.

"Yeah," Jase growled. "Sometime." Then his brows drew together in a quick frown as he leaned closer to Amy for a moment. "You've been drinking!"

Amy bristled. "I didn't know there was a law against it!"

"Who the hell bought you a beer?" he muttered as Ray moved back behind the bar with a commiserating smile for Amy.

"Don't shoot, I'll confess," she retorted sardonically. "Your friend Maggie poured a can of beer down my throat while we discussed the general cowardice of your sex. Only one tiny beer. See? I can walk a perfectly straight line." She stalked dramatically across the wooden floor and spun around to confront him. "And for the record, Mr. Lassiter, I am not accountable to you for such things."

Jase bit back a retort as he studied her challenging expression. "What time will you be serving dinner?" he asked very politely.

Satisfied that she had made her point, Amy relented. She stepped across to the bar and picked up her sack of groceries. "Your presence will be required around five o'clock," she told him haughtily.

Jase looked blank. "My presence? Dinner is at five?"

"No, five is when I'll need you to behead the fish. Fresh or not, I can't bear the thought of cooking the poor thing with its head on. Those little beady eyes are so reproachful!" She marched out the door.

"Amy, wait, where are you going?"

"To put the food away!"

"I'll be home in a few minutes," Jase said quickly. "Then we can go swimming or something."

Amy didn't respond. She was already moving rapidly down the street toward Jase's home. He stood, one hand braced against the bamboo that framed the entrance to The Serpent, and watched her until she turned up the lane that led to the house. Slender and supple, he thought, remembering how she had felt underneath him the previous night. Strong-willed and intelligent. Deeply female. And she needed him.

Or was it he who needed her?

God help him if that were the case. He didn't need anything else on his list of things he wanted but couldn't have.

Men had been known to go insane out here when their lists of such items got too long.

"She's gettin' to you, boss," Ray murmured behind him, not without sympathy.

"I know."

"That's asking for trouble."

"Damn it! I *know!*" Jase gritted softly. "Take care of things for me here, Ray. I'm going home." Without glancing back, he started down the steps.

Ray shook his head in rueful acceptance of the vagaries of fate. For a man like Jase Lassiter a woman like Amy could ultimately prove more disastrous than the rum. Why couldn't she have been just another souvenir hunter? Jase handled that type without any trouble at all. Tonight's home-cooked meal might cost a hell of a lot more than his boss could afford.

In Jase's kitchen Amy began unpacking the sack of groceries, anxious to get everything into the refrigerator as soon a possible. The humidity and the heat would spoil food quickly. She was hauling out the paper-wrapped length of fish when the crumpled piece of paper that had been so rudely tossed into the sack by the passing stranger flopped out.

Amy was about to toss it into the garbage with disgust when she noticed the scrawled writing. Slowly, with a sensation of anxious dismay and excitement, she carefully unfolded the note. It was short, to the point, and there was no question about the fact that it had been meant for her.

*No. 53. North end of the dock. Bring the mask. Come alone or no deal. Dawn tomorrow.*

D.H.

Amy's hands were trembling so badly that the note nearly slipped from her fingers. Grimly she clutched it more tightly and tried to think. This was the contact. This was what she had been waiting for. Now what?

Her mind refused to clear. The only thought that stood out was that she had better hide the note. If Jase saw it he would start making all the decisions about what to do next. Amy knew him well enough to be absolutely certain that he would take charge completely.

And that might ruin everything.

Hastily she hurried down the hall to her bedroom and stuffed the note into a corner of her suitcase under a pair of Italian-designed bikini briefs. There, she thought, dusting her hands symbolically, now she could have time to think about it before deciding what to do next. She heard Jase at the front door just as she slammed the suitcase closed.

"Amy?"

"In the bedroom. I'll be right out, Jase." Damn, she thought explosively as her foot accidentally caught on the edge of the sisal matting and nearly sent her sprawling. She was going to have to be extra careful. Her nerves had suddenly shifted into high gear. The specter of her anxiety-induced clumsiness was hovering near. Amy took several deep breaths as she made her way back down the hall. She thought she had herself under control as she rounded the corner and stepped into the kitchen.

But the look she caught in Jase's eyes as she swung through the doorway was enough to halt her in her tracks. It only lasted a few seconds, but there was an aching hunger in that turquoise gaze that pierced her soul.

The realization that this man's vulnerability upset her far more than the scrawled note in her suitcase hit Amy like a tidal wave. What was happening to her out here at the end of the world?

# *Six*

"Jase," Amy said firmly a few hours later as she watched him savor a bite of succulent poached fish, "everyone on this island seems to know where I slept last night."

"On Saint Clair we keep secrets about our pasts, not about the present. This fish is fantastic, Amy. Did you poach it in wine?"

"Are you trying to tell me you bragged about what happened last night?" she demanded, bristling.

"What do you think?" He reached for another helping of salad—his third.

"I...I'd like to think you wouldn't be that juvenile about the whole thing," she got out irately. Her temper had been somewhat uncertain since she had received the note that afternoon, and she knew it. Amy decided she had just cause. Events were starting to get out of hand.

"All men are boys at heart." Jase grinned easily, but the teasing expression vanished in a split second as he saw the color leave Amy's cheeks. "Honey, don't look at me like that. I'm only joking. Of course I didn't discuss last night with the rest of the island. For God's sake, calm down. I've told you, Saint Clair is a small place."

Amy didn't feel mollified. "Jase, the situation is very uncomfortable for me. I appreciate the fact that you were only trying to help last night..."

"You're woman enough to know I wasn't exactly being altruistic," he contradicted bluntly, eyes narrowing as he studied her. "What's the matter, Amy? You've been getting more and more high-strung all evening. In another few minutes I'll be rescuing falling wineglasses again."

"It isn't amusing!"

"I know, I'm sorry. Honey, tell me what's wrong. Are you worrying about making contact with Haley? Afraid he won't show up after all and you'll have made the trip out here for nothing?"

Amy swallowed and reached for her glass of wine as she thought of the crumpled note in her suitcase. "I suppose that's part of it," she mumbled.

He nodded as if that explained her unstable mood. "How long will you wait for him to show?" he asked in a too-casual tone.

"I'm not sure." Damn it, why should she feel guilty about lying to Jase? After all, the meeting with Dirk Haley was entirely her own concern. It was the business that had brought her to Saint Clair. The relationship with Jase was strictly a secondary matter. Wasn't it? She owed him nothing, not even explanations.

"A week? Two weeks?"

"I told you, I don't know! Why, Jase? Does it matter?"

He stared at her. "Unfortunately, yes."

"What do you mean, 'unfortunately'? Have you got another tourist scheduled to arrive soon? Will I be in the way in a few days?" she demanded bitterly.

"You're really upset about what happened last night, aren't you?" he shot back wonderingly.

"Yes!" That much was the truth. Every time she rethought last night, she got upset. "I didn't come to Saint Clair to have an affair."

Jase looked down at the food on his plate. "I realize that. You didn't come here to fix me a home-cooked meal either, did you?"

"No," she sighed.

He looked up, smiling tentatively. "Amy, this is the best food I've had in so long I can't remember. If I promise not to assault you tonight, would you please stop scolding me and let me enjoy it in peace?"

Amy's mouth fell open at the outrageous request. And then, out of nowhere, the laughter bubbled up inside. It gleamed in her sea-gray eyes and curved her expressive mouth. "When it comes to the crunch, the man chooses food over sex! I have the feeling I should be insulted!"

"It was a tough choice," Jase allowed, grinning back at her.

"Thanks!"

But the mood of the evening had been lightened. And in spite of the mess in which she had found herself, Amy was glad to have the downward spiral temporarily halted. She *did* want Jase to enjoy the meal, she realized. She took a strange satisfaction in watching him savor the good home-cooked food. When dinner was over, he thanked her as if she had just furnished him with a priceless treasure.

"Think of it as a souvenir of the States," she instructed dryly as they washed the dishes and prepared to wander over to The Serpent.

His mouth crooked wryly. "Yeah, I will."

Amy scowled briefly as she rinsed the last dish. "It needn't be a once-a-decade experience," she told him briskly. "If you moved back to the States, I'm sure you could eat like this regularly."

He hesitated and then said quietly, "I decided a long time ago that there's nothing for me back there. Come on, honey, let's go. Ray will be wondering what happened to us."

"I'll take him a slice of the coconut cream pie."

"He'll be your slave forever," Jase complained.

"Sounds useful," she retorted brightly, trying not to think about his very final-sounding pronouncement on the subject of returning to the US. Why should it matter to her?

"You don't need another slave," Jase told her whimsically, reaching out to catch her face between his palms. "You've got me."

"There's something very unservile about you," she whispered, standing quite still. The physical awareness that seemed to be always there between them pulled at her more strongly, and Amy knew she should be fighting it.

"I'm trying," he promised in a husky whisper, bending his head slowly to brush her mouth with his own.

"You...you said you wouldn't assault me tonight." Amy's eyelashes flickered down as she watched his intent features through them. What did she really want from him tonight?

"A man will make a lot of rash promises when he's hungry." Jase dropped a small, warm kiss on the tip of her nose. "Amy...?"

"I think we'd better be going, Jase," she managed with an effort. She could hardly tell him there was little point in going to The Serpent this evening, that the contact she sought had been made already earlier that day. Right now The Serpent seemed a kind of haven, a place where she could put off making the crucial decision of how she would spend the night.

With a stifled groan of reluctance Jase released her. "Okay, honey. Let's go. Ray's going to be more excited about that slice of pie than he was about the stack of Victorian erotica!"

The evening passed uneventfully as Amy knew it would. She did watch for the rangy, blond-haired man's appearance, but no one resembling the stranger on the quay showed up at The Serpent. Why the secrecy? she wondered.

What in the world was so special about the mask? And what was she going to do at dawn tomorrow morning?

Long before dawn, however, another situation had to be confronted.

"Let's go home, honey," Jase said shortly after midnight, reaching for her hand with the comfortable expectation of a man who intends to go home to bed with his woman and doesn't really anticipate any problem. "It's getting late and it's obvious Haley won't show tonight."

He pushed aside his glass of rum without finishing it, and it occurred to Amy that he hadn't had as much of the potent alcohol tonight as he'd had the night before. A part of her insisted on approving the voluntary cutback. She didn't want to see Jase Lassiter fall victim to the heat and the rum of Saint Clair. On the other hand, it was highly unlikely that Jase would be a victim of anything or anyone, she told herself as she got to her feet. He didn't need her concern!

"Jase," she began with determination, "I've been thinking that there's really no reason I can't go back to the Marina Inn tonight. Whoever ransacked the place isn't likely to return. Probably just a drunk fisherman looking for some cash."

"Hush, Amy." Jase cradled her against his side, his arm snugly around her shoulders.

"Damn it, Jase, don't tell me to hush! I'm trying to explain that there's no need for me to go home with you!" Amy felt trapped and her nerves, which had quieted during the evening, came awake with that sense of restless anxiety she knew so well.

"Amy, I want you," he told her, the sherry of his voice flowing over her as he came to a halt and cupped her shoulders with his hands. His harsh, rugged face was deeply serious as he looked down at her. In the shadowy light emanating from the bar, Amy could see the need and the desire in his brilliant turquoise eyes. "I need you," he whispered simply. "Please don't fight me tonight."

"Jase, needing someone isn't enough," she tried to say, feeling helpless herself beneath the pull of that need. "Everything happened too fast for me last night. I couldn't think."

"But today you've had a chance to think, is that it? Honey, I meant what I said earlier this evening. I won't force you into my bed. I have a hunger for you that won't let up, but I won't force you."

"Oh, Jase," she groaned, feeling wretched at the evidence of his honest desire. "A relationship has to amount to more than sheer physical attraction."

"If ours did amount to more than that, we'd both be in a hell of a lot of trouble, wouldn't we?" he countered grimly. "We're from two different worlds, you and I. The best we can hope to have is a relationship based on mutual desire."

The blunt words chilled her. Amy stepped back, feeling shaky and appalled at the savage truth of what he was saying. Desperately she sought for something rational and sophisticated to say. "Yes, yes, I suppose you're quite right. All I can say is that the kind of relationship possible for us is not one I want." She turned on her heel and started down the lane that led to his house. "I'll get my suitcase and go back to the Marina Inn tonight."

"Amy, no!" The words were grouped out behind her, and an instant later Jase had caught up with her, his hand reaching out to manacle her wrist. She sensed the effort he was making to control himself before he spoke again. "All right, Amy. You win. I would give everything I owned if you would come to my bed willingly tonight, but I won't push it. But I have to insist that you stay in my home. Please understand how nervous I would be about sending you back to the inn. If you can't accept the fact that I need you and want you tonight, at least accept the fact that I'd be damned worried about you if you went back there."

She realized that it was all she could do to deny his

desire; she didn't have the strength to deny the lesser request too. "All right, Jase. I'll stay."

An hour later, as she lay alone in her own bed, listening to the rustle of the palm fronds outside her window, Amy acknowledged the depths of the quicksand in which she was getting mired.

What in the world had led her to insist on cooking Jase a decent meal tonight? She could have survived quite well on another couple of days of greasy food. The urge to feed a man properly was as strange to her as the ease with which she'd wound up in Jase's bed the previous evening. There was something uncomfortably primitive and essentially female about the action that disturbed her now on a very fundamental level.

But the two primitive reactions were only part of a growing list of inexplicable emotions, and they were all highly dangerous. Amy stirred restlessly in bed and finally tossed back the covers to pad across the floor and stand in front of the window. She wouldn't go out on the veranda tonight. Jase might still be awake, and if he sensed her presence out there, he would be sure to join her. And Amy knew exactly where that would lead.

The breeze off the ocean tasted and smelled good, she decided, as it lightly tousled the skirts of the burgundy nightgown she wore. Some aspects of paradise were very attractive, and therein lay the danger. It could be so attractive that it would sap a man's ambition and spirit. Even a man like Jase couldn't hold out forever against the enervating lure of it.

She thought about Maggie's philosophy of men and women. What would have happened to Jase if ten years ago a woman had tried to domesticate him? If his ex-wife had realized that a home without children might be quite satisfying with a man like Jase?

Amy knew she was an idiot to torture herself with such thoughts. Jase no longer seemed to be concerned with his own future. He lived in the moment, taking what became available here on Saint Clair and not asking for more. Asking for more, he had implied, would be asking for hell.

Didn't Jase realize that what he had asked of her tonight when he'd wanted her to share his bed could easily put her in a similar state? If she were to go into his room now, she would be asking for the hell of falling in love with a man who had already said the relationship was impossible.

The wrong place at the wrong time. And the wrong people into the bargain.

But the urge to give this particular man the one thing he asked of her was too overwhelming to ignore. Her eyes were wide open as she stepped through the window and onto the veranda. Open figuratively and literally. Tomorrow morning she would not be able to say she didn't know what had come over her.

At the open window of his room Amy paused, trying to make out the shadows within. The sheet that covered Jase to the waist was a white patch in the darkness, beckoning her closer. His tanned, smoothly muscled torso was visible above the white edge as she moved into the room on silent feet. Was he awake? He didn't stir as she approached.

"Jase?" His name was a near-silent whisper on her lips as she walked slowly to the edge of the bed. He didn't move. He was sprawled on the bed in an arrogant, utterly relaxed manner, his hair tousled and dark against the white pillow. He was lying on his stomach, his face turned away from her. Amy wanted to reach out and run her fingers through the heavy mahogany pelt of his hair.

Cautiously she sank down onto the edge of the bed, not quite knowing how to go about making him aware of her presence. She put out a hand and touched his broad shoulder with her fingertips.

"It's about time you got here," Jase muttered thickly. "I was going out of my head." He turned on his side with a speed that indicated he'd never been asleep at all. Flinging an arm around her waist, he tumbled her down beside him, covering her legs with one of his own as he bent his head to kiss her startled mouth.

"Ah, Jase, you're an arrogant, greedy man and I shouldn't be here," Amy breathed, her arms going around his neck as his hand found the hardening tip of her breast.

"I know, I know. But don't ask me to let you go now that you are here. I couldn't do it!" He cut off her next words by filling her mouth with his thrusting, searching tongue as if he had been starving for the taste of her.

She felt the weight of him crushing her against the bed, and the satiny skirts of her nightgown seemed to willingly wrap the rough length of his thigh.

His hard, naked frame pressed down on her, excitingly masculine against her softness. The words he groaned into her mouth and then into her ear were thick with desire and the hunger she had sensed in him.

She was dimly aware that he was trying to hold himself in check tonight. He was trying to make the pace of their lovemaking a slow and voluptuous one. The fact that the action seemed to strain his willpower thrilled her. Amy realized that she, too, was feeling somewhat greedy and arrogant. She wanted Jase to be compelled by her, to be enthralled by her, to be overwhelmed. There was a primitive delight in knowing she had a spark of the primeval feminine power. One of the greatest gifts Jase gave her in the throes of their lovemaking was a sense of that power.

Strong, exquisitely sensitive hands traveled down her body, removing the beautiful gown with care. When she was free of it, Jase raised himself on his elbow to gaze down at her. Amy lay slightly curved against him, her hair flowing back over his arm, one leg arched at the knee. She splayed her fingertips against his chest, glorying in the feel of him.

Then he shifted, eyes gleaming in the shadows, and knelt between her legs.

"Jase?"

"I want to learn every inch of you, sweetheart." Leaning

forward, he braced himself on his arms and began dropping slow, heated kisses across her stomach. Amy sighed with mounting desire. His teasing, exciting mouth moved lower, taking tiny erotic nips along her thigh until she thought she would go crazy with the level of her own passion. Time ceased to flow in its normal pattern. The night glowed.

Jase's fingers found the ultrasensitive core of her first, and then she gasped his name aloud as he replaced his hand with his lips.

"Jase, oh, Jase!"

She began to twist beneath him, her passion suddenly an ungovernable thing. Desperately she clung to his shoulders, trying to pull him up along her body and into her softness. Reluctantly he allowed himself to be urged into the final embrace, but when Amy felt the heavy, waiting hardness of him at the gate of her femininity, she knew he was more than ready himself.

Still he forced her to accept his deliberately slow pace, filling her with leisurely power. When she tried to arch her hips and draw him into her more quickly, he slipped a hand beneath her buttocks and held her still.

"We're not going to do *everything* your way tonight," he taunted with provocative roughness.

"You're a beast," she whispered, digging her nails into the tanned skin of his shoulders.

"But you'll tame me eventually, won't you, Beauty?"

The damp, satiny warmth of her received him eagerly, even though his hardness seemed to fill her completely. As ready as she was for him, Jase's body managed to shock her, just as it had the night before. Would it always be like this? No, not always. She could not have Jase for always. Amy frantically pushed the haunting thought aside and clutched at the man above her.

Then all flickering thoughts of the future vanished as Jase established a pulsing, incredibly erotic rhythm. Amy gave herself up to it completely, twining her legs around his hips and her arms around his neck.

"Amy, sweet Amy! My God, woman, you consume me!"

When the rippling, shivering culmination of her passion took her, Amy could barely breath under the force of it. She was aware of Jase locking her to him and knew he was taking a fierce satisfaction in her own pleasure. Then he was surging more quickly against her, and the soft explosion caught him up before it had released Amy.

A long time later Jase stirred beside her, turquoise eyes narrowed in lazy satisfaction. "I'm not going to ask why you came in here tonight, Amy. But thank you. I needed you."

She lay quietly in the circle of his arms as he drifted off to sleep. They had both been right every step of the way. She shouldn't have sought out his bed. She probably should never have come to Saint Clair. Heaven help her, she was in love with a man she could never have. Jase Lassiter had given up on commitments and civilization and everything else that she herself valued.

Amy was aware of the time crawling past on the ceiling of the room. The pattern of the night shadows changed slowly but inevitably. She dozed at odd intervals, aware of the heavy, utterly satiated sleep of the man beside her.

It wasn't until the first vague light of dawn began to lighten the sky outside the window that Amy remembered the note in her suitcase.

The real business of her visit to Saint Clair had to be dealt with this morning, she realized suddenly. And Jase could not be a part of it.

Slowly, with infinite care and a kind of sadness, Amy slipped out of his bed. At the window she turned to glance once more at the sleeping form of the man who had made such passionate love to her during the night. Soon she would have to say good-bye to him. After she had finished her task here on the island, there would be no reason to stay. Her souvenir of the visit to Saint Clair would be the memories of Jase. The knowledge tugged at her heart.

Picking up the nightgown she had worn to his room, Amy hurried out onto the veranda and into her own bedroom. There she dressed in haste, pulling on jeans and a boat-neck T-shirt. Then she grabbed the roomy handbag she had brought with her to Saint Clair and let herself out of Jase's house.

Dawn on Saint Clair was the one pleasantly cool time of day. The air was not yet heavy with humidity, which would intensify later. The sky was wonderfully, brilliantly, clear. The ocean seemed more peaceful at this hour, too, and there were few people moving around the docks. Sometime during the night the Navy ship had left.

She strode along the quay, the leather strap of the large purse hanging over her shoulder. No one paid her any attention as she made her way to number fifty-three. The small building was a dilapidated old wooden structure, probably a storage locker. Scanning the area, Amy searched anxiously for the tall man with the blond hair.

For the first time she was able to put the memories of the night out of her head long enough to feel nervous. She really knew nothing about Dirk Haley except that he claimed to have been a friend of Ty's. There was no reason to doubt that part from the evidence he had provided in his short cables.

But why the secrecy of their meeting? Why had he been so insistent on having her come alone? She was glad she had taken the one precaution of not bringing the mask with her. Dirk Haley would provide her with the truth first, and then she would decide whether or not to hand over the mask.

He came around the corner of the old building with a silent suddenness that startled her. For a second they gazed at each other assessingly. Amy felt her pulse racing anxiously as she took in the blond hair, hard gray eyes and rangy build of the man in front of her. He was dressed in jeans and an old battered leather flight jacket. That caught her attention for some reason. It was pleasantly cool this morning, but not cool enough to require a leather jacket. He was a man who might have been handsome in a boyish way if it hadn't been for the coldness of his gray eyes. There was a hard, sullen slant to his mouth that vanished instantly when he smiled with a too-easy charm. It reminded her of Ty.

"Amy Shannon?" he drawled in a cool, faint southern accent. The gray eyes flickered over her and lingered on the large purse hanging from her shoulder.

"That's right. You're Dirk Haley?" She found herself wanting to step back from him and resisted the urge. She must keep cool and remain poised and self-confident. She was here to bargain.

"At your service. Bring the mask?"

"We have some talking to do first," she reminded him steadily, instinctively clutching the bag more tightly. He saw the small gesture and nodded once. "The mask rightfully belongs to Ty's son. I want to know why it's so valuable to you and I want to know where Ty is today."

Dirk Haley leaned against the wall of the old storage building and regarded her coolly. "Why didn't his wife come?"

"That's not important. I'm here in her place."

He nodded again. "I figured out who you were by listening to some bar gossip. You must be a hot little thing. Not on the island more than a day and already making it with one of the locals. Picked an important one too. Lassiter's a force to be reckoned with on Saint Clair, I'm told. For what that's worth!" Haley added with a dry chuckle. "Big fish in a small pond. But then, it doesn't take much to be important out here. Just some money and a slightly dangerous reputation. I'm going to make myself into a similar pillar of the community, but I think I'll pick a different island. Something tells me Saint Clair isn't big enough for Lassiter and me both. That's okay. There are a lot of islands left."

Amy experienced a frisson of genuine fear as she

watched his face. Ignoring the insult, she asked softly, "Is the mask going to buy you that status, Mr. Haley?"

"Yes, Miss Shannon," he retorted in mockingly polite tones, "the mask is going to buy me that. Also a new name, a new passport and a few other essentials of life out here. I'm afraid I really can't allow you to take it back to Ty's kid."

"What's so important about it?" she persisted, her fingers whitening as she held on to the strap of her bag for dear life. Good Lord, what had she gotten into? Jase would be furious. Ludicrous as it was, that was the main thought that seemed to be dominating her mind at that moment.

What the hell was she doing standing out here all alone on a deserted dock, dealing with a man who was turning out to be very much more dangerous than she'd expected? She could almost hear Jase demanding the answer to that question now. Thank heaven she hadn't brought the mask with her. It might very well turn out to be her ticket out of this uneasy situation.

"I think you'd be happier not knowing why I want that damned mask," Haley drawled. "Something tells me you might not approve."

"I want to know about it and I want to know about Ty!" She managed to keep her voice cool, injecting a touch of self-confident arrogance into it.

"Murdock is dead," Haley told her carelessly.

Amy drew a deep breath. "Are you certain?"

The slow, menacing smile he gave her was frightening. "Very sure."

Something clicked in her head and Amy stared at him, wide-eyed. "Did you kill him?"

He straightened away from the wall with a studied casualness that made her take a step backward. Real fear coursed through her veins now. "No, I didn't kill him, but I'm not particularly sorry he's dead. He presented something of a problem."

"What problem?"

"You are full of questions, aren't you, Miss Shannon?"

"I want to know for certain what happened to Ty Murdock!"

"He's dead, I told you! You want proof?" Amy flinched automatically as he reached inside the flight jacket. But what he withdrew was only a US passport. With an arched brow he handed it to her.

Hand shaking, Amy reached for the passport and flipped it open. It was Ty's. The sardonic, handsome face smiled up at her, the familiar dark eyes full of mocking charm. A boy who had never really grown into a man. A boy who had wanted to go on playing boyish games. One of those games must have caused his death. She could think of no other reason for Dirk Haley to have Ty's passport. Amy felt no real emotion as she gazed down at the picture of her nephew's father, only a kind of sadness for the infant son waiting back in California. Her sister had been right. It was best to tell Craig that his father had intended to return someday, that the man had been killed on some exotic adventure. Who knows, Amy thought, perhaps it is the truth.

Slowly she raised her head and handed the passport back to Haley.

"You can keep it," he told her. "I only brought it along because it was the one proof I had of his death. I couldn't very well bring his head in a sack, could I?"

"You're a very cold-blooded man, Mr. Haley," Amy noted distantly.

"I'm a survivor. Unlike Murdock. Now, let's have that mask." He reached for the purse slung over her shoulder, but Amy stepped back once more, gathering her courage. "I'm afraid I don't have it with me."

"The hell you don't!" he ground out savagely. "Where is it?"

"It's hidden. I meant what I said. That mask is my nephew's only legacy from his father. I want to know the true value of it before I decide what to do with it."

"You never did intend to hand it over, did you?" he

hissed with a perception that surprised her. "You lying little bitch! You only struck the bargain because you wanted me to tell you why the mask is important!"

"If...if you can prove you have a right to the mask, I'm willing to turn it over," Amy protested, very scared. "Otherwise I think it should go to Craig."

The gun appeared in his hand as if out of nowhere. One moment Haley's palm was empty, the next it flashed with the lethal metal nose of a revolver that was pointed at her.

The shock of it was stunning. Amy stood rooted to the spot for an instant, and then blindly she whirled around, as if to run. It was pointless to run from a bullet, her embattled brain warned her, but there was nothing else to do. Perhaps he wouldn't kill her until he had the mask!

In any event she never got beyond the edge of the old storage locker. Haley's palm clamped over her mouth and the muzzle of the gun was cold and hard near her ear.

"You don't really think I'm going to let some lying, scheming female cheat me out of what I want, now do you?" he gritted, compelling her to move back against him. "That mask is mine and I'm going to get it without playing any more of your stupid games! Get in the boat."

Amy tried to go limp in his grasp, but he held her easily, nearly tossing her headlong into a large cruiser tied up alongside the quay. She opened her mouth to scream as he temporarily released her, but he lifted the gun threateningly.

"I won't kill you, at least not yet," he muttered, "but I'll use this thing as a club if you don't keep still. Unless you want to spend the next couple of hours unconscious, you'd better behave."

Haley never took his eyes off her as he loosened the boat from its moorings. Then he shoved her into the cabin and locked the door from the outside. Amy watched helplessly as the engines started and the relative safety of Saint Clair slipped out of reach.

# Seven

Amy sat huddled in the cabin as Dirk Haley guided the large cruiser to the far end of Saint Clair. She watched the coastline as it drifted past outside the window and wondered dully what Haley intended. A quick search of the sparsely furnished cabin had yielded nothing useful, not even a kitchen knife. What next?

Saint Clair was virtually uninhabited outside of its single town, so it was not surprising that when Haley finally anchored the boat in a cove, Amy saw no sign of life ashore. When he unlocked the cabin door, she swung around to glare at him, struggling to conceal her fear.

"Looks like we're going to have to do this the hard way," he muttered, shifting the gun to his left hand and reaching for her arm. "Come on."

"Killing me isn't going to do you any good." Her mouth was suddenly dry as he yanked her out of the cabin and up on deck. "I'm your only link to that mask!" She had to keep calm, keep bargaining. It was her only hope.

"You're my link to the mask, all right, but not in the

way you think. You'd better hope you made a good impression on Lassiter while you were in his bed."

"What are you talking about?" she managed, a new fear taking shape in the pit of her stomach. Her hands were trembling and she stumbled awkwardly as he pulled her across the deck to the small ladder that hung over the side.

"You're my key to getting that mask, but I'm not going to send you back for it. Lassiter knows where it is, too, doesn't he? I thought so," Haley added in brutal satisfaction as he saw the betraying tension in her expression. "Well, we're going to find out if he thinks enough of his new playmate to trade that mask for her. Your best hope is that he doesn't know what the thing's worth. Because if he does, I can tell you right now he won't give it up just to get your warm body back in his bed. He'll be able to buy all the warm bodies he needs if he learns the value of that thing. Come on! Quit stalling. Get into the dinghy."

Amy nearly fell going over the side into the quietly rocking little boat that trailed the cruiser. She'd never felt so clumsy in her life. What would Haley do if her nervous awkwardness resulted in the dinghy tipping over? Or should she try to tip it deliberately?

That feeble plan was crushed almost at once.

"Put your hands behind your back," Haley growled roughly, reaching for a coil of rope in the bottom of the small boat. With a few savage twists he immobilized her wrists. Any thought of trying to deliberately overturn the dinghy died. She would probably drown herself if she tried such a thing, now that her hands were tied. Even if she could make it to shore, it wasn't likely she would do so alone. Haley would be right behind her.

In deadly silence he rowed them both to shore. There Haley forced her quickly out of the boat and into the shallow water. Amy waded toward the sliver of sandy beach, her sandals heavy and uncomfortable as they became waterlogged.

"I want to make sure I can find you when I get back,"

Haley drawled coldly, pushing her toward the trunk of a palm tree. There he lashed her uncomfortably, hand and foot, securing her to the tree. "Don't run off now, will you? It's going to be interesting to see what Lassiter does. Is he going to be smart enough to figure out that the mask is worth a hell of a lot more than you are? Better hope not."

Amy watched in dismay as Dirk Haley rowed himself back to the cruiser, climbed aboard and started the engines. In a few minutes the big boat was leaving the cove, heading back toward town. Amy sagged back against the rough palm trunk, trying desperately to think.

How well did she really know Jase Lassiter? What *would* he do when confronted with the ultimatum Haley intended to deliver? She had only met the man a couple of days ago, and now her fate was in his hands. The hands of a man who had willingly separated himself from civilization and its code of behavior years ago.

It would be obvious to Jase when Haley contacted him that the mask must be worth a great deal. Would he try to keep it for himself?

The sun had risen rapidly in the sky, and the heat of the day was beginning to make itself felt. Amy wasted a lot of energy struggling with her bonds before deciding that Dirk Haley had tied them with the skill of an expert. How had Ty Murdock gotten mixed up with such a man? She could well believe Ty had gone looking for adventure and a life of excitement, but until now she hadn't really believed he could have become an outlaw. There was no doubt, however, that Haley was operating far outside the law. If he had been a friend of Ty's, that meant Murdock had fallen quite low before his search for excitement had finally killed him.

She thought of her nephew and her sister. Melissa had fabricated tales that she could tell her son about his father when the child was old enough to ask questions. Now Amy fabricated tales that she could tell her sister. If she got out of this mess alive, did she really want to go back to Melissa with the full story of what had become of Ty Murdock? What good would it do Melissa to know that the man she had loved had become, in all probability, a renegade?

If she got out of this alive.

Amy tried to concentrate on deep breathing to calm herself. There was no doubt that murder would come easily to Haley. Ty's death had obviously meant little to him—had simply solved a problem. What made that damn mask so valuable?

The palm to which she had been tied was one of a small grove which straggled down to the tiny beach. Flanking the grove and extending out into the sea to form a natural harbor were huge arms of chunky lava, frozen forever into craggy, bizarre formations. Occasionally jets of water spouted into the air, seeming to come from the joining of the arms on dry land. The plumes, she guessed, were evidence of natural caverns and tunnels which had their openings below the water line. With the ebb and flow of the waves, water was forced into them to erupt at the opposite end, on the surface of the rocks.

When the distant sound of a boat's engine caught her attention, a new tide of fear washed through her. Haley was on his way back to the cove. Had he confronted Jase? What would be her fate now?

She waited, every fiber of her being tight with tension as Haley anchored the cruiser once more in the cove. He came over the side and rowed to shore in the dinghy, his gun clearly visible now that he'd taken off the flight jacket.

"Curious, are you?" he mocked as he loosened her bonds and dragged her back toward the boat. "So am I. We'll soon find out how much Lassiter thinks of you. Or how much he knows about that mask!"

"What did you do?" she whispered as he forced her back into the dinghy.

"Sent a message through one of the men working at the dock."

"What kind of message?"

"Just that I had something of his that I would be willing to exchange for something he had in his possession. I wrote down a brief description of how to find this cove and added that if he didn't come alone, I would be forced to destroy the, er, object in my possession."

Amy sucked in her breath as he casually explained that he would kill her. "Did you do this sort of thing a lot with Ty?" she asked bitterly.

"Ty and I had some good times together before we parted company. Made a lot of money and spent it."

"Did he...did he ever mention his wife or his son?" For the life of her she didn't know what made her ask that question.

"Just once. The night he told me about the mask and how he had sent it back to the States for safekeeping. Said it was going to be his pension plan," Haley told her, forcing her up the boat ladder ahead of him.

"He meant to return someday?" she pressed, needing to know the answer for Melissa's sake.

"How the hell should I know? He was an unpredictable bastard," Haley said unconcernedly. "Sit down in that deck chair. I want you very visible when Lassiter arrives. Don't want him doing anything rash, like trying to sink the boat with a few shots below the waterline. He'll be a bit more cautious if he can see you're aboard."

Would Jase show? Amy glanced toward the horizon, her eye sweeping the entrance to the cove. Yes, she thought suddenly. He'll come for me. She knew that with perfect clarity. For some inexplicable reason she had trusted him from the beginning. As Maggie had said, women were the real risk-takers. Who else but a woman would be crazy enough to instinctively trust someone she had known for such a short time? Amy shook her head in wonder. It was a miracle the human race had survived, with half its members willing to take such crazy chances with the other half. Or perhaps that was the reason the race *had* survived!

Haley lapsed into a brooding, uncommunicative silence.

He fixed himself a cup of coffee but didn't offer her one as she sat, hands still tied behind her back, on the deck of the boat. The sun was beating down on her now, and Amy was aware of the perspiration soaking the T-shirt she wore. God, it was hot out here on the ocean in the full glare of the sun. She was going to be burned. Which wouldn't matter a whole lot if she didn't get out of this alive, she reminded herself gloomily.

Where was Jase?

She sensed Haley's increasing tension and it fed her own. If there was one thing worse than confronting a man with a gun, it was confronting a nervous man with a gun. She sincerely hoped he didn't become as clumsy as she did when she got nervous!

The muted roar of the launch was audible before it came into view around the jutting shoreline. Haley heard it at once, emerging from the shadow of the cabin to watch along with Amy as the craft cruised slowly into the calm water of the cove. Jase was at the helm and he was alone. There could be no doubt about that. The boat had no concealing cabin in which someone else might be hiding.

"Well, I'll be damned. The fool decided to play it straight," Haley muttered in triumphant relief. For the first time Amy realized just how uncertain the man had been about what Jase would do. Probably worrying that the other man would behave as he himself would have done in a similar situation, Amy thought disgustedly. There was no doubt that Dirk Haley wouldn't have valued a woman's life above possession of that mask. She could have told him Jase was different.

She would have put her money on Jase any day. She loved him.

The engines of the motor launch shut off a moment later, though it was still some distance away.

"Amy, are you all right?" Jase called.

From where she was sitting she could see only that his face was set in grim, unreadable lines.

"Answer him," Haley snapped, prodding her shoulder with the gun.

"Yes. Yes, Jase, I'm all right." Her voice was weak, even to her own ears, but Jase seemed to hear her.

"Did you bring the mask?" Haley shouted.

For the first time Jase, who had been standing on the right side of the launch, lifted his right arm. In his hand was the end of a length of rope, and dangling at the other end of the rope was the mask. Tied to it was a heavy-looking metal weight. The mask swung lazily just above the surface of the water.

"I've got it. But as you can see, the only thing keeping it safe is my grip on the rope. The water's quite deep over here, Haley. You'd need diving gear and a lot of time to find it on the bottom if this rope slipped out of my hand. And it will slip out of my hand if you hurt Amy or try to take a potshot at me."

Haley swore a short, violent oath. "I'm willing to deal, Lassiter. You can have the woman. All I want is the mask."

"You can have it," Jase assured him. "But it goes to the bottom if anything happens to Amy."

"Cruise closer and I'll let her step into your boat as you hand me the mask," Haley instructed quickly.

Jase's mouth curved disdainfully, "I'm not quite that stupid, Haley. As soon as you have the mask, you'll shoot us both. I get the uneasy feeling you're not the type to be comfortable at the thought of having left witnesses behind."

"You're not in much of a bargaining position, Lassiter! I'll kill her if you don't hand over that mask and you know it."

"I know it. I also know the mask means more to you than anything else in the immediate vicinity. I've got an alternate suggestion." Jase waited coolly for the other man's response.

"Let's hear it."

"Put Amy over the side. Let her swim to shore. When

she's safe, I'll cruise past your boat and hand you the mask. You'll still have me to shoot if you don't like the way the trade goes."

"Are you armed?" Haley demanded after a pause.

"No."

"Prove it." Haley waited grimly.

Slowly, never letting go of the dangling mask, Jase peeled off the tan shirt he was wearing. A moment later he stood naked from the waist up, wearing only a pair of snug-fitting khaki slacks. It was obvious he wasn't concealing a gun.

Haley considered the situation, and Amy sensed that his tension was increasing. She kept still, not daring to distract him. "All right, Lassiter, you've got a deal."

Amy leaped to her feet. "No, Jase! He'll kill you."

Haley grabbed at her arm, yanking her back against him. "Shut up," he hissed angrily.

"Amy, do as he says. Go over the side and swim to shore," Jase called hurriedly.

"But, Jase...!"

"Amy!" Jase's voice was suddenly full of the heavy authority it had held when he had broken up the fight in his bar. "I'm telling you to go over the side and swim to shore. No arguments. Move, woman!"

She fell silent, staring across the expanse of water, her eyes wide with mute appeal. He was ordering her to follow the plan of action he'd worked out. Jase was not a stupid man. Perhaps he knew what he was doing. She felt Haley tearing impatiently at the rope that bound her wrists. A moment later she was free. He pushed her viciously.

"Go on, get out of here. I don't want to wait around any longer than I have to, damn it! Swim to shore."

With one last helpless glance at Jase's hard, unyielding expression, Amy shakily swung her leg over the side of the boat and dropped into the water. The pleasant coolness was a welcome relief from the heat of the blazing sun, but she wasn't particularly grateful for it. All she could think about as she obediently struck out for shore was that it was her fault Jase was in such terrible danger. What a fool she had been to think she could handle the unknown quantity of Dirk Haley.

A few minutes later her feet found the sandy bottom and she waded ashore, the wet clothing dragging at her limbs. Dripping wet, she turned to view the scene on the water.

As soon as she looked in his direction, Jase waved her into the palm grove to her right. He wanted her out of target range, she realized. But what about him?

He must have some plan, she told herself over and over again as she trotted obediently into the grove. Surely he won't just let himself get shot after he hands over the mask. She hurried into the cover of the palms.

The shot rang out the moment she moved into the grove. Amy whirled, horrified, to stare in the direction of the two boats. "Oh, my God! Jase!" He was nowhere in sight.

She could see Dirk Haley's figure poised at the stern of the cruiser, the barrel of his gun swinging back and forth as he scanned the water. Even as Amy watched, he fired again and again into the sea.

Jase must have deliberately gone overboard, Amy thought frantically. Had he hoped to swim underwater to shore? Haley was certain to spot him as he came out of the sea. Jase would be a perfect target as he waded ashore. Or was he trying to hold his breath and fool Haley into thinking he'd been killed?

The only other alternative that Amy could imagine was that Jase actually had been killed. Perhaps Haley had hit him just as Jase had gone over the side. "No," she whispered, refusing to accept that possibility. No. She couldn't bear that thought.

Again Haley fired into the water and then spun around, his gaze searching rapidly for her on the beach. She saw the wild, infuriated expression on his face just as he raised the gun and pointed it in her direction. Could he see her through the cover of the palms? She glanced toward the craggy lava arm to her right.

Instinct alone sent her diving behind the shelter of the rocky outcropping. An instant later two shots pinged off the rock, and Amy closed her eyes, crouching.

"Amy!"

Jase's voice brought her eyes open in a hurry. "Jase! My God! How did you get here?" she breathed, fascinated by the sight of him, half naked and soaking wet. He was about five yards away from her and he seemed to have emerged from the middle of the craggy arm of land that framed that side of the cove. From the boat Haley wouldn't yet be able to see him. Another shot hit the wall of rock behind her. "I thought you were in the water. I was afraid—" She broke off, unable to even say the words aloud.

"I know this island a hell of a lot better than Haley," Jase got out tightly as he crawled quickly toward her. "There's an undersea cavern that opens down below the waterline at the edge of the cove. The other end opens over there." He nodded with his chin toward a stretch of rock, confirming her earlier guess. "I've swum here a lot."

Amy could see nothing, but she could vaguely hear the echo of water rushing into the bottom of the cave.

"This island is all volcanic and there are a lot of odd formations like that around here." He drew himself into a crouching position beside her, keeping out of sight. "Are you okay?"

"Yes. Oh, Jase, I'm so sorry. I made such a mess of things," she wailed.

"You sure as hell did," he agreed, showing a marked lack of sympathy. "And we're not out of it yet. Haley's madder than a wet hen."

"That's putting it mildly," she breathed as another shot struck the rock. "What did you do with the mask?"

"Dropped it overboard when I jumped out of the boat," he told her carelessly. "Which means we've got a problem. Haley didn't get the mask, but he's got two witnesses to a kidnapping and assault charge. Even out here in the backwater islands we don't look on attempted murder as a joke.'' Another shot chipped off a sliver of rock and sent it whizzing past Amy's head. ''Come on, we've got to get out of here.''

Without waiting for her acquiescence, Jase pulled her after him as he led the way across the rough volcanic rock. ''Stay low.''

On her hands and knees Amy did as instructed, trying to ignore what the rough surface was doing to both portions of her anatomy. If they had to travel much distance in this style, her palms were going to be in shreds, she thought ruefully.

''He's stopped shooting,'' Amy observed a few minutes later as Jase reached the end of the volcanic outcropping and dropped lightly down onto the sandy beach on the far side. He reached up to help her.

''That's probably because he's busy rowing himself to shore,'' Jase explained grimly, catching her fingers and turning them over to look at her badly scratched palms. ''Damn! Look at your hands.''

She snatched her fingers away. ''I'm sure yours aren't in any better condition. We can compare our dishwater hands together later. What are we going to do now?'' She glanced worriedly back over her shoulder but could see nothing. The tumble of volcanic rock shielded them from Dirk Haley.

''What any sensible person does when dealing with an armed gunman: We run.'' Grabbing her wrist, Jase suited action to words, pulling her across the sand and into the tangle of palm trees and ferns beyond.

''You think he's coming after us?'' she panted, trying not to stumble as they pelted through the undergrowth. Overhead several angry birds screeched their disapproval of the activity on the ground.

''I haven't heard him start the boat's engines. So yes, I think we have to assume the worst,'' Jase told her dryly.

"Maybe...maybe he doesn't know you made it to shore," Amy suggested in a hopeful tone.

"Maybe." Jase sounded skeptical. "He'll figure out there are still two of us soon enough, though. We're leaving a path a mile wide."

Crushed ferns and broken leaves were indeed marking their wake. Amy cast a despairing glance behind her and then concentrated on saving her energy. Already she was getting short of breath. Just when she was beginning to think she couldn't go much farther, the distant sound of pursuit began.

"The birds," Jase muttered, glancing back over his shoulder in the direction they had come.

The birds, which had screeched so disapprovingly when they had plunged into the jungle, were once again setting up a raucous protest. Haley must have found the point at which his prey had started inland.

"Jase," Amy pleaded, swinging around to face him honestly, "I don't think I can go much farther. Maybe it would be better if I tried to hide. You could keep going without me...." Even as she stood there, gasping for breath, Amy could feel her knees trembling. "I'll only hold you back."

Instead of either a plea to keep on trying or a reluctant agreement that she might be right, Amy got a narrow-eyed, savagely intimidating expression in response. Jase's turquoise eyes burned brilliantly and threateningly. "You will keep running until I say you can stop. Is that clear? You were stupid enough to get yourself into this mess, so we have to assume you're probably not bright enough to get yourself out. Therefore you will obey orders. Run, Amy, or I will take a belt to your backside when this is all over, I swear it."

Fear and intimidation, Amy discovered, were underrated motivators. She was amazed at the renewed energy she felt as Jase turned around and yanked her after him, plunging deeper into the jungle growth. She supposed ultimately she would simply collapse, but in the meantime her legs kept moving. The only thing that made it possible for her to go as far as she did was the fact that the undergrowth was really too thick for an outright dash. Several times they had to slow as the ferns and greenery became more lush.

"Are...are we just running blindly?" she finally managed to gasp out as the pace slowed once again. "Or do you have a destination in mind?" she added with sarcastic emphasis. She still hadn't forgiven Jase for his threat, effective as it had been.

He flicked her a faintly amused glance. "I have a destination in mind. But we need to get there with a little time to spare. Come on, let's get moving."

"Oh, God," she groaned, but she grabbed for air and started moving as quickly as possible after him. The sound of pursuit in the distance sent a spurt of adrenaline through her. "Why doesn't he just give up," she mumbled, "take the opportunity to escape in the boat?"

"Because he knows what I'll do to him when I eventually find him," Jase retorted bluntly. "He knows his best bet is to make sure I'm dead."

"Oh." Amy decided she didn't have breath enough to ask him exactly what he would do to Dirk Haley.

The jungle began to thicken around them. Huge ferns the size of small trees arched overhead, and gigantic tropical blossoms occasionally hit Amy in the face. If the situation hadn't been so desperate, she would have been entranced by the lush greenery around her.

"Just a little farther, Amy."

She didn't respond. She didn't have breath enough left to answer. Then the faint sound of rushing water caught her attention. A few moments later Jase pulled her through a natural gate of tall, waving ferns and into a scene that could have been created by an artist trying to paint a seductive vision of a tropical island paradise. In fact, Amy thought suddenly, it had been painted by such an artist. This was the place Ray had depicted in his latest painting.

As Jase came to a halt, Amy stared, gasping for breath

and trying to take in the incredibly lush spectacle. At the far end of the jungle glade a wall of water cascaded down, veiling the shadowy entrance to a huge rock grotto. A wide pool captured the downpour of the waterfall. All around, the foliage grew with a luxuriance that seemed surreal.

"Jase, it's fantastic," Amy whispered, panting.

"It's also a dead end," he returned practically. "Which is something Haley should realize as soon as he sets foot inside the entrance. He'll think he has us cornered."

"Then why are we here?" she demanded quizzically, looking up at him.

"Because we're going to try to turn the whole place into a trap. It's our only chance, Amy." He released her arm to reach down and begin rolling up the wet cuff of his khaki trousers. As Amy watched in amazement, he revealed a long length of ultrathin nylon rope wound up his calf to the knee. Thrust between the coils of the rope was a wicked-looking knife.

"I thought you told Haley you were unarmed," she remarked dryly.

"I lied."

"That's funny," she managed with a weak grin, still drawing in great gulps of air. "I trust you implicitly."

He gave her a short, level glance as he removed the nylon rope and lowered the cuff of his trousers. "You can. Haley shouldn't. But then, I'm sure he doesn't."

"Sounds fair enough to me. Now what?"

"Now we set a trap and hope Haley is so anxious to get us that he'll step into it." Jase was already coiling the nylon rope in a strange fashion, forming an elaborate knot that secured the wide loop at the bottom.

"You're going to rope him like a calf?" she asked in disbelief.

"Not quite. I never had any experience as a cowboy. I'd probably miss!" he retorted, laying the loop of the rope out at the entrance to the clearing. "But some of the islanders have developed their own methods for catching two-footed game.''

''You think he'll come in through the same entrance we did?'' Amy asked dubiously.

''He won't have much choice. There's no other way into the grotto, and as soon as he sees that there's a cave behind the waterfall, he's going to think we're hiding in it—I hope.'' The last two words were spoken in an almost inaudible mutter as Jase strung an end of the rope into a thicket of ferns and fastened it to a small palm trunk. Then he walked across the mossy entrance and tugged at the other end of the rope.

''Where are you going to be, Jase?'' Amy demanded suddenly as she realized that he intended to activate the trap from the concealment of the shrubbery.

''Here, behind these ferns. I can use this rock as a partial blind. You're going to be over there in that thicket beside the waterfall. I don't want you hiding in the grotto itself, because it's too obvious. The first place Haley will look if something goes wrong here at the entrance is inside the cave.''

''But, Jase, you'll be within five feet of him when he comes through that bunch of ferns. If he sees you, he'll have you at point-blank range.''

''Let's hope I'm good at looking like a part of the landscape,'' he growled. ''Now listen, Amy. If I don't get him up here, I think he'll head straight for the grotto. As soon as he goes behind the waterfall to find you, make a dash for the exit, understand? Run and keep on running. That grotto extends quite a distance, and with any luck he'll waste so much time searching it that you'll have a chance.''

''I won't leave you behind,'' she insisted stubbornly, furious that he should even suggest such a thing.

''Why not? You did this morning, didn't you?'' he shot back cruelly.

Amy went white, unbearably hurt that he should misconstrue the situation deliberately. Wordlessly she stared at him, her eyes full of pain.

"Oh, hell, I didn't mean that the way it sounded," he groaned. "Go on, get over into that thicket. Bury yourself as deep as you can." The distant sound of disturbed birds grew closer. "One way or another this is going to be over pretty damn quick. *Move,* Amy!"

There was nothing to argue about. Amy spun around and did as ordered. She scrambled toward the dense foliage to one side of the grotto entrance.

"Go through the water so there won't be any footprints around the edge to lead him to you," Jase called softly after her.

Obediently she stepped into the bubbling pool and waded toward her destination, sticking close to the edge. She could see that toward the center the water was very deep. At the far end she turned to glance back at Jase. He was already out of sight. For a moment she was tempted to run back to his side and take her chances there. The only thing that stopped her was the knowledge that Jase would be furious. With a sigh she edged her way deeply into the mass of green that formed a massive wall beside the grotto. As soon as she had penetrated a couple of feet, she realized that there was a real wall of rock behind the heavy undergrowth. Jase was right. They were in a dead-end canyon. The rock wall extended on either side toward the entrance, where Jase was concealed.

The rush of the waterfall was almost deafening this close. She had a glimpse of the black yawning grotto beyond and was glad that Jase had decided they shouldn't try to use it as a hiding place. It seemed dark and eerie. She'd rather take her chances in the open.

The rising clamor of birds was canceled out by the roar of the falling water, so Amy didn't have any warning a few minutes later when Dirk Haley suddenly appeared just outside the entrance of the tropical canyon. She was crouched low, peering intently in that direction, and was startled when his trouser leg came into her line of vision. She could see little of him because of the depths of her own concealment, but it was obvious he was still beyond the range of the loop trap Jase had set.

Oh, Lord, she thought helplessly, if Haley saw Jase first, there would be no chance at all for the man she loved. He would be a sitting duck at that range. Silently she tried to talk Haley into the clearing. It was obvious he was hesitating, trying to assess the situation.

"Come on, Haley," she whispered, as if trying to exert her will over him. "Another couple of steps. That's it."

The bit of trouser leg in her field of vision shifted cautiously. Amy thought the man must be searching the canyon, perhaps sensing the trap. What was needed, she realized suddenly, was a little push. Something to convince him it was worth his while to walk toward the grotto. Why was he suddenly being so cautious? He must suspect something. They mustn't lose him now!

If Haley decided that they were in the grotto, he might decide to outwait them. How long could she and Jase stay huddled silently in their respective niches?

"Lassiter!"

The birds renewed their scolding as Haley called Jase's name.

"Lassiter, you and the woman haven't got a chance."

But Haley didn't move into the trap. Damn it, Amy thought desperately, this is all my fault. Any second now Haley would decide to try outwaiting his quarry, or perhaps he would catch a glimpse of Jase in hiding. Jase was so close to the other man! All it would take would be a breeze catching the concealing foliage or a bird landing on a branch and making it sway.

It was the thought of Jase's imminent danger that made up Amy's mind. Without giving herself time to think, she leaped to her feet and dashed through the waterfall and into the dark grotto. For a few vital seconds she presented a target Haley couldn't resist.

He fired once, more out of reflex than anything else, and then he raced forward, straight into the trap Jase had set.

It was Amy's natural clumsiness that saved her life. Her foot struck a small protrusion as she ran through the pounding water. The jolt sent her into a stumbling spill. She wound up flat on her stomach as Haley's bullet whistled over her head and struck a far corner of the cave. For a long moment she lay where she had fallen, grateful for the first time in her life for her physical awkwardness.

Haley's scream of startled rage, penetrating even through the noise of the waterfall, made her scramble back to her feet. Bracing herself with one hand against the clammy rock of the grotto, she tried to peer through the cascading water. When she could see nothing, she dared inch back out the entrance.

The battle taking place on the floor of the canyon was the most violent spectacle she had ever seen. It was far different from the brawl the drunken sailors had waged in The Serpent. This one, she thought in horror, came under the heading of "Life or Death."

It was obvious Jase had caught one of Haley's ankles in the loop of hidden rope and jerked the other man off his feet. Then he must have leaped from hiding to take advantage of the one chance that would be available.

The two men flailed viciously at each other on the ground. Amy's pulse pounded and her mouth was dry with the shock of the battle, but she made herself run toward the pair. Somewhere on the scene there was still a gun to be reckoned with.

She saw the weapon within inches of Haley's scrabbling hand. The flash of the knife in Jase's fingers registered simultaneously on Amy's consciousness. But Haley was strong, managing to hold Jase temporarily at bay as he tried for the gun.

Then she had it, scooping up the heavy weight of the cold metal in her palm and instantly stepping back out of reach. When Haley saw his chance at the weapon disappear, he tried for Jase's throat instead.

But Jase, who was half underneath the other man, twisted his weight to one side. When Haley automatically shifted to compensate for the change, Jase rolled over rapidly, pinning him. An instant later he held the point of the knife at the base of Haley's neck.

"Move and I'll slit your throat," Jase snarled.

Haley lay still, his chest heaving with the effort he had been exerting. In sullen fury he regarded the man who held the knife. Apparently he believed the threat of chilled rage in Jase's brilliant turquoise eyes.

Amy also remained quite still, momentarily immobilized by the violence she had witnessed. The male of the species, she decided half hysterically, had a streak of savagery that rivaled in sheer primitiveness the female's primeval propensity for risk-taking.

Here, in the tropical forest, civilization suddenly seemed very far removed.

# *Eight*

"What are we going to do with him?" Amy shouted above the roar of the motor launch engines. She glanced disgustedly at the stern of the small craft, where Dirk Haley crouched sullenly, securely bound. He had said almost nothing during the trek back to the beach, but Amy had the feeling he'd remained alert to even the slightest possibility of escape.

"We'll dump him in Cowper's lap," Jase told her, concentrating on guiding the launch out of the cove. "He can figure out what to do with him."

"Cowper?" Amy frowned and then remembered. "Oh, yes. The local government man you once threatened me with."

Jase's gaze slid sideways to focus on her innocent expression. "I never threatened you with Cowper," Jase growled. She could barely hear him above the engine sound.

"Sure you did," she retorted breezily, leaning complacently against the bulkhead. "You were going to make me go to him the night my room was searched, remember? If I didn't go home with you, I was going to have to explain the whole situation to Fred Cowper. I call that a threat."

"Given the way things turned out, I should have gone through with the idea. We'd probably both be sleeping peacefully in bed right now if we'd turned the whole mess over to the proper authorities."

Amy chose to ignore that bit of hindsight. "It must have been Haley who searched my room that night."

Haley flashed her an icy glance from the stern and then continued his disinterested perusal of the horizon.

"Maybe Cowper or someone higher up can find out what's so important about that damn mask." Jase guided the little craft just beyond the breakers, hugging the shoreline as close as possible. "We can get it off the bottom of that cove with a tank of air."

"That will be exciting," Amy said enthusiastically, receiving another sidelong glance from the man at the helm. "I want to go with you when you retrieve it."

"You're really feeling your oats now that this is all over, aren't you?" Jase drawled coolly. "Have you already forgotten how close you came to getting us both killed?"

That sobered Amy at once. Impulsively she touched his arm, eyes instantly full of apology. "Oh, Jase, of course I haven't forgotten. I'm so sorry for getting you involved in all this. I had no right to do that. It was my problem and I should have kept innocent bystanders out of the situation."

"Oh, for God's sake!" he growled in deep annoyance. "I didn't mean you shouldn't have involved me! You know damn well I meant to be involved, right from the beginning! What I meant was that you had no business not keeping me fully involved and informed! Why in God's name didn't you tell me about that note from him?" He gave a short nod toward Haley in the rear.

"Because I knew you probably wouldn't have let me meet him alone," Amy tried to explain, keeping her tone rational. It was becoming increasingly obvious that Jase was at the end of his patience.

"Full marks for second-guessing me on that issue," he gritted. "You're damn right I wouldn't have let you meet him alone. We wouldn't have had to go through this morning's exercise if I'd known what was happening."

"But, Jase, I had to find out what I could about that mask! That's what I came to Saint Clair to do. It was the whole reason for my trip!"

"And if you'd gotten yourself killed? What good would that have done, Amy? There wouldn't have been any answers at all in that event, would there?"

Amy bristled. "I didn't know it was going to be this dangerous, Jase. For heaven's sake! I'm not an idiot!"

"I'll form my own opinion on that subject!" he countered rudely.

Thoroughly annoyed in her own right now, Amy shot him a scorching glance. "If you think so little of my intelligence then we can only conclude your own intelligence level must be rather low. Only one idiot would be dumb enough to take another idiot..." She trailed off quickly, furious with herself for having let her temper get the better of her. It was the strain, she decided bleakly. She'd been under too much strain.

"Only one idiot would be dumb enough to take another idiot to bed?" Jase concluded for her coolly. "You may be right."

Amy swallowed, knowing she was in the wrong. "Jase, I really am sorry," she said. It was difficult to get the right apologetic tone into her voice when she was trying to make herself heard above the engine.'

"Save it," he ordered brusquely. "You can tell me how sorry you are after we get back to town."

Amy lapsed into a silence that was almost as sullen as their captive's. It didn't seem to bother Jase at all. He appeared to have his mind on other matters. Amy studied his hard profile. I've fallen in love with him, she thought wretchedly. He can yell at me all he wants and I will try to yell back, but ultimately I'll wind up trying to placate and pacify. He had saved her life that morning. In a way that action seemed to reinforce the claim his physical possession had staked. She shifted uneasily, bracing herself with both hands on the frame of the launch's windshield.

It was the first time she had admitted to herself that she felt such a claim, and Amy found it unnerving, even frightening. For her own sake she had to think of her relationship with Jase Lassiter as an affair, doomed to end when she left Saint Clair. It would be hard enough to recover from the pain of loving a man she could not have. But love, at least, was a civilized emotion. Given time and a great deal of distance, Amy was realistic enough to know she would eventually be able to put the memories of Jase into a far corner of her mind where they could fade quietly. Time and distance could cure an emotion as gentle and civilized as love.

This other feeling, however, this sensation of being claimed, of being bound, was anything but civilized. How long would this more primitive emotion last once she was off Saint Clair? A lifetime? Amy shivered under the heat of the tropical sun.

The quay was a welcoming sight a few minutes later. Already bustling with the business of the day, it looked pleasantly normal to Amy. There were questions and a lot of interested glances as Jase tied the launch up and urged his prisoner ashore.

"Been fishing already this morning, Lassiter?" asked a man on a neighboring boat. He eyed Haley.

"Just taking the tourists on a tour of the island," Jase retorted dryly.

"Anything to help build the tourist trade," the other man chuckled, sheathing a fishing knife he'd been wielding. "Want some help?"

"I think I can handle it. Thanks. Seen Cowper this morning?"

"Believe it or not, he's actually in his office today. Saw him half an hour ago when I went for breakfast."

"That's a switch!" Jase muttered, prodding Haley ahead of him. "Let's go, Amy. Fred's going to have a lot of questions for both of us."

Obediently she walked beside him, her clothing dried but stiff and uncomfortable from the seawater dunking. Haley stared straight ahead, impassive. He didn't try any further resistance as Jase marched him up the street toward a small, weathered building not far from the Marina Inn. There had once been a sign stenciled on the front door, Amy saw, but all that was left of the identifying marks were the top half of a capital *U* and the bottom half of an *S*.

Jase shoved open the door of the office, revealing an old government gray-metal desk piled high with aging papers, a broken swivel chair and a wall full of filing cabinets. There was also an ancient teletype machine in the corner, clicking away merrily. A man of about fifty, portly and with hair the color of his desk, hunched over the machine, reading the message that was coming across. He glanced up as Jase entered with Haley and Amy.

"Jase! What the hell are you doing here? Who have you got there?"

"Morning, Fred. I've brought you a little work, I'm afraid."

"It never rains but it pours," Fred Cowper quoted ruefully, tearing off the paper that had emerged from the teletype machine. "Haven't had a thing to do in three months, you know. Nothing at all since I had to go down to the dock and pick up that fool trying to ship unsprayed fruit off the island. Then this morning I find all kinds of excitement waiting for me. You know how I hate excitement," he added with a gloomy sigh.

"Sorry about that." Jase smiled wryly. "I've had a little too much of it myself this morning. Meet Dirk Haley." He pushed Haley farther into the room. "Kidnapper extraordinaire. Attempted murder, assault with a deadly weapon and a few other things I'm sure we can think of between us. A general all-around nuisance.''

''Well, I'll be damned.'' Fred Cowper sank squeakily into the old swivel chair and stared up at Haley as if fascinated. ''I'll be damned,'' he repeated and glanced down at the torn sheet of teletype paper in his hand. ''Dirk Haley, a.k.a. Roger Henrick, Joe Mellon and Harry Dickson. Six foot one inch, blond, blue eyes, one hundred seventy-five pounds.'' He glanced up, smiling benignly at Jase.''*That* Dirk Haley, do you suppose?''

''Have I just spent the past couple of hours doing your job for nothing?'' Jase demanded, one brow arched.

''Why not? Nothing is a good description of what the government pays me. You might as well work for the same minimum wage. Tell me how you spent your morning, pal.'' He listened attentively as Jase gave a quick summary of the events, and then Fred nodded contentedly. ''You have just done me one hell of a favor. You have made it possible for me to go fishing again this afternoon. And here I was thinking I'd have to spend the whole day watching folks come and go down at the dock.''

''You going to tell us about this little bit of coincidence? Jase asked curiously as Cowper surged out of his chair to take charge of the prisoner.

The older man was about to answer as he shoved Haley into a rusty-looking cell at the far end of the room when the door to the old office swung open once more and another man stood on the threshold.

''I think I'll just let him explain,'' Fred Cowper said cheerfully as he slammed the door of the small cell shut. ''Allow me to make introductions. This here is...''

''Introductions aren't really necessary, are they, Amy?'' the newcomer said easily as he lounged against the doorjamb with easy male insouciance.

The color drained from Amy's cheeks as she stared at the man in front of her. The sardonic, masculine twist of the mouth, the faintly amused dark-brown eyes, the handsome, tanned features and the lean, tall frame all formed an entirely too-familiar picture. There was an infant back in San Francisco who would one day look a lot like this.

"Hello, Ty," she said quietly. "I was under the impression you were dead." Instinctively, not even bothering to question her motive, Amy took a small step that brought her a little closer to Jase. She was vaguely aware of the sudden, intense stillness of the man beside her. Then Jase's arm came out to rest possessively across her shoulders. He waited, saying nothing, but never taking his eyes off Ty Murdock.

"I'm afraid the report was a little exaggerated." Ty smiled, glancing derisively at the prisoner. Haley was staring, almost as stunned as Amy, at the newcomer. "Surprised to see me, Dirk? Didn't I tell you once that the only way to survive out here is to stay unpredictable? You, I'm afraid, are very, very predictable. Couldn't resist the mask, could you?"

"You always were a bastard, Murdock," Haley muttered, and then sank down on the small cot, apparently bored with the whole proceeding.

"I think," Jase finally said very softly, "that I'd like some explanations."

"You're not the only one," Fred Cowper murmured coolly. "Okay, Murdock, I've verified your credentials, I've received the description of the wanted man and I have delivered said man into your care. With a little help from my friends, of course. Let's hear it. What's this all about?" There was a thread of cold steel beneath the pleasant drawl, and it occurred to Amy that Fred Cowper has probably done a few other things in his time than pick up people who were trying to ship unsprayed fruit off the island. Another man with an interesting past who had washed up on Saint Clair.

Ty shrugged, folding his arms across his chest. His eyes were on Amy as he talked. "Haley and I used to work together. We both had the same employer: Uncle Sam. But a few months ago Dirk decided to go into business for himself. He wanted me to go renegade with him and I played along for a while. Then he started getting suspicious of me.'' Ty flicked an amused glance at the man in the cell. ''Or did you just decide that you didn't want to split the take two ways, Dirk? You always were a greedy SOB.'' The dark eyes went back to Amy's taut face. ''At any rate he pulled a disappearing act in Hong Kong after kindly arranging to have me taken permanently off his trail. But I managed to miss the appointment he had set up for me with a few street thugs. Unfortunately, by the time I had realized who had set me up and why, Haley had skipped. We didn't have any idea where to start looking for him. A man can get almost as lost as he wants out here in the Pacific.''

''Unless he gets too greedy,'' Fred Cowper drawled.

Ty grinned briefly. ''Exactly. I had told him about the mask I'd sent to San Francisco. At the time I had some vague idea of using the lure of the mask as a trap, something my superiors could watch in case anything unexpected happened to me. It was to be bait to draw Haley out into the open in case we lost him at some point. Well, needless to day, I survived the unexpected.'' He broke off to allow the full impact of the understatement to be felt.

Typical Ty Murdock, Amy thought fleetingly: ultramacho, ultracool. Ty wanted everyone to understand that he'd almost been killed but had survived by his own ingenuity and physical ability. Her hand clenched into an impatient ball at her side.

''Haley had disappeared,'' Murdock went on, drawing out the story for his attentive listeners. ''All we could do was watch and wait. One of the people the department kept an eye on was my ex-wife in San Francisco. We knew Haley wouldn't be able to get into the States without us knowing it, so if he decided to go after the mask, he'd have to get Melissa to send it to him. Or he'd have to convince her to bring it to him wherever he was.''

"But it wasn't Melissa who came out to the South Pacific with the mask," Amy interjected stiffly. "It was me."

Ty inclined his head, mouth turning upward at one corner in a gesture that Amy remembered well. "It was you. But the guy assigned to watch Melissa didn't know to keep an eye on you, too, so we lost track of the situation for a couple of days. By the time someone in San Francisco had figured out that you'd left for Saint Clair and probably had the mask with you, things were getting out of hand."

"When did you realize it was Amy who had decided to bring the mask to Haley?" Jase asked very quietly.

"Yesterday," Ty admitted. "I got here this morning."

"As you said," Jase said dryly, "things were already getting out of hand by the time you folks figured out what was happening." His turquoise eyes went cold and hard. "Amy damned near got killed this morning, Murdock."

Murdock's dark gaze slid away from Jase's implacable face. He gave Amy one of his easy, charming grins. "Sounds like you've had a little excitement in your life lately, Amy. How did you like it? An interesting change for you, hmmm?"

Before Amy could even think of a reply, Jase exploded beside her. He was across the room, slamming Ty against the wall in one swift movement that left Amy and Fred Cowper blinking in amazement.

"Around here, Murdock," Jase ground out as he pinned the other man to the wall, "we don't call it a 'little excitement' when a woman gets kidnapped and shot at. We call it attempted murder. We may be a bit rustic here in the islands, but we do draw the line in a few matters. As far as I'm concerned, you're partly to blame for what almost happened to Amy this morning. Keep that in mind when you start making little jokes, okay? I'm not feeling in a humorous mood." He released his victim and stalked over to Amy, who looked up at him anxiously.

"Jase?" She didn't even glance at Murdock, who was smiling laconically as he straightened his shirt.

"Let's go," Jase ordered brusquely. "I'm taking you home." He took her arm and started for the door, ignoring the other two men.

"Just a second, Jase," Fred Cowper interrupted gently but with an air of command. "We'll need to pick up Haley's cruiser this afternoon and take a look at the scene. You'll have to show us where that particular cove is located."

Jase nodded once. "I'll be back after I take Amy home," he muttered.

"Hey, one more thing," Murdock called after the pair as they went through the door. "What about the mask? Where did it end up?"

"Under about thirty feet of water," Jase told him bluntly. "You'll have a lot of fun looking for it, I'm sure. It'll put some excitement in your life." He slammed the old door behind him.

A heavy silence reigned between Amy and Jase as they walked back toward the old sea captain's home. Amy didn't know what her companion was thinking about, but she knew what her own overriding impression of the morning was. In a soft, sad voice she said it aloud. "He didn't even ask about Craig. His own son. He didn't even ask about him."

Jase roused himself from his own private thoughts. "You knew what kind of father he was, Amy. You found out a long time ago, remember?"

"Yes," she whispered, thinking of little Craig and Melissa. What would she tell them? "Maybe I'll tell them he's dead anyway."

Jase drew a deep breath. "We'll worry about it later," he instructed forcefully. "Right now I want to fix those hands of yours. They're a mess from crawling on that lava. Then you should get some rest."

"I'm not tired," she replied automatically.

"You have to be exhausted."

"Why do I have to be exhausted? We ran quite a ways,

but I've had a chance to recover from that. I'll just wash off these cuts on my hands and maybe take a shower. Then I'll change clothes and I'll be as good as new."

Jase yanked her to a stop in the middle of the street, a fierce expression marking his brows and tightening the lines at the corners of his mouth. "You're exhausted," he ground out. "You will take a nap this afternoon while I show Cowper where that cove is. Do I make myself clear?"

She stared up at him, not fully comprehending the vehemence in his voice. Instinct, however, told her this wasn't the time to argue. "Yes, Jase," she said meekly.

He eyed her for a minute as if not certain he could trust the meekness, then he tugged her along toward the house. "We'll see to your hands and then I'll go back to Cowper's office. Might as well get the rest of the formalities over with. The sooner everything is cleaned up, the sooner Murdock will be leaving Saint Clair."

Amy thought about that last sentence all during the somewhat painful first aid on her palms. Jase wanted Murdock off the island. Jase had made quite a scene in Cowper's office, threatening Ty and half accusing him of being responsible for the mess in which Amy had found herself. Jase didn't like Ty Murdock at all.

Which was rather surprising in a way, Amy decided objectively. Actually the two men shared a number of traits and a similar background. They were both graduates of a harsh school. Living in the rough corners of the world had left its mark on both of them. Neither sought the solace and comfort of civilization as she knew it, and neither would have been at home in it.

Then Maggie's words came back to her, reminding her that men weren't naturally at home anywhere. They needed to be domesticated by women. But domestication hadn't taken with Ty Murdock. He had returned to the wild, seeking freedom and adventure.

Was it too late for a woman to try her hand at domesticating Jase?

Probably. He himself was convinced that his present life was the only one in which he could now fit. Amy looked at his red-brown head bent attentively over her palm as he swabbed the jagged scratches. A rush of warm, gentle love and affection went through her. It had nothing at all to do with physical desire, but it was somehow part of the same spectrum of emotion.

"Jase, you saved my life today. I don't know how to thank you."

He glanced up sharply. "You can thank me by never getting yourself into such a stupid situation again."

Amy's brow arched as some of the warm affection she was feeling gave way to a natural defensiveness. "So gallant," she murmured.

"I'm not interested in being gallant, I'm interested in not having to rescue you from another mess like the one you were in this morning." he muttered, swiping a little roughly at the last of her scratches.

"Ouch!"

Instantly he cradled her palm within his own. When his eyes met hers the turquoise gaze was filled with an intensity that astonished her. "Amy, I got the living hell scared out of me today. Please don't ever do that to me again!"

Amy relented, lifting her wounded palm to the side of his face. "No, Jase. Never again. I'm sorry I caused you so much trouble."

"Amy..." His teeth snapped together almost audibly in silent frustration. He caught her face between his hands and pulled her to him for a quick, hard kiss. Then he lifted his head slightly. "Stop apologizing, for God's sake, and go take your shower. Let's just be glad it's all over."

She nodded, sliding off the stool where she had been perched while he had tended her hands. "What would we have done today if Haley hadn't stepped into your trap?" she asked rhetorically, shaking her head as she moved toward the bathroom.

"I don't even want to think about it," Jase confided

gruffly, watching her move through the bathroom door. "If he hadn't lost his patience and run toward the grotto when he did...!"

Amy froze, one hand on the doorjamb. She didn't turn around. She didn't *dare* turn around. For the first time she realized that Jase hadn't known she'd made a target out of herself back there in the jungle. She hadn't been in his line of sight, she thought, chewing on her lip. He hadn't known what had made Dirk Haley rush forward into the tropical glen.

Some things, she decided, unsticking herself from the doorjamb, were better left unexplained. Very carefully she shut the bathroom door behind her and began undressing. She felt as if she'd had as close a call just then as she'd had out in the jungle. Her mouth twitched ruefully as she turned on the shower and stepped beneath it. What would Jase have said if he'd known the full truth? It didn't bear contemplation. Zealously, Amy began scrubbing the jungle mud and dried seawater off her body.

When Jase left the house half an hour later, Amy waited until she heard the front door close and then bounced out of bed, searching for her clothing. As if anyone could nap after the sort of experience she'd been through, she thought disgustedly as she pulled on clean jeans and a striped dolman-sleeved blouse.

But she hadn't felt up to arguing with Jase when he'd ordered her to bed, so Amy had done as instructed, crawling between the sheets without demur. Her obedience had seemed to please Jase, and Amy decided rather humorously that it was because he hadn't had much experience with that sort of feminine behavior. He couldn't, for example, tell when it was feigned, apparently.

From the veranda she watched him disappear into Cowper's office down the street. Some time later the three men left the quay in Jase's launch, heading back to the cove that had been the scene of the action. Even from a distance, Amy could tell that Jase was ignoring Ty Murdock as much as possible. He really didn't like the man. Well, that made two of them, she thought with a sigh as she turned back to the window that led into her bedroom. She didn't much like Ty Murdock either.

She had been right two years ago not to take a risk on him. It was sad that Melissa's instincts hadn't been sharper.

Superficially, Amy decided as she stuffed some money into her back pocket and started down the street toward Maggie's grocery shop, Jase and Ty had a lot in common. And although she could list those superficial similarities quite readily, Amy knew the resemblance was deceptive.

The two men were very dissimilar in a fundamental way. Amy couldn't yet put a name to the elemental difference between the two men, but she sensed it as surely as she sensed the heat of the Saint Clair sun.

"Good afternoon, Maggie. Got any more strange vegetables for me to try today?" Amy asked chattily as she stepped inside the relative coolness of the little grocery store.

Maggie raised her neat head from the year-old fashion magazine she was reading and grinned. "What do you think about this new tuxedo look? This magazine says it's going to be all the rage this season."

Amy stepped over to the counter and glanced down at it. "I think that refers to last season, Maggie. The tuxedo look has come and gone back in California."

"Oh, well, we're always a few years behind out here on Saint Clair." Maggie tossed the magazine aside and got to her feet, going to the locker where she kept the beer. "Have one?" She held up a can invitingly.

"Sounds good." Amy glanced down a row of canned goods. "Got any reasonably fresh baking powder? I'm thinking of making biscuits tonight."

"You're going to drive Jase crazy." Maggie chuckled, popping the tops on the cans. "That man won't know what hit him. Here." She handed over a can. "What do you suppose is going to happen to him when you leave, Amy?"

Amy frowned. "I'm not exactly changing his whole life by feeding him biscuits and honey, Maggie. After I'm gone he'll sit in The Serpent and wait for the next unsuspecting female tourist!" The image was very depressing.

Maggie shrugged and swallowed a large sip of beer. "Think you'll ever come back?"

"To Saint Clair? I doubt it." Amy's voice trailed off wistfully and she tried to focus her attention on the aisles of dusty cans and packages. "Got any honey?"

"Yup. Friend of mine has a couple of hives at the other end of the island. Keeps me supplied. Heard you got yourself into a bit of trouble this morning. What happened?"

"It's a long story. Jase came and got me out of the mess, though," Amy explained with a tiny smile.

"So I heard. Who's the fellow Cowper's got locked up?"

"He's named Dirk Haley."

"Ah," Maggie nodded wisely. "That's the one Jase was telling folks to be on the lookout for."

Amy glanced up in astonishment. "He was?" She hadn't known Jase had made inquiries.

"Yeah, but no one realized Haley was the guy on the cruiser. Must have been using a different name. Hardly surprising out here. Lots of folks do. Glad you're okay, though."

"I'm fine," Amy agreed weakly.

"So who's the other stranger? The one who left on Jase's launch along with Fred Cowper?"

"He's the man who came to pick up Haley," Amy said slowly. "Apparently the US government's been looking for him for a while."

She spent the next couple of hours explaining the complicated story to a very interested Maggie, who stored up all the details so that they could, in turn, be related to other interested people. Amy didn't worry at all that she might be giving away information the authorities would rather not have had spread around. After all, Murdock and his cronies had been quite willing to use Melissa and the mask as bait for their trap. They deserved to have the whole story become public knowledge. It was little enough retribution for what had almost happened to Melissa. It could so easily have been her sister who had come out to Saint Clair and nearly gotten herself killed, Amy thought grimly. Besides, it didn't matter what information she gave out. Nothing this juicy would have stayed secret on Saint Clair for long.

"That was pretty smart of Jase to take along the rope and knife," Maggie laughed, enjoying the tale enormously. "But it fits. Don't see him walking blindly into a mess like that without taking a few precautions."

"That grotto area where he set up the trap is fantastic, Maggie. If Saint Clair ever does develop its tourist trade, you can definitely list it as one of the local sights." Amy sipped her beer thoughtfully, remembering the fantasy world of the tropical grotto.

"I have some nice memories of that place, myself," Maggie murmured softly. "My husband and I used to go there now and then. Not sure I'd want a bunch of tourists stomping through it."

Amy laughed and set down her empty beer can, reaching for the sack of groceries Maggie had packed. "That's the problem with a tourist economy, Maggie: You've got to expect a certain amount of stomping around. Thanks for the beer. I'll see you later."

"How long are you staying on the island?" Maggie called after her.

Amy's smile faded as she faced the question she had been pushing aside since she had begun to realize that her business on Saint Clair was finished. "I don't know, Maggie. I don't have any reason to stay too much longer."

"Don't you?" Maggie smiled benignly. "Think about it while you're whipping up biscuits for Jase tonight."

Amy hurried away, not wanting to think about that at all. She was trying so hard not to think about it, in fact, that she almost collided with Ty Murdock, who stood directly in her path on the quay.

"Whoa, Amy, where are you going in such a hurry?" he drawled softly, steadying her with two hands on her shoulders.

"Ty!" She stepped back in surprise, not liking the touch of his fingers. "Are you and Fred and Jase through already?"

He nodded toward the side of the quay where Haley's blue and white oceangoing cruiser was tied up. "Everything's taken care of except the small matter of getting that mask back."

"Where's Jase?"

"I left him and Fred back at Cowper's office." Ty lifted one shoulder dismissively. "I had other things to do. I wanted to talk to you, Amy, and I figured it was going to be tough getting past Lassiter to do it. So I came looking on my own. Someone said they'd seen you heading toward the grocery store down there."

"I see. We don't really have much to talk about, do we, Ty?" she responded carefully.

"Don't we? You came a hell of a long way because of that mask, honey," he said in a persuasive tone. "I couldn't believe it when I learned that it was you and not Melissa who had left for Saint Clair. Why, honey? What brought you out here to Saint Clair looking for answers? Were you looking for me?"

"Ty, I really don't know what to say," Amy began a little desperately. "It's all so complicated now and I..."

He took the sack of groceries out of her arms. "Come on, honey. Let me buy you a drink. It's the least I can do for old time's sake, hmmm? But I think we'll go into another bar besides Lassiter's. I can do without him hovering over my shoulder, glaring at me every time I look at you."

Helplessly, reminding herself that answers about Ty Murdock were indeed the real reason she had come so many thousands of miles across the Pacific, Amy allowed herself to be led inside the shaded confines of a dockside tavern named Cromwell's.

On the veranda of The Serpent, a little more than a block away, Jase stood with his hands shoved into the back pockets of his khaki slacks and watched the pair disappear into the other bar. He stood very still, realizing he didn't dare take his hands out of his pockets because his fingers were trembling.

Finally, his self-control stretched to the breaking point, he turned on his heel and stalked into The Serpent, heading for his usual seat at the end of the bar. Ray didn't ask any questions immediately. Unasked, he opened a new bottle of rum and poured a drink, sliding it over in front of his boss.

"Did you find her?" he finally inquired, leaning one elbow on the top of the bar.

"Yeah, I found her. She was just coming out of Maggie's with a load of groceries."

"Then why do you look as if you just lost your best friend?" Ray flicked at a piece of lemon peel that had landed on the bar.

"Because Murdock intercepted her and took her into Cromwell's for a drink and God knows what else," Jase rasped, reaching for his glass of rum.

"So? She bought the groceries for your dinner, not his," Ray pointed out, concealing a smile. He'd never seen Jase like this over a woman. "I mean, she couldn't have bought the groceries for his dinner because he's staying at the Marina Inn and they don't have kitchens there. You're the one with the kitchen."

"Is this an example of the kind of analysis I can expect from a shrink without a diploma hanging behind the bar?" Jase gritted sarcastically.

"Sorry," Ray said instantly, realizing he'd trespassed the invisible boundary. "Are you really worried, Jase?"

"He's the one she came several thousand miles to find

out about. I just happened to be someone who got in her way.''

Ray lit a cigarette while he considered that. ''You saved her life,'' he said finally.

''I don't want her gratitude!'' Jase inhaled deeply, closing his eyes briefly. ''Besides, this afternoon I discovered just how I saved her life. We made Haley tell us his version of the story, and do you know what he happened to mention in passing?'' Jase glared at his employee.

''Haven't the foggiest.''

''He casually stated that as he was standing at the entrance to the grotto area he saw Amy dash from where I'd hidden her, straight through the waterfall. *That's* what made him run forward into the trap I'd set,'' Jase growled. ''It was sheer luck he didn't hit her when he fired into the cave. Sheer, blind, tourist luck! And she must have made the dash on purpose, to draw him out for me.''

Ray winced at the savage tone. ''She's okay, Jase,'' he tried to say reassuringly. ''You got her out of the mess.''

''She's going to be in a much worse situation when I get my hands on her. I've never felt like beating a woman before,'' Jase added wonderingly, somewhat shocked by the depths of his own feelings on the subject.

''Is that why you went looking for her when you got back with Cowper a few minutes ago? You were planning on beating her?'' Ray grinned.

''Let's just say I thought I'd express my views on the matter in no uncertain terms. She had no business risking her neck like that. Haley would have wandered into the trap, given a few more minutes. He couldn't have resisted searching that grotto. He had to know we were in there.''

''Amy's not as good as you are at guessing what people like Haley will do, Jase. She was probably afraid for you, afraid he wouldn't step into the rope.'' He eyed his boss's knuckles as they closed around the glass of rum. They were turning white with the force of Jase's grip. ''If you want a little free advice from your underpaid analyst...''

"What advice?" Jase growled.

"Beating her at this particular juncture may not be your smartest move." Ray smiled. "It might make Murdock look very pleasant by comparison!"

Jase swore something short, harsh and derived from the barnyard. Slowly he unwound his fingers from the rum glass and got to his feet.

"Where are you going?" Ray demanded.

"I'm going to rescue my dinner." Jase headed for the exit of The Serpent and started down the street toward Cromwell's.

# *Nine*

Three minutes after he'd seated her at a table and ordered drinks, Amy had decided what was motivating Ty Murdock. She glanced down at the glass of plain tonic water she'd ordered and then lifted a speculative gaze to his face.

"This drink isn't for old times' sake at all, is it, Ty? You're indulging yourself in still another fantasy, aren't you?"

He leaned back in his chair, every inch the tough, cynical, faintly amused playboy. "Running into you again after all this time does have a certain element of fantasy about it."

Amy shifted impatiently, automatically taking in some of the waterfront atmosphere in which Cromwell's specialized. She didn't like this place as much as The Serpent. Cromwell's catered to the same assorted crowd of visiting sailors, fishermen, locals and a few brave tourists, but the place seemed alien to Amy. It made her uneasy. Then she remembered that that was how she'd felt the first night at The Serpent. It helped to know the proprietor, she thought wryly. And the bartender. Here she felt very much alone in a totally masculine haunt. The man behind the bar had nodded curiously at her when she'd entered with Ty, however, so perhaps he knew who she was. It seemed that most everyone on the island did now.

"Ty, I'm talking about a different kind of fantasy than you are, and I think you know it. For you the real pleasure in seeing me is the kick your ego is getting at the idea that I came all this way on a romantic goose chase. You think I traveled several thousand miles across the Pacific to find out what had happened to a man I couldn't forget, right?"

"Didn't you?" He half smiled, his dark eyes moving over her with the beginning traces of desire. "You're here, Amy, and that says a lot."

"Ty, this is going to come as something of a shock to you, but I didn't come to Saint Clair to satisfy my own personal curiosity about you. I came to find out the truth about what happened to Craig's father. Your son is a year old now, Ty. Doesn't that interest you at all?"

"Craig was a mistake," he said quietly.

"One Melissa ended up paying for. You sure as hell didn't stick around to support her, either emotionally or financially! You got off scot-free, didn't you? Walked away from all the responsibilities. No worrying about doctor's fees or mowing the lawn or changing diapers or wondering if Craig will do all right in school!"

"Amy, I wasn't cut out for that kind of life and you know it," he shot back harshly.

"Oh, I know it. I knew it two years ago. That's why I wouldn't marry you when you asked me! I just wish my sister had had the same realization."

"So do I, Amy, so do I," Ty said wearily, lifting his drink. "Do you want to know what really happened between Melissa and me? I'll tell you. After you turned me down she was very sweet. Soft and feminine and loving. All the things you wouldn't be for me. Is it so very strange that I found her, well, comforting?"

"You mean she was balm for your wounded ego and you used her to try to teach me a lesson for having the gall to turn down your proposal of marriage," Amy said tightly. "Talk about behaving like a boy! Ty, you're so proud of your male prowess, but the truth is you've never really become a man. You handle the real responsibilities of life like a boy. You walk away from them!"

He sat forward sharply, reaching across the table to snag her wrist in one large hand. The dark eyes glittered. For a moment Ty Murdock reminded Amy very much of Dirk Haley. She felt her nerves go into high gear, shudders of fear sparking through her.

"Look, Amy," he ground out, "what happened between Melissa and me was just one of those things. You were always the important one to me. We could have had something special, you and I. If you hadn't been so damned cautious—if you'd let yourself love me the way Melissa did—everything would have been different!"

"Nothing would have been different and you know it. If I hadn't been so damned *cautious,* I'd have wound up just like Melissa. No man is ever going to put me in that position, Ty Murdock. Especially not one who would do what you've done to Melissa!"

His mouth tightened. "You're really not interested in my side of the mess, are you? Do you know how it feels to wake up one morning and find yourself trapped with a wife and a baby on the way? To see your whole life going down the tubes? Life is too short to waste it stranded in a suburb. I need to be free. I need to be constantly testing myself, finding out how good I am at surviving. My job is like a chess game with an element of real danger thrown in to spice it up. Nothing Melissa offered could match the lifestyle I've got now."

"I know," Amy said quietly. "She was offering you a home. Don't you see, Ty? Things would have been the same if I had accepted your proposal of marriage. Because a home is all I had to offer too."

"We could have worked something out."

Amy shook her head. "No. If I had given you the son you claimed you wanted, I would have wound up raising him alone. Which is exactly the way Melissa is raising the son you gave her. He's a beautiful baby, Ty. He looks a lot like you."

"Don't try to pull those particular strings, Amy," he snapped. "It won't work. I could never go back and stay. It's better for both Melissa and Craig if I don't try."

For the first time since he had collected her on the street and brought her into Cromwell's, Amy managed a tight, sad smile. "I couldn't agree with you more. I didn't come out here to find you and drag you home, Ty. We honestly wondered if you were still alive. Melissa needed to know, you see, because someday she's going to have to explain you to your son."

He scowled. "Tell him the truth!"

"We were trying to avoid having to tell him that his father is a bastard."

"Why, you little...!" The fingers around Amy's wrist tightened painfully for an instant as Ty's face turned murderous. Amy stifled the instinct to flinch, sitting very still as she waited for whatever came next. Then, in a gesture of disgust, Ty released her, flinging back into his chair. The dark eyes regarded her broodingly. "So what are you going to tell Melissa when you get home?"

Amy shrugged. "I was thinking of telling her that you were dead."

"That could be inconvenient if I ever happened to turn up in San Francisco again," he pointed out maliciously.

"If you should make the mistake of showing up on her doorstep, you will find yourself dealing with a man who understands responsibility. Melissa is getting married soon, Ty. One of the responsibilities Adam understands is how to protect his family. He won't let you over the threshold. He won't let you hurt her or your son. Why do you think I'm the one who had to come to Saint Clair to find out the truth about that mask and about what became of you? Adam wouldn't think of letting Melissa come on her own. And to tell you the truth, she didn't want to come. She's over you, Ty. The home she once offered to you has been offered to another man who's had the sense to grab it with both hands. Adam will be formally adopting Craig as soon as possible."

"Adopting him!" It was one of the few times, perhaps the only time, when Amy had ever seen Ty Murdock lose his composure. He stared at her, dumbfounded. Then he recovered almost immediately. "Well, maybe that's the best way to handle it."

"I'm inclined to agree," she said dryly. She got to her feet and reached for the bag of groceries on the chair beside her. "Good-bye, Ty. I won't say it's been a pleasure, but it has been enlightening. It would be interesting to see how much you like your free and adventuresome life-style twenty years from now, when you're slowing down physically and the women don't find you quite so charming. Adam and Melissa's son will be in college by then. He may turn out to resemble you physically, but you can bet his parents are going to see to it that he doesn't become another case of arrested development like his biological father! He'll grow up to be a man, not a boy who wants to play boyish games forever." She took a step forward to leave and then her eyes fell on Jase, who had just arrived at the entrance. He was staring at her with an expression she couldn't define. It was somewhere between fury and fear, and there was a good deal of pure, masculine frustration thrown in.

As she halted beside the table, Ty got up beside her, putting a restraining hand on her shoulder. He hadn't yet spotted Jase. "Amy, listen to me. Forget about Melissa and Craig and everyone else back in San Francisco. Out here you learn to live only in the present, not the future. And right now there's only you and me. Let me show you what you missed two years ago. I'll take you to dinner and then we can spend the night together. It'll be good, Amy, I promise."

Jase was moving forward, crossing the room with his efficient, lithe stride. The fury was now dominating his features.

"I'm afraid that's impossible, Ty," Amy said carefully, her nerves quivering as she faced Jase. She'd had enough excitement for one day, she told herself anxiously. The last thing she needed was another round of male violence. "I've already got dinner plans. And I have plans for after dinner as well."

Ty's head swung around to follow the direction of her gaze. His eyes narrowed. "Are you really sleeping with Lassiter?"

Amy jumped slightly as Jase came down upon them. Her elbow struck the glass of tonic water, which she hadn't finished, and it teetered precariously on the edge of the table. Instantly, Jase was reaching out to right it, the gesture automatic. His full attention was on Ty Murdock, not the glass of water he'd just rescued.

"Yes," he ground out in answer to Ty's question "She's sleeping with me. And the groceries in that sack are for the dinner she's fixing for me tonight. Furthermore I'm the one who saved her life today. All things considered, Murdock, you don't have any claim on her at all. Come near her again and I'll break your neck. Let's go, Amy."

He lifted the grocery sack out of her hands, cradling it in the crook of his arm. With his free hand he encircled her wrist and led her out of Cromwell's.

Amy didn't protest as she was hauled unceremoniously along the waterfront. She had to trot in order to keep up with Jase's long strides, and her wrist ached a little from the tight grip in which he held it. Still, her overwhelming feeling was one of relief. She was putting Ty Murdock behind her forever and the knowledge was pleasant.

Jase didn't speak until they had reached the house. As he pushed open the kitchen door and set the grocery sack down on the counter, he released his captive to face her with a hard, narrow stare.

"You don't want him, Amy."

"No," she agreed readily, her lips trembling in a gentle smile.

"He's an SOB."

"Yes."

"Your sister and her kid don't need him either. No one needs a man like that."

"Very true," Amy said, the soft smile widening a little.

"I don't want you near him again."

"I understand, Jase. Believe me, I don't want to go near him again."

His turquoise eyes were suddenly very brilliant. "I found out what you did at the grotto this morning, Amy. Haley described the way you made a target out of yourself."

"Oh," she gasped.

"I was furious. I was thinking of beating you, in fact. But Ray talked me out of it."

"Did he?" Amy held her breath as he came closer. Desire was shimmering to life between them once more. She thought she would melt beneath the turquoise fire of his eyes.

"Ray said," Jase explained carefully, searching her face, "that if I succumbed to the temptation of whaling the living daylights out of you, you might decide Murdock looked good in comparison."

Amy lifted her hands to cradle his face. "Ray was wrong. You aren't at all like Murdock. And nothing you did could make him look good in comparison to yourself." She stood on tiptoe and brushed her lips against his. "I would still cook your dinner for you tonight, even if you did decide to beat me." She smiled.

"And you'd still spend the night in my bed?" he persisted, his sherry-dark voice flowing over her as he found the clip in her hair.

"Yes." Amy wrapped her arms around his neck and

tilted her head back as her spice-colored hair fell free. From beneath lowered lashes her eyes teased him lovingly. "But under those circumstances we might have to make a few changes in the normal routine."

"What do you mean?"

"Well, if my backside was sufficiently uncomfortable, I suppose I'd have to be the one on top when we made love, instead of the one on the bottom."

"I get the feeling you're not taking my masculine outrage very seriously," he groaned, pulling her close to nuzzle her neck.

"I'm using my feminine wiles to overcome your masculine outrage."

"Your wiles seem to be working. I'm feeling less and less outraged." He tickled the nape of her neck with his lips. "God, Amy, I want you. Right now I feel as if I either have to beat you or make love to you. One way or another I've got to put my mark on you."

"Do I get to choose which technique you use?" she taunted.

He bent down abruptly and scooped her up into his arms, his expression taut and hard with desire. "No. No, I don't think you do. You've been driving me crazy all day long, ever since I woke up this morning and found you gone. When I got that message from Haley I nearly went out of my mind with worry. I no sooner get that mess straightened out than Murdock has to show up. One way and another it's been a very trying sort of day!"

As he spoke he was carrying her through the kitchen and out into the living room. He sat down with her on the sofa, letting her rest across his thighs to lie cradled in his arms. Jase stared down at her as she nestled against him. He was aware of the high level of his own frustration and knew that it wasn't merely physical in nature.

The frustration he was experiencing tonight wasn't going to be pacified by making Amy his once more. What he felt was a far more serious form of dissatisfaction. And it had its roots in plain fear. Amy had accomplished her business on Saint Clair. There was nothing to keep her with him now, and Jase wanted to lash out violently against that knowledge. He had nothing to offer to induce her to stay, and he knew it.

His hands trembled as he began undressing her. Willingly he let the passion of the moment push the unsettling, hopeless thoughts out of his mind. There was no point thinking about tomorrow. Hadn't he learned that lesson a long time ago?

But with Amy he found himself tempted again and again to do exactly that: think about the future. *Fantasize about the future* would be a better description, he told himself. Amy was right. Men did like to indulge in their fantasies. He had to keep reminding himself that she was from a different world, one he had cut himself off from years ago. Contemplating a future with her was very much a fantasy.

He could feel her fingertips toying with the buttons of his shirt as he slid off her blouse. Her touch made him groan, and the evidence of his desire seemed to encourage her. She had his shirt off shortly after her own had fallen to the floor. Then he felt the faint sting of her nails as they circled his flat, male nipples and tugged sensuously at the hair of his chest. Her mouth began to wander across the bare skin of his shoulder, and he experienced a sharp tremor as she used her teeth to nip enticingly.

The delicate curve of her breast filled his palm, and he grazed the budding nipple lightly, fiercely excited when it began to harden beneath his touch. When the tip of each breast had hardened to his satisfaction, Jase settled her back against the end of the sofa, sprawling aggressively on top of her. Then he lowered his head to taste the buds he had cultivated.

The scent of her invaded his senses as he stabbed at each nipple with the tip of his tongue. He would never forget the fragrance of her, Jase thought distantly. It would be imprinted on him for the rest of his life. That thought made him long to leave her with a memory of himself that she would never be able to evade.

"I want you to think of me when you go home to San Francisco," he heard himself rasp. "I want you to see me, feel me, be aware of me every time you look at another man. I want to be in the way every time you think of going to bed with someone else!"

"Oh, Jase, you're cruel," Amy whispered.

"I know. With you I can't seem to help it. You do something to me, sweetheart, bring out the part of me that's been safely buried for a long time." He slid down along her body, dropping warm, damp kisses on her stomach. Then he plunged his fingers beneath the waistband of her jeans.

With a quick, impatient yank he unsnapped the fastening and slid down the zipper. Shoving his palms down the full curve of her hips, he tugged off the jeans with a touch of desperation. He knew even as he did it that this wasn't the way he had envisioned making love to her. He had wanted to make it romantic and civilized, with all the nuances she would remember as sophisticated and exciting.

But he couldn't shake the sense of desperation, the almost violent desire to force himself on her. The thought that he would be losing her soon impelled him this afternoon as he made love to her in the airy living room.

She didn't resist him, didn't try to slow him or ask him to go more gently. Her willing acceptance of his mastery increased his restless desire even as it fed his satisfaction. She seemed to be as caught up in the urgent, primitive passion as he was, and that knowledge made his head reel.

His hands clenched into the rounded globes of her buttocks, and Jase caught his breath as his blood raced. He heard the soft moan at the back of her throat as he buried his lips in the hollow of her shoulder.

Then she was shakily undoing the fastening of his slacks and he drew himself slightly away so that she could finish undressing him.

"Amy, Amy, I want you so!"

"Yes, Jase. Oh, *yes!*"

He kicked off the slacks and then came back down on her, hungrily parting her thighs so that he could indulge himself fully in the scent and heat of her. When her fingers locked roughly in his hair, Jase gloried in the knowledge that he could make this one woman come so beautifully, excitingly alive. The way she surrendered to his touch was unlike anything he had ever known.

With infinite wonderment he probed the secrets of her body, searching out the most sensitive places and teasing the welcoming flesh until Amy was writhing and twisting beneath him.

He raised his head to look at her. Her eyes were shut tightly and her lips were parted and moist as she panted in her excitement. She moaned softly, arching her hips into his hand, pleading with her body for the satisfaction he promised.

Entranced, Jase fit his hand to the damp, throbbing heart of her desire and marveled at the heat of her. "You're on fire for me, honey. Molten fire."

"Come to me, Jase," she whispered throatily, pulling at his shoulders. "Come close to me. Please."

As he slid slowly up to take what she offered, Jase felt her soft, tender hands move down his waist. When she captured his manhood in her fingers, he growled his need, whispering short, blunt words of encouragement in her ear.

Her hands teased him, just as he had been teasing her, promising everything, enticing with reckless abandon.

"Guide me," he ordered huskily. "Put me inside, honey. Show me where you want me to go."

Instead of doing as he commanded, however, Amy held him in exquisite captivity. Her palms cupped him and her fingers explored with gentle excitement.

"Amy!"

Still she teased and provoked and taunted. Her legs shifted languidly alongside his, making him fully aware of the satin softness next to his own hair-roughened thigh.

"Sweetheart, you can't keep me out in the cold any longer," he vowed.

He thrust himself easily through the soft restraint of her hands, finding the waiting promise of her womanhood and plunging deeply into the dark velvet warmth.

Beneath him Amy gasped as she always did when he made her his. He felt her body accommodating him, closing around him, and in that moment Jase experienced again the overwhelming urge to give her a child. His child. He let the fantasy take hold, just as he had let it take hold the other times he had made love to her. He longed to satisfy her as a woman, to make it possible for her to experience the physical pleasure of lovemaking. But on a deeper level he wanted so much more. He wanted to know that he had left a fertile seed in her as a talisman against the future.

The fantasy of making Amy pregnant was too strong to resist. The urge to father a child had lain dormant for ten years, and now that it had surged to the surface again, Jase was unable to banish it. When he held Amy in his arms he could think of nothing else.

But the fantasy was not a sophisticated, civilized one. It was not a languid, jaded thing that could be drawn out and spun into endless nuances that, in turn, extended the love-making.

With Amy beneath him and the fantasy in his head, everything seemed to explode for Jase in a white heat. He took his woman in a storm of need and desire, exulting in her equally explosive response. When he felt the delicious tremors take hold, rippling through her, he knew she had found her own satisfaction. That knowledge unloosed his own.

Arching heavily against her, Jase gave himself up to the pulsating release, crying out Amy's name in an agony of fulfillment as he collapsed against her breasts.

It was a long time before Amy stirred, aware of the masculine weight that was still crushing her into the cushions of the sofa. Slowly her lashes lifted and a soft smile played at the corner of her mouth as she met Jase's eyes. "Beautiful," she murmured, stroking the mahogany hair back off his forehead. He looked at her questioningly. "Your eyes," she whispered. "You have the most beautiful eyes in the whole world. I've never seen anything quite like them."

He smiled reluctantly, forcing himself to adopt a bantering tone. "The better to see you with, my dear."

"If you're going to play that game, I'd better not go on listing your best attributes," she complained. "It could get embarrassing."

"Don't be shy."

"Fishing for compliments?" she teased, luxuriating in the gentle aftermath of their passion. These special moments would not last long, and she wanted to store up the tenderness and the memories. They were unique and they would remain so for the rest of her life. Amy knew that beyond a shadow of a doubt. Jase had succeeded in doing what he'd wanted to do: He'd imprinted her body with his own. She would never forget him. But then, she'd known that after their first night together.

"I'll trade you compliment for compliment," Jase suggested helpfully. "In exchange for telling me I have beautiful eyes, I will tell you that yours are the color of the sea in the morning or after a storm."

Amy glowed, even though it was only a game. "That's pretty good. Let me see. You have terrific shoulders. Not bulky like a weight lifter's, but strong and sleek. Must be all that swimming."

"And you," he murmured, bending close for a second to touch the tip of his tongue to one of her nipples, "have the nicest breasts. Soft and sensitive. Just like the rest of you."

Amy smiled and let her hand trail down to his thigh. "You have a tight, lean waist. No fat. Not bad for a man who makes a living running a bar," she added approvingly.

"And your tummy has the cutest little curve to it," he countered.

"You've got good legs too," she tried.

"Your legs feel unbelievably exciting when they're wrapped around me," he drawled, eyes gleaming. Then he put out a hand and sank his fingers into her buttock. "But if I had to choose the part I like best..."

"I told you this could get embarrassing!"

"Never!" he vowed, touching her mouth with his own in a slow, satisfied kiss. "Nothing about you is cause for embarrassment! Except, perhaps, the way I react to you!"

"Oh, no," she protested on a soft note of laughter. "I like that part best."

"You like to see me lose all control?"

"Umm. Gives me a feeling of power."

He stared down at her, the humor fading from his eyes as he studied her face intently. "I'm the one with the feeling of power. But it's all a fantasy, isn't it?"

"What? Jase, what's wrong?" Amy looked up at him uncomprehendingly as he sat up beside her.

At once he turned back, slapping her lightly on the rump. "Up and at 'em, woman. I've done my manly duty, asserted myself forcefully and put you firmly in your place. Now I'm staring."

"Banishing me to the kitchen?" she pouted.

"Right after a shower," he confirmed, reaching down to help her to her feet. "What did you get for dinner?"

"Sex and food. Is that all you ever think of?"

"Mankind's two most basic motivators." He lunged, grabbing her lightly around the waist and tossing her over one of the shoulders she had recently been admiring. "Let's hit the showers, lady. Then you can hit the stove. You didn't answer my question. What did you get me for dinner?"

"How long has it been since you've had biscuits and honey and old-fashioned chicken potpie?"

"Oh, God, I've salivating already."

The fantasy they had created in the aftermath of their passion, that of being two happy lovers without a care in the world or a future to consider, persisted right through dinner. Amy was aware that she was deliberately trying to prolong it, and it seemed that Jase was willing to go along with the illusion.

She was watching him down the last biscuit when she remembered something.

"What's wrong?" Jase asked instantly, seeing the line of her brows.

"I was just wondering—did anyone ever find out what really was so valuable about that mask?"

Jase hesitated. "Murdock let Haley think it held a list of US agents operating in the Pacific. He implied that he intended to sell the list to the highest bidder someday if he ever found himself in need of money or leverage."

"And is there such a list inside?"

"Murdock says no. He said he was only using it as bait for Haley. The only value in that mask is whatever sentimental value it might hold for Melissa's son someday. I can get it off the bottom for you, Amy, if you really want to take it back."

She thought about it. She had come so far to find out the secret of the mask and to discover what had happened to Ty Murdock. Now she knew the answers to both questions. "No," she said finally, "don't both retrieving it for me. Craig will have a new father soon—a real one, I hope. He doesn't need any souvenirs from a man like Ty Murdock."

"Are you going to tell Melissa the truth about Murdock? That he's still alive?"

"Yes. It's probably best. But it won't make any difference. She's very much in love with Adam and I don't think she'd give up the reality of his love for the illusion of Ty's."

"And you, Amy?"

"I haven't had any illusions about Ty Murdock from the beginning, Jase," she said very steadily. The only illusions I'm entertaining at the moment, she thought bleakly, are about you.

She didn't know for certain when or where the fantasy had been born, but it blazed now in her head, full-blown and in living, breathing color. The fantasy was a mental image of Jase surrounded by a comfortable home, enveloped in her love, living a normal, civilized sort of life.

This was the man for whom she wanted to create a home.

She had finally chosen a man, and in her incredible clumsiness she had selected a man who had already cut himself off from civilization. A man who had no real interest in a home.

# *Ten*

The fragile web of illusion that had been constructed between Jase and Amy in the heat of passion began to fade as soon as dinner was over. Reality returned all too quickly.

Amy knew what was happening, what was going wrong on her side of things. She could only guess at the reasons for Jase's increasingly dark mood.

From her perspective it was simple enough to define the reasons for her deteriorating sense of well-being. As the rosy illusion of happiness faded, she was forced to face the inevitable question: How long could she extend her stay on Saint Clair now that her business had been accomplished? The question was ringing through her head as she walked beside Jase to The Serpent after dinner. How long could she stretch out the painfully thin excuse of taking a couple of extra days to see the island before she boarded the plane home?

How long did she really want to stretch out that excuse? The longer she stayed with Jase, the harder the final parting would be. She was doing herself no favors by lingering on Saint Clair.

As if by mutual agreement, neither she nor Jase had talked openly about the date of her impending departure. But the prospect of it yawned before Amy like a vast chasm of emptiness. Jase, she suspected, was following his own hammered-out philosophy of taking each day as it came. He would take what she had to give for as long as she was willing. She knew he rarely thought in terms of the future. It was the way he had learned to survive emotionally during the past ten years and it worked for him. She had no right to criticize it. Nevertheless the realization of how basically different they were on even this fundamental level was depressing.

The crowd in The Serpent was beginning to get lively. There was another Navy ship in the harbor, and in addition to the sailors who had already found the place, a number of locals had turned out for a beer and a little gossip about the day's events. Fred Cowper was seated at one table with a couple of fishermen Amy had seen on the docks. All three nodded in a friendly fashion as Jase led her to a table on the waterfront side.

Ray smiled cheerfully, bringing a glass of red wine for Amy and a glass of rum on ice for his boss. Amy held out a small sack she'd brought with her. "Here you go, Ray. Dessert."

His smile broadened into a grin as he grabbed the package enthusiastically and tore it open. "Chocolate chip cookies! My favorite!"

"You said coconut cream pie was your favorite," Jase grunted, lifting his glass of rum and taking a long sip.

"That was because Amy gave it to me on Thursday. On Thursdays, coconut cream pie *is* my favorite. However, today is another day. When did you make them, Amy? You've been fairly busy today, from what I hear."

"I mixed them up just before dinner and stuck them in the oven while we were eating," she said gently.

"How many has Jase already eaten?" Ray demanded.

"Don't worry, I didn't get any more than you did," his boss informed him dryly.

"Gee, he's in a swell mood this evening, isn't he?" Ray observed to Amy as he wolfed down the cookies. "Maybe you didn't feed him enough of these cookies. They're delicious."

"Thanks, Ray."

She watched him as he hurried back to his post at the bar. Beside her, Jase lounged deeply into the high-backed wicker chair and drank rum with an intensity that disturbed her. He'd cut back on the rum during the past couple of days, and now it seemed he was intent on making up for lost time. Amy's unease was shot through with a strange kind of anger.

"Are you just going to sit here in The Serpent every night for the rest of your life and drink rum?" she muttered when she couldn't stand the silent drinking any longer.

He flicked her a sidelong glance, his attention chiefly on the entrance of the bar. "Maybe. Does it matter?"

Her mouth tightened under the cool rebuff. She glanced around the interior of the bar, anxious to take her mind off the tension that was building steadily between herself and Jase.

The Serpent no longer seemed the dangerous and alien place it had been that first night, she thought wonderingly. Perhaps because she now knew some of the people in it, at least by sight. Actually she had made tentative friendships with two or three of the locals by now, friendships she would never have expected to establish in the beginning. She thought of Maggie with her practical philosophy and the cheerful, easygoing Ray with the painting. Saint Clair hadn't turned out to be quite the way she had imagined. There were some nice people here.

"What are you thinking about, Amy?" Jase broke a long stretch of silence with his quiet question. He had almost finished the rum and had nodded his head at Ray to signal that he wanted another.

Amy eyed the disappearing rum. "I was thinking about the future of the tourist trade here on Saint Clair," she answered evasively. "The Serpent could become quite a nightspot if the cruise ships start calling here."

"Yeah, I guess it could." Jase didn't appear too interested in the possibility.

"Don't you ever think about the future, Jase?" she whispered, feeling somewhat desperate.

"Not if I can avoid it. No percentage in it."

Ray brought another glass of rum, his expression politely blank now instead of cheerful. Amy got the impression he didn't approve of his boss's renewed interest in the stuff.

Conversation dwindled again. Amy's fingers flexed nervously around the stem of her wineglass, and she consciously tried to relax them, not wanting the embarrassment of another spill. What was happening? She wanted these last few hours with Jase to be perfect, as special as possible. She needed the memories so badly. Instead everything was becoming incomprehensible and unmanageable. Tears sparkled for an instant in her eyes before she hastily blinked them away.

When her vision cleared, it revealed impending disaster. Ty Murdock was swaggering into The Serpent, plainly having put in some drinking time elsewhere before arriving. Even Amy sensed the new variety of tension that suddenly flared to life in the man beside her. She didn't need to be told that trouble was brewing. Uneasily she watched as Ty hooked one booted foot over the brass rung of the bar and ordered a drink. His dark gaze swept the room.

"Oh, hell," Jase muttered in disgust. "Just what I needed tonight."

He settled even deeper into the shadows of the wicker chair, studying the other man with a cool, meditative perusal that increased Amy's sensation of doom a thousandfold.

"Jase?" He ignored her anxious gaze. "Jase, I don't want any trouble tonight."

But she could feel the masculine challenge hovering in the air between the two men, and she had no idea of how to dissolve it. Out here the normal rules of polite behavior didn't always apply. A jolt of panic raced through her. "Jase, he's not doing anything. Just having a drink, for God's sake."

That got his attention briefly. "That's all I'm doing too. Having a drink. But there's one fundamental difference."

"What's that?"

"I'm having my drink with you," he explained very politely, as if she weren't very bright. "Your old friend Murdock knows damn well I took you home and made love to you this afternoon right after I plucked you out from under his nose. He'd had similar plans himself. Now he's had a few drinks and a little time to think about it. He's not in a friendly mood, honey. Don't blame me for what happens next."

"Stop it!" she hissed, alarmed at the fatalistic way he seemed to be preparing for a fight, even anticipating it with a strange pleasure. "Don't say things like that. He couldn't possibly know we spent the afternoon..." Her voice trailed off as Ty's gaze settled broodingly on their table. A flush rose into her cheeks.

"Couldn't know that we spent the afternoon in bed? Sure he does. He knows damn well that's exactly what I had in mind when I dragged you out of Cromwell's. He's probably been drinking steadily since then, running the picture of you in my arms through his head over and over again."

"Jase!" Amy's shock was plain.

"Men and their fantasies, honey, remember?" he drawled mockingly.

"Jase, please, I don't want a fight."

"He's spoiling for one. By now he'll have convinced himself he has to prove he's man enough to demolish the lover you chose over him. And he'll want you to witness the proof of his manhood."

"You can't be serious! That's childish! Immature! Stupid."

"Men are like that sometimes. You're the one who keeps telling me that."

"All right, I'll admit Ty's capable of doing something immature, like starting a brawl to prove his manhood, but I expect better behavior out of you, do you hear me?" she began in a sturdy, lecturing tone.

"Why should you expect anything more sophisticated from me? I'm just another male who washed ashore on Saint Clair. Another male who walked away from your civilized world a long time ago."

Amy glared at him, feeling helpless to avert disaster. "You're spoiling for a fight, too, aren't you? You're actually hoping he'll start something!"

"You're turning into a fair amateur shrink. Stick around out here in the Pacific long enough and you'll get to be an accomplished one. Goes with the territory."

Out of the corner of her eye Amy saw Murdock down the last of his drink and start purposefully across the room. There was elemental male hostility in every line of his body.

Beside her, Jase didn't move, but she felt the coiled tension in him and wanted to shriek aloud in her frustration. "Jase, this is crazy. Don't let it get out of hand. It's up to you to control the situation!"

"I'll control it." He wasn't paying her even the slightest attention now, his whole awareness centered on Murdock, who halted beside the table in cool challenge.

"Had enough of playing around with the second string, Amy? My offer for the evening is still open, you know. Be glad to show you the difference between the men and the boys." The words were aimed at Amy, but there was no doubt that the taunt was directed at Jase.

"Ty, please," Amy began weakly.

"I think it's time you left, Murdock," Jase said coldly, cutting across Amy's plea for reason.

"When I leave tonight, I'll be taking Amy with me," Ty drawled insolently. "I'm going to show her what she missed two years ago."

"She knows she didn't miss much," Jase returned smoothly. He was practically motionless. Only the brilliant turquoise eyes burned with the fires of his counterchallenge. "And she's not going anywhere with you. Get lost, Murdock."

Ty's eyes narrowed as he hooked his thumbs in his belt and stood with his feet braced slightly apart. "I knew her a long time before you did, Lassiter. Tonight I'm going to renew old acquaintances. Come on, Amy."

"Ty! No!" she gasped, startled when he abruptly reached down and took hold of her arm, jerking her to her feet. Almost predictably the action caused her left hand to flail out in the direction of the half-filled wineglass. When it toppled over Jase made no effort at all to catch it. The red wine ran across the table and dripped to the floor, totally unnoticed.

"I told you if you came near her again I'd break your neck," Jase reminded his opponent. There was a wealth of anticipation in his voice, and Amy winced as she heard it. Jase wanted this fight every bit as much as Murdock did. She was furious at both of them and utterly helpless.

"Please let me go, Ty," she begged softly, turning pleading eyes up to him.

"You heard the lady."

Then, with horrifying swiftness, Amy was released. The two men exploded into a vicious brawl before her eyes. Jase had come up out of his chair in one swift motion, his fist aimed at Ty's chin.

Instantly, having achieved his purpose of goading the other man into the battle, Murdock released his pawn and barely managed to avoid the blow Jase had launched. It landed on his shoulder, knocking him backward into a sprawl. Jase rushed in, seeking the advantage.

"Oh, my God," Amy breathed, her hand going to her mouth as she backed up instinctively.

The rest of The Serpent's clientele moved respectfully aside, watching the spectacle with great interest. At the table nearest Amy she could see two men laying down bets on the outcome. Others cheered on the action. Ray stood watching from the other side of the bar, making no move to dig out the hose he had used the night the sailors had gotten into a brawl.

"Someone stop them!" Amy yelled furiously. No one paid her any attention. Jase and Ty were locked in savage combat. Tables were overturned, chairs were sent crashing, glassware shattered. It was chaos, and Amy's emotional reaction hovered somewhere between hysteria and fury. Fury won out.

As the two men rolled across the floor and the sickening thud of fists striking flesh reached her ears, she turned desperately toward where Ray stood impassively behind the bar.

"Ray, do something! Stop them! Use the hose," she cried.

"This is Jase's fight," Ray pointed out philosophically, as if she didn't understand the finer nuances of these things. "He'll settle it."

"Don't be ridiculous! They're trying to kill each other!"

"Jase will be okay," he assured her.

"I want it stopped!" she yelled.

"Jase would probably kill *me* if I tried to interfere," Ray explained gently. "At the very least I'd lose my job."

"Well, I don't have a job to lose! Give me that hose!" Amy plunged behind the bar, grabbing for the garden hose coiled underneath the sink.

"Hey, wait a minute," Ray managed, seeing her intention.

But she already had the water turned on. With shaking

hands she aimed the blast toward the two men, knotted together on the floor in front of the bar.

There was a mingled shout of laughter from the onlookers as the cold water showered over the pair. Jase and Ty broke apart, both drenched and both seeking the source of the water with furious eyes. They stared in astonishment as they saw Amy wielding the hose.

"For God's sake, Amy," Jase gasped, his chest heaving as he caught his breath. "What the hell do you think you're doing?"

"Stop spraying that goddamned water!" Ty gritted, trying to roll aside to avoid the spray she was still aiming at them.

With a wrench Amy reached beneath the sink and turned off the hose. Holding the dripping end in one hand, she stood behind the bar and glared at Jase. "I swear I'll turn it on again if the two of you don't stop acting like a couple of cowboys fresh off the trail! I want you to know I have never been so humiliated in my entire life! A couple of real macho types, aren't you? Have you both proved your manhood now? Honest to God, you should both be ashamed of yourselves. If this is what you think it takes to prove your manhood, I've got news for you: Right now you both look like two young punks. A couple of boys out to show the world they're still boys. Not *men*—boys! This is all part of the fantasy, isn't it? Have a few drinks and then get into a bar fight over a woman!"

"Amy," Jase tried to say, dabbing at his bleeding mouth with the back of his hand, "put down the hose."

"I will not put down the hose until I've had my say!" she shouted, aware that everyone else in the bar was thoroughly enjoying the scene. She focused on Jase's stony face. "Is this how you're going to spend the rest of your life, Jase Lassiter? Drinking more and more rum? Getting into meaningless fights over the occasional lady tourist? Trying to prove your manhood by taking on other men like Ty Murdock who haven't grown up yet either?"

"Amy..." Surprisingly it was Ray who attempted to interrupt this time. She ignored him, continuing her tirade with unabated ardor.

"Listen to me, Jase Lassiter," she went on forcefully, the words tumbling over themselves as she spoke without stopping to sort out her thoughts. "I'm going to give you a choice. A real choice between a home and a future made up of a succession of nights like this one. Are you listening to me? I'm offering you a home, complete with home-cooked meals and slippers by the hearth and...and a woman in your bed every night. I'm offering you a future, not just a present. I'm offering you something steady and real and lasting. I'm offering you everything I have to give a man. I've never been willing to take that risk with any other person. When you decide whether or not you're interested in taking me up on my offer, come and find me. I'm taking the plane home to San Francisco in the morning!"

Throwing down the hose, Amy turned and strode out of the room full of stunned men. She looked neither to the right nor the left and totally ignored the pair of bleeding, bruised men on the floor. Once out in the street she hurried toward Jase's house.

When she reached it she raced to her bedroom, collecting her clothing and shoving it into the suitcase. Not pausing for an instant, she let herself back out into the warm night, hurrying toward the Marina Inn.

"Well, well, Miss Shannon," Sam the desk clerk said cheerfully as he looked up from a centerfold to find his old customer standing in front of him. "What can I do for you this evening?" He ran interested eyes over her disheveled appearance but refrained from making any inquiries about it.

"You can give me my old room back, Sam, and you can see to it that I am not disturbed by *anyone* at all this evening!"

"Yes, ma'am," he murmured, reaching for a wad of keys. "Here, take all the extra keys to one-oh-five. That way I won't have any to give out in case someone comes asking."

She smiled wryly. "In other words you'll be off the hook?"

"You got it. Have a good evening, Miss Shannon. How long you plan on staying?"

"I'll be leaving at dawn."

"The six-thirty flight?" he asked warily.

"Yes." Amy turned and made her way up the stairs, dragging her suitcase behind her. Slowly the adrenaline that had been pounding through her bloodstream began to slacken, leaving behind a weary depression for which there was no cure.

She had taken her chance. There was nothing else she could do. It was up to Jase now. She didn't need to be told that the odds were against his deciding to take her up on her offer. He'd decided a long time ago that a cozy, stable home life wasn't for him.

Why did it have to be this man? she asked herself hopelessly as she undressed and crawled into bed wearing the champagne-colored nightgown. Why couldn't she have found herself someone who wanted what she had to offer? Why did her heart insist on trying to take the risk with a man who was probably beyond the reach of any woman's domesticating talents?

It wasn't fair, but since when had life ever been fair?

Amy fell into an exhausted sleep and dreamed of a man with turquoise eyes who would not be gentled or tamed by a woman's hand. For the remainder of the night she chased him, offering every inducement she could think of, but to no avail. In the morning she awoke as tired as she had been when she'd tumbled into bed. No one had bothered her during the night.

Which meant she had probably lost her gamble.

Wearily she packed for the flight home, trusting to luck that there would be an empty seat on the jet that left for the States once each day. There were seldom many passen-

she didn't let it show. She acted as if Adam could handle him with one hand tied behind his back should the necessity arise. Amy watched her sister's lovely face and realized it wasn't an act put on for Adam's sake. Melissa really did trust this man to look after her. And perhaps, in a real showdown, Adam would be the winner. His motivation would be a lot stronger, and that counted for a great deal. Besides, Amy didn't think Ty would ever be back.

"I left the mask at the bottom of the cove, Melissa. It has no intrinsic worth, apparently, and I decided Craig didn't need it."

"No," Melissa agreed, watching her sister play with the happy, dark-haired child. "No, he doesn't need any reminders of Ty. Adam is his real father in all the important meanings of the word."

Craig gurgled cheerfully, smiling enticingly up at his aunt as she bounced him on her knee.

"One of these days that young man is going to have some brothers and sisters," Adam grinned proudly. "He'll have all the family he needs."

Amy glanced up and caught her sister's eye. More children, Melissa? she asked silently. Are you really willing to take that risk again? Even for this man? But she didn't have to ask the question aloud. The affirmative answer was in Melissa's eyes.

"When are you going back to work?" Melissa asked, pouring more coffee for all three of the adults at the table.

"Tomorrow. Today I really felt the jet lag."

"You look beat," Adam told her bluntly. "Are you sure it's just the jet lag?"

"I'm fine," she assured him, summoning a smile. She had given them only the briefest description of her association with Jase Lassiter, not implying at all that he had become her lover during the time she had spent on Saint Clair. But she was aware of Melissa's half-curious, half-speculative glance.

It wasn't until the next day, when Melissa showed up

with Craig at Shannon's Sensuous Chic Boutique near Union Square, offering to take her sister to lunch, that Amy got the questions.

"Tell me about him, Amy," Melissa ordered as they ate stuffed croissant sandwiches in a neighboring shop. "What happened out there on Saint Clair?"

"I found a man I wanted to make a home with," Amy replied quietly. "He apparently didn't want any part of the process." Under her sister's blunt probing, Amy told her the whole story, feeling strangely relieved when it was concluded. "I suppose I'm lucky he had enough sense of honor not to let me take the risk, hmmm?" she ended half humorously.

"Oh, Amy, I'm so sorry," Melissa whispered sympathetically. "You have so much to give and you've been cautious for so long. To finally take the chance and then have it all thrown back in your face...!"

"I'll survive. Women do, you know. Look at you and little Craig. A woman named Maggie told me that it's the female of the species that keeps the race going. We're the ones who take the biggest chances."

Melissa smiled lamely.. "She may have a point. A little hard on us, but I guess it does work toward the survival of the species. She's right about one thing: I can't picture a man willingly taking the chance of getting himself pregnant!"

Amy laughed, remembering Maggie's similar words. Then she sobered as she realized her sister was staring at her in consternation. "What is it, Mel?"

"Speaking of getting pregnant," Melissa began with heavy emphasis.

"Oh!" Amy blinked and then looked away, flushing at the very direct question. "No, there's nothing to worry about, Mel."

Her sister arched an eyebrow. "I know you don't make a habit of carrying contraceptives around with you, Amy.

Are you telling me this Jase Lassiter was, er, fully prepared for entertaining lady tourists?"

"Melissa, don't be crude. Just take my word for it. On that issue I'm perfectly safe."

Fortunately, Craig chose that particular moment to spit out a large chunk of liver pâté-stuffed croissant. Amy, who was holding him at the time, grabbed for a napkin.

"You know, Amy, you'd make a good mother," Melissa observed easily as they prepared to leave. "Look how well you handle Craig. The two of you get along great together."

"Uh-huh. That's because we both know that we're not stuck with each other. As soon as the socializing's over, we get to go our separate ways." Amy chuckled, mopping up the liver pâté from the corners of Craig's mouth. He giggled delightedly and grabbed for the napkin.

"I don't think you're quite the coward you believe yourself to be when it comes to kids," Melissa observed softly. "Tell me something. When you went to bed with Jase, did you really think about protecting yourself?"

The red stain on Amy's cheekbones was answer enough. "Let's go, Mel, I'm late getting back to the shop." Firmly she handed her nephew over to his mother.

Melissa sighed, getting to her feet as she put her son into his stroller. "For a woman as cautious of real romance as you are, you're sure in a funny business!"

The days wore on, falling back into their normal pattern. Thoughts of Jase and Saint Clair seemed to hover as close as ever, although Amy did her best to put them out of her mind. But when night fell, she went to bed wondering if Jase was sitting in his corner of The Serpent, watching for lady tourists who were looking for a "souvenir" of the islands.

Was her relationship with him no more than a pleasant memory for Jase now? Please, God, she thought, let it have meant something more to him than that. She might not be able to have him, but a part of Amy wanted Jase to remember her. Just as she would always remember him.

A few weeks after her return to San Francisco, Amy conceded that time was not as great a cure-all for heartache as she had supposed. How long did it take to get a man out of one's head? She forced herself into a faster-paced routine, accepting invitations, attending concerts, working late. But no matter how crowded her days, her nights seemed emptier than ever.

It was Melissa who finally took charge one afternoon. "Amy, you look awful. Something's wrong."

"I'm just a little tired, Mel."

"Well, you can't use jet lag as an excuse any longer. You've been back over three weeks now. And I don't think you're just pining away from unrequited love either."

Amy arched an eyebrow. "I should hope not!"

"I think you should see your doctor."

"Don't be ridiculous! There's nothing wrong with me."

"Not just any doctor, Amy. I think you should see Dr. Carson," Melissa stated.

"My gynecologist? Whatever for? I just had my yearly physical a few months ago!"

"You know very well what for, Amy Shannon. You're a big girl now. How long?"

"How long what?" Amy demanded, puzzled.

"How long since...?" Melissa let the question trail off as a clerk hurried over to ask Amy a question.

By the time she had finished answering the clerk's question, Amy had figured out what it was her sister was trying to ask. "Oh, no, Mel," she whispered, suddenly feeling weak. "That's impossible. I can't be. He *promised!*"

"Men," stated Melissa with the voice of experience, "have made promises like that to women for the past several thousand years. Probably longer. And women," she continued, "have believed those promises for the same length of time, even though they ought to have known better."

"But, Mel, you don't understand. Jase said he couldn't...I mean, he said he'd been told he would never be able to..."

A week later Amy sat in the consultation room of her gynecologist and tried to explain the same thing to the middle-aged women on the other side of the desk.

"I can't be pregnant," Amy concluded huskily, pleading for confirmation.

With a sympathetic expression Dr. Jessica Carson strove to explain the facts of life to her twenty-eight-year-old patient. "Having a low sperm count is not the same thing as being sterile, Amy. Far from it. I can introduce you to any number of couples who gave up and adopted children, only to turn around and create their own baby a few months later. The odds may not be in favor of a man getting a woman pregnant if his count is low, but that is not to say it's impossible."

Amy stared at her, stricken. With ringing clarity she remembered the scene in her bedroom the morning after she had first gone to bed with Jase. She had been in a panic and he had been anxious to calm her down.

What were the odds that his soothing story had been a complete fabrication, that he had made it up just to keep her conveniently where he wanted her: in bed?

Amy was trembling as she left the doctor's office. Jase had tricked her. In her panic and hurt and anxiety, that was the only fact that seemed to blaze forth.

Jase had used her, knowing he would never see her again. Just like so many other men, he hadn't cared about the consequences of his actions. All that had concerned him was having a convenient and willing lover for a while.

And like so many women before her, Amy had been left to deal with the results of her own recklessness.

A fury unlike anything she had ever known took root in the depths of her soul.

# Eleven

San Francisco was suddenly teaming with babies. Amy saw babies everywhere she went during the next few days. Ahead of her on escalators in the department stores, they rode snuggled in special backpacks. The elevator in her apartment building always seemed to be crowded with strollers filled with toddlers. Babies gazed up at her as they sat on their mothers' laps beside Amy on the bus. Infants lazed contentedly in grocery store carts, riding through the checkout line with the rest of the items in the baskets. Never had she been so aware of babies. Normally she had paid little attention to children, aside from Craig. Now she couldn't seem to avoid them.

It was psychological, Amy knew. She told herself again and again that the shock of her own pregnancy had made her overly aware of the babies around her. My God, she thought over and over again, what am I going to do? One thing was certain, she had to stop stumbling unwittingly into the infant departments of the large stores and staring, fascinated, at every child under the age of two. She couldn't even sleep nights because of the dreams full of babies.

A week after Dr. Carson had given her the news, Amy sat at her sister's kitchen table and repeated the lament dully. "Mel, I'm going out of my mind," she whispered honestly. "I just can't seem to think straight. What on earth am I going to do?"

"Well, there is one very definite way out," Mel said gently as she poured the coffee. "And you know it as well as I do. Every woman has the option."

Amy stared at her sister, eyes dark and ravaged as she acknowledged the truth. "An abortion?" she made herself ask. Why was it such a difficult word? "I keep telling myself I'm not going to let a man trap me, but..." She broke off, shaking her head uncomprehendingly. "I refuse to let myself be used and then abandoned to raise a child alone. But an abortion? Mel, I just can't *think!* What's wrong with me?" she ended, softly pleading.

Melissa watched her sister warily as the coffee cup in Amy's hand clattered awkwardly on the saucer. Her sister's natural propensity for clumsiness had increased several degrees lately. Amy was living on her nerves, and it showed.

"Who," Mel finally pointed out gently, "abandoned whom in this instance?"

Amy stared at her, stunned. "What are you suggesting? That I run back to Saint Clair and demand marriage?"

"Why not?"

"I will not beg a man for marriage," Amy seethed. "If Jase had wanted me he would have come after me. If you want to know the truth, I think he was rather relieved to see me go. Our relationship was hopeless and we both knew it, right from the start. The wrong place, the wrong time and the wrong people. He told me that, Mel. He said I was exactly the wrong sort of woman for him," she concluded wistfully.

"Well, you were even, weren't you? You thought he was exactly the wrong sort of man for you!"

"How could I have been so stupid?" Amy wondered aloud, not for the first time since she had returned to San Francisco.

"Will you at least consider the possibility of an abortion?" her sister asked very gently.

Amy scowled at her.

"I got that far, you know," Melissa confided quietly.

"No! I didn't know! Mel, are you telling me you almost had an abortion when you discovered you were pregnant with Craig? I didn't realize...!"

"I knew things probably weren't going to work out between myself and Ty. I think I knew from the very beginning. He was everything you said he was, unreliable, undependable, untrustworthy and uncaring. I knew he didn't really want a baby. I panicked when I realized I was pregnant and scheduled an abortion."

"What happened?"

Melissa's mouth turned downward wryly. "This is going to sound crazy, but I canceled the appointment at the last minute, because I felt like an idiot. It's incredible what feeling like an idiot does to your common sense."

"I don't understand," Amy said weakly.

"I walked into the waiting room at the clinic and discovered that almost every other female present was about fourteen years old!"

"Oh, my God!" Amy stared at her.

"Exactly," Melissa continued emphatically. "They looked at me as if to say, 'I'm only fourteen, so I've got an excuse for being here. All fourteen-year-olds make mistakes. You're almost thirty. What the hell's your excuse for getting into trouble?' I tell you, Amy, it was mortifying," Melissa ended with a rueful chuckle. "There I was, going through one of the most traumatic moments in my life, and my initial reaction was old-fashioned embarrassment over the obvious fact of my own stupidity. Crazy. But it was enough to drive me back out of the clinic to rethink the whole matter."

"And obviously you changed your mind entirely." Amy

shook her head and then rested her brow on her palm in an attitude of weary frustration. "I wish I could think this through clearly. But I can't seem to approach it rationally. I keep remembering that Jase *lied* to me. He told me he couldn't get me pregnant!"

"Was that before or after you'd taken the risk?" Melissa inquired softly.

Amy flushed, her cheeks hoisting flags of brilliant color.

"Do you want me to call Dr. Carson and have her set up an appointment for you at the clinic?" Melissa asked matter-of-factly. "It's only four-thirty. She's probably still at her office this afternoon."

Amy felt the mounting pressure and was afraid she would lose her self-control completely. Was that what she wanted? An abortion? Why weren't there more options for a woman in this situation? Life could be so unfair! But that undeniable fact didn't give her the right to be unfair to the small growing life within her. This was Jase's child she was carrying, not a medical specimen. No, not just Jase's child, her child. With sudden decision, Amy looked up at her sister.

"No, Mel. Abortion is not an option, not for me."

"There is one possibility you're overlooking. Dr. Carson could put you in touch with the social agencies that could arrange for adoption."

"Adoption," Amy repeated blankly. Yes, that was a possibility. But why was it almost as hard to think about as abortion had been?

Melissa's eyes were alight with deep comprehension. She knew, even if Amy hadn't yet realized it, what her sister's final decision would be. "Still going through with the cocktail party you had planned for next Friday?" she inquired practically as her sister got to her feet and reached for her small red leather shoulder bag.

"Of course I'm going through with it," Amy snapped. "I must keep my life as normal as possible. I will not let this...this *situation* disrupt it!"

There was no way, however, to ignore the situation.

Sooner or later the decision had to be made. She knew she ought to call Dr. Carson and start the adoption proceedings.

But the next morning something came up at one of the two boutiques she owned, something that seemed to require her immediate presence and somehow, by three o'clock, Amy hadn't yet called Dr. Carson. She told herself that she'd wait one more day. Somehow the call didn't get made the next day, either.

Two days after that she accidentally blundered into the newborn department of one of the huge department stores on Union Square. Blankly she stood looking at a beautiful layette done in yellow and white lace. Her mind pictured a baby in the tiny crib, a baby with turquoise eyes. Her knees went weak.

Abruptly she realized she was weak all over. Her head was ringing and her stomach started to churn. Good Lord, she was going to faint right there in the baby department!

The horror of that kept her going on wobbly feet until she managed to find the ladies' room. En route through the newborn department, she accidentally knocked over two plush teddy bears and a gift box of dress booties. Amy didn't even notice the small disasters she left behind. All she could think about was getting to the ladies' room before she disgraced herself. Half an hour later, having managed to recover sufficiently to get herself out of the store, Amy glanced at a clock. It was getting late in the day. Too late to phone Dr. Carson.

Twenty-four hours after the incident in the baby department, Amy left work early, taking herself to a nearby cafe for a cup of tea and a private talk with herself.

It had been nearly a week now and she still hadn't made the appointment with Dr. Carson to discuss the possibility of putting her baby up for adoption. Amy sipped tea, staring at the rain-slicked sidewalk and forced herself to face facts.

There were no more good excuses left for putting off the phone call. There never had been any good excuses. The past week had been an exercise in deliberate procrastination, and it was time she faced up to what that really meant.

A part of her refused to take the one escape route offered. A part of her wanted Jase Lassiter's baby.

It was almost a relief to admit it. With a long, weary sigh Amy took another swallow of the tea and wondered what came next. She had been resisting the thought of being a mother for so long that it was difficult now to think logically about it. But she had no choice. The feminine heart of her, the part of her that still loved Jase, couldn't deal with the prospect of losing the seed of their union.

However, that decision, as straightforward and positive as it was, didn't clear up the muddiness of her feelings toward Jase. There was still the fact that he'd undoubtedly lied to her, still the fact that he hadn't wanted to make a home with her and still the fact that he hadn't followed her back to San Francisco. She might want his child, but the rage she felt toward Jase was unabated. It was the fiery, chaotic, half-hysterical fury that only a woman in love can experience. He had taken what she'd given, but he had rejected the future she offered.

Amy went back to the office of Shannon's Sensuous Chic Boutique, pushed aside a pile of frothy blue bikini panties that were stacked on her desk and reached for the phone. When Melissa came on the line, Amy told her of the decision she had made.

"You won't be alone, Amy," Melissa assured her with deep understanding. "I'll be there, just as you were there with me."

"Thanks, Mel. Thank you very much."

There was a long silence while each woman considered the future, and then Melissa said practically, "I'll see you at the cocktail party Friday."

"Oh, Lord," Amy groaned. "With all this decision-making, I'd forgotten all about it!"

Amy dressed for her cocktail party Friday evening with care and determination. She wanted to look her best, wanted to show herself that she was a woman in charge of her own destiny. Continuing with her normal round of activities, including entertaining, was a silent statement to the world that she was in control of herself and her future. Having the baby was a conscious decision, just as it had been a conscious decision to go into business for herself. She could manage her own life. For the first time in days Amy's nerves began to settle down. She didn't knock over a single glass as she set the glassware out on a buffet table. She didn't even drop a loaded tray of canapés.

When all was in readiness, she automatically checked her appearance in the mirrored wall behind the dining area. She was wearing blue tonight, a curious shade of turquoise blue. The dress was a sensation of tiny pleats with a fitted bodice, which emphasized the gentle curves of her breasts. The skirt fell over her rounded hips, flaring gracefully at the knee when she walked. Long Renaissance sleeves ended just below the elbow. Her spice-colored hair was swept into an easy, sophisticated knot, and she had kept her makeup to a minimum. The tiny heels of her black shoes were marked with gold. Amy frowned consideringly at the picture she made, and her hand went to her stomach. How much longer before she should start shopping for maternity clothes? The ringing of the doorbell drew her attention, and Amy went to answer it with a smile on her lips.

Within an hour the apartment was filled with friends. Amy circulated easily, the gracious hostess in full command of herself and the party. No one but Melissa and Adam knew of her pregnancy, and she decided to wait before telling anyone else. The result was that she moved through the crowded living room feeling as if she had a special secret carefully hidden from the others. It put a sparkle of amusement in her eyes and a smile of contentment on her lips.

"You look more relaxed tonight than you have since you returned from Saint Clair," Adam observed as he and Melissa stood chatting with Amy beside the buffet table.

"You mean I haven't knocked over anything or dropped a platter of food on the floor?"

Adam chuckled ruefully, smiling down at Melissa. "Mel here explained that you've always been a little on the, uh, klutzy side."

"Only when I get nervous," Amy said, grinning. She was about to help herself to a glass of wine when the doorbell rang again. Hesitating, she took a quick sip and made a face. It didn't taste very good for some reason. Another quirk of pregnancy? Perhaps it was just as well, she thought as she excused herself to answer the door. She'd read somewhere that it was probably best to avoid alcohol during pregnancy.

The glass was still in her hand when she opened the door with a welcoming smile. An instant later it fell to the floor from nerveless fingers as Amy realized who was standing on the threshold.

"Jase!"

He stood there, larger than life, in familiar khaki clothes. The mahogany-colored hair was carefully combed and was damp from the San Francisco fog. His only concession to the weather appeared to be an old trench coat that lay over one arm. Standing there in the carpeted hall, Jase looked out of place, a little rough and clearly unaccustomed to the sophistication of the city. He also looked bigger than Amy remembered, taller and more intense, more intimidating. She stood frozen with shock.

"Amy?" The familiar turquoise eyes moved over her with a stark hunger, a hunger Amy remembered well. The sherry-rich sound of his voice broke her paralysis. Without hesitation she brought up her palm in a short, violent arc.

The sharp crack of her hand against the side of his face turned the head of everyone in the room.

It also turned Jase's head. In fact the totally unexpected blow sent him staggering back a pace into the hall. Amy followed, shutting the door to her apartment firmly behind her. As he stared at her, his fingers going to the red welt she had left on his cheek, Amy faced him, her hands on her hips.

"I'm pregnant, you bastard! And it's all your fault! What the hell are you going to do about it?"

Jase just stood there, his eyes riveted to her face as she glared up at him. He couldn't think of anything to say except the obvious.

"Amy, that's impossible! You can't be pregnant," he whispered, still too stunned to think straight. Of all the welcomes he'd imagined, this was the last kind he'd expected. It was as if the fantasy that had been in his head that last night when he'd made love to Amy had suddenly taken complete hold of his senses. She *couldn't* be pregnant!

"Tell that to my gynecologist!" Amy hissed. "But don't bother trying to give her that story about the low sperm count because it won't wash. How could you lie to me like that, Jase? I trusted you! I *trusted* you with my life, in fact. How could you lie to me?"

He swallowed, trying to recover his self-control. He seemed able to respond only to one thing at a time. "Amy, I didn't lie to you," he said. "I've never lied to you."

"You're going to have the sheer arrogance to stand there and tell me you really didn't think you could get me pregnant?" she demanded, enraged.

"Are you going to have the sheer arrogance to stand there and tell me I *did* get you pregnant?" he retaliated.

Amy blanched, her eyes widening in shock as she realized for the first time that if he was telling the truth, if he really believed that he couldn't get a woman pregnant, then it followed that he wouldn't believe her when she accused him of fathering her child. "Oh, my God," she whispered. "Oh, my God."

The door opened behind her before the stark silence could be broken. Melissa and Adam came through, shutting it again behind them. Melissa was holding the wineglass Amy had dropped on the carpet, and Adam still clutched a stained paper towel. They both looked at Jase.

"Is this the father, Amy?" Melissa asked, never taking her assessing gaze off Jase.

"Yes," Amy managed shakily. "But he doesn't believe me. Isn't that funny, Mel? The one possibility I hadn't considered. That he was telling the truth and that he wouldn't believe me if I told him I was pregnant." Summoning a brave smile, which came out rather strangely, she turned and opened the door to her apartment. Instantly, Melissa was at her side, unobtrusively moving to lend her silent support as Amy faced a roomful of curious guests.

Out in the hall Adam considered the tall man standing in front of him. Jase was gazing blankly at the closed door. "You look," Adam said conversationally, "as if you could use a drink."

"You may be right."

"Come on inside and I'll get you one," Adam opened the door and stood waiting.

Jase looked into the crowded room, dazzled momentarily by the cheerful noise, the fashionable clothing and the prospect of seeing Amy again. "I'm, uh, not used to this sort of thing," he explained wryly to the stranger holding the door.

"Amy says you can handle a bar full of drunken sailors back on Saint Clair. Dealing with a room full of partying San Franciscans should be a snap for you."

Jase hesitated. "Amy talks about me?"

"Incessantly." Adam grinned dryly. "When she isn't talking about the baby, that is."

"The baby." Adam repeated the words as if they were a foreign language.

"Come on, I'll get you that drink." Adam smiled. "I'm Adam Trembach, by the way."

Jase decided he could like Adam Trembach very easily. "Jase Lassiter."

Adam chuckled. "I know."

Twenty minutes later Jase found a relatively quiet corner of the room, a Scotch and soda in his hand. There hadn't been any rum at the liquor table. So he'd made himself the Scotch and soda while Adam refurbished his Manhattan. The two men stood quietly, sipping their drinks and watching the lively crowd. A few of the more curious guests came over to introduce themselves. Adam handled them diplomatically, making the introductions and then banishing each guest in turn.

"You've got a nice touch," Jase drawled as Adam gently sent a streaked blonde in a black skintight gown on her way. "I could use you for a bouncer at The Serpent."

Adam laughed. "Something tells me it would take more than casual diplomacy to deal with the crowd you get on Saint Clair."

"Oh, I don't know. The crowd's changing a little. Just before I left the island yesterday, a friend told me that one of the cruise lines was making inquiries about putting Saint Clair on its list of ports of call."

But even as he spoke, Jase's attention was only partially on the conversation he was trying to hold with Adam. He couldn't take his eyes of Amy. She moved across the room, chatting with her guests, laughing at the easy jokes of some of the men, making sure everyone had plenty of the excellent food and drink.

Although she hid it fairly well, Jase could see that she was getting through the evening on her nerves alone, and God knew that made her an accident waiting to happen. He watched the painstaking care she took whenever she handed a glass to someone. When she passed around an hors d'oeuvre tray she did it with both hands, although it obviously wasn't very heavy.

She was pregnant.

"I beg your pardon?" Adam said politely.

Jase realized he must have mumbled something aloud. He reddened. "I said I can't believe she's pregnant," he muttered.

"Oh, she is. No doubt about it. Mel's spent the past couple of weeks laying her options on the line for her. There aren't that many for a woman, you know. Adoption, abortion or keep the kid."

"An abortion!"

"Umm," Adam nodded as if they were discussing the weather. "But Amy wouldn't even think about that possibility. Or adoption either. It was pretty traumatic for her. She's just beginning to relax. Been edgy ever since she got back from Saint Clair, you know."

"She gets that way when she's a little anxious. She gets a bit clumsy," Jase explained almost affectionately. "I spent half the time she was on Saint Clair rescuing falling glasses of wine."

"Did you?" Adam's voice was politely neutral.

"She *can't* be pregnant," Jase repeated disbelievingly as he recalled how he'd spent the other half of the time with Amy on Saint Clair. This time Adam said nothing. It was hardly something a woman like Amy would make up, Jase thought uncertainly. In the few days they'd had together, he'd come to know her. He'd trusted her in a way he hadn't ever trusted a woman before in his life. And she trusted him. She'd believed him that morning when he'd explained to her that she hadn't taken the risk she thought she had by sleeping with him. And she'd trusted him with her life. She'd known he would save her from Haley, she'd told him later.

And she'd trusted him enough to offer him a home.

Jase had come several thousand miles and through a couple of different cultural climates to claim the home she had offered. But never in his wildest dreams had he expected that home to include a baby.

The evening seemed to drag on interminably. Jase was beginning to think Amy's party would never end, and then, quite suddenly, long before he was ready to face her alone, it was over. Even Melissa and Adam were saying good-bye, the last ones out the door.

Amy shut the door behind her sister and Adam and then turned to confront the only person left in the room. Jase saw the tension in her over-bright eyes and noticed the way she clung to the doorknob, her hands behind her back as she faced him. My God, he thought, she's so very vulnerable. She puts on such a bold air, but underneath she's so very soft and vulnerable. Instinctively he took a step toward her, setting down his empty glass on a nearby end table.

She halted him with her stark words. "Why did you come, Jase?"

He looked at her. "Isn't it obvious, Amy? I came for you. I came to find you. You talked about a home...."

Her mouth twisted bitterly as she carefully moved away from the door. "Well, I'm sure you've had some second thoughts during the evening, haven't you? That home I offered now comes equipped with another man's baby. I'm sure you'll want to reconsider the proposition under those circumstances. After all, it's not as if you have to feel any sense of responsibility...Jase!" She broke off her brittle monologue with a startled gasp as he crossed the room in three swift strides and seized her around the waist.

He lifted her just far enough off the ground so that she was forced to meet him eye to eye. His tightly drawn face was only inches from her own, and his gaze burned with a frightening intensity. Amy held her breath, more terrified than she would have believed possible.

"Another man's baby, Amy?" he demanded in a voice that was deadly calm.

"Th-that's what you believe, isn't it? That it must be another man's child I'm carrying? You really don't think you got me pregnant, do you?" she whispered, searching his face.

"Has there been anyone else since you came back from Saint Clair?" he asked savagely, his strong hands still clamped around her waist.

"No," she blurted, tentatively trying to steady herself by putting her hands on his shoulders. The feel of him was so comfortingly familiar. But his expression was anything but comforting.

"And you weren't pregnant when you came to Saint Clair?" he persisted.

"Jase, there's been no one else for years." Her mouth was dry as she stated the truth. Her gray-green eyes were wide, reflecting her nervousness as well as her underlying honesty.

"Then that leaves me, doesn't it?" Jase said coolly.

Amy lowered her lashes despairingly. "Yes."

"Then we'd better see about getting married as soon as possible, hadn't we?" he asked as he slowly lowered her to her feet.

"Jase! Are you saying you believe me? You believe the baby's yours?"

"Would you lie to me about a thing like this, Amy?"

"Oh, no, Jase. Never. I couldn't lie about this," she breathed, unable to absorb the implications of what he was saying.

"And do you really think I'd lie to you?" he went on, curling his hands around the curve of her shoulders. "Do you think I was lying that morning when I told you I was sure I couldn't get you pregnant?"

She let out a deep breath. "No," Amy admitted. "I know you believed it yourself when you told me. But when I got back to San Francisco and realized that I was going to have a baby, I nearly went crazy. I was so angry at you, so hurt that you hadn't followed me home. The thought that you had deliberately used me, without any regard for the consequences I would have to face alone, left me so furious I haven't been able to think straight. On top of that, I felt so utterly *stupid!*"

"Because you'd trusted me?"

She nodded numbly. "It was more than that. I was angry because I'd believed you, but I was just as furious with myself because that first night I hadn't even worried about the future. I didn't have any excuse at all for the first night, Jase," she said huskily.

His hands lifted to cradle her face. "Sweetheart, you couldn't have felt any more stupid than I did that night in The Serpent when I tried to take Murdock apart and you turned the hose on both of us. I listened to you offering me a home in front of fifty witnesses and I just let you walk out the door."

She waited uncertainly. "And the next morning? Jase, the next morning you said you didn't think you could make it back in the States. Right from the very beginning you'd told me I was all wrong."

"You were the only *right* thing that's happened to me in over ten years. Maybe in my whole life," he rasped. "Honey, please believe me. I really did think I had no business trying to follow you back to San Francisco. I told myself you were better off without me, that you'd get over the affair in time and you'd be glad I hadn't tried to take you up on your offer. Amy, I have nothing to offer you in return, don't you see?"

She smiled tremulously. "I wouldn't say that. I seem to have brought home one heck of a souvenir from Saint Clair."

"Oh, *Amy!*" He groaned heavily, pulling her against him, his mouth in her hair. He was silent for a long moment, savoring the feel of her and the wonder of what she had told him. "Are we really going to have a baby?"

"I think," she said, her words muffled against the fabric of his shirt, "that you'd better have a talk with my gynecologist."

His hands moved along her back. "I believe you, sweetheart. I'm not doubting what you've told me."

She lifted her head. "I know. But you're bound to have a few questions on the matter. I sure as hell did!"

He gave a husky, half-choked laugh. "I'll bet you did. God, Amy, I'm so sorry—" He clipped off the words, shaking his head ruefully. "No, I'm not sorry. How could I be sorry? Back on Saint Clair I told you I'd give anything in the world to be able to make you pregnant, to watch you growing nice and round with my baby. I'd give up any hope of ever having a real family. How can I even think of saying I'm sorry when I've finally got everything I've ever wanted?

What I'm sorry about is that you had to come back to the States and face the whole thing alone.''

Amy stood silently in his grasp, thinking of what she'd been through during the past few weeks. After a moment he went on slowly. ''Adam said Melissa talked to you about giving up the baby, but you wouldn't do it.'' He scanned her face as if searching for something very crucial. ''Why not?''

She gathered her courage. ''For the same reason that I stood in front of fifty customers in The Serpent and made a fool of myself by offering you a home. Because I love you, Jase.''

''Oh, God, Amy.''

''Why did you come several thousand miles to take up an offer from a woman who was totally wrong for you?'' she whispered, touching the side of his cheek delicately with her fingertips.

He smiled crookedly, eyes gleaming. ''Because I love you. And love seems to make a man selfish and possessive and determined to try anything. I've spent these past few weeks telling myself that if I really cared for you, I'd stay out of your life. But I woke up two days ago with a hangover that nearly killed me, and I suddenly realized that, whether it was in your best interests or not, I didn't think I could live another day without you. I had to find out if the offer was still open.''

''The offer would have remained open for the rest of my life,'' she told him, her voice husky with the passion of the words.

''Even though you were ready to take my head off the moment I appeared?'' he teased softly.

''I suspect that it's a part of loving to want to clobber the beloved one occasionally.''

His smile widened into a very male grin. ''I remember the day I wanted to beat you for risking your neck in front of Haley's gun!''

"Now we know which of us is the more dangerous. I followed through on my impulse to clobber you."

"While I restrained myself? Ummm, you're probably right," he mused, nuzzling the nape of her neck with his warm mouth. "But then, they always say the female of the species is more dangerous than the male."

"She has to be tough. She's the one who takes the biggest risks," Amy explained complacently.

She lifted her head, inviting his kiss. Jase accepted the invitation with all the hunger and passion that was in him. He took her mouth, setting his seal on her once more. Then he lifted her head, turquoise eyes deep and brooding.

"It's not going to be easy, you know, Amy. The only thing I know how to do is run a place like The Serpent. After the baby is born, I'm going to take my family back to Saint Clair. Does that worry you?"

Amy stared at him, some of the rosy glow that had enveloped her beginning to fade as the first hint of reality seeped back. "Jase, there's no need to go back to Saint Clair. I make enough in my boutiques to support all three of us. There will be plenty of time for you to look around and find something here in San Francisco that suits you."

He sighed, unwilling to dampen the warm wonder of the moment. "I came to take you back to Saint Clair with me, Amy, not to settle down in San Francisco. I don't fit into city life anymore. I can't come back."

She silenced him with her palm against his mouth, her lips curving in gentle denial. "We have months and months ahead of us to talk about it, Jase. We'll worry about it after the baby is born. I love you."

"And I love you!" He shuddered with the force of his feeling as he pulled her close once more. "My woman, my wife, the mother of my child. My God, how I love you!" The kiss he gave her was reverent. "I've spent so many nights wanting you, sweetheart. So many nights..."

She twined her arms around his neck. "I'm here now."

"In my arms," he whispered disbelievingly. "And pregnant. Oh, God, Amy, I'll be so careful with you, but I've got to have you again."

Her eyes glowed. "You don't have to be *that* careful," she teased lovingly. "I haven't suddenly become a fragile piece of crystal."

"Haven't you?"

And he made love to her that night as if she were indeed made of delicate crystal. At least he did so until the obvious evidence of the passion he remembered so well convinced him that Amy wouldn't shatter in his hands.

He was the one who felt shattered when it was all over. Shattered and then made whole.

# *Twelve*

After Jase's first conference with Dr. Jessica Carson, Amy privately decided she would never forget the idiotic grin he wore when he emerged from her consultation room.

"It seems," he explained very carefully to a wryly amused Amy, "that there are very few certainties when it comes to dealing with the physiology of human beings. Especially the reproductive physiology."

"Tell me about it," she mocked, remembering her own shock upon hearing Dr. Carson explain a few of the scientific facts of life.

"She says," Jase went on, looking pleasantly dazed, "that it might even happen again."

"Oh, Lord," Amy groaned, "you don't have to look so awestruck with the wonder of your own power!" But secretly she was delighted. It wasn't until she had faced Jase the night before at the party that it had occurred to her how easily he could have denied his responsibility. In all good conscience he could have chosen to believe the doctor's verdict of ten years ago and refused to accept that he was the father of Amy's child. His trust in her the previous night would warm her for the rest of her life.

As she lay in his arms the night after he'd had the consultation with Dr. Carson, Amy told him very seriously how much his unquestioned trust had meant. Jase grinned, putting a hand on her still-flat stomach with possessive pleasure.

"Amy, I love you. I'd trust you with my life and my honor, and as it turned out, I was able to trust you with the life of my child. What more could a man ask of a woman?"

He drew her closer, his fingers seeking the lace hem of the elegant nightgown she wore. Slowly he probed the feminine shape of her, enjoying the curve of her thigh and the swell of her hip. His lovemaking, Amy had discovered the night before, was now tinged with a new kind of tenderness, a luxuriously gentle passion, as if Jase now knew he had all the time in the world. She nestled closer, seeking his warmth.

His kisses were deep, drugging things, filling her mouth and then showering across her breasts. When he claimed her totally, forcing his knee gently but firmly between her thighs and fitting himself solidly to her softness, it was a clear act of possession, but there was no doubt that Jase was as enthralled as the woman he possessed.

They were married the day following Jase's first visit with Dr. Carson. Melissa and Adam were the only ones in attendance, and afterward they took the newlyweds out to dinner.

"You'll be able to take Melissa and me out to dinner next month," Adam announced expansively, pouring the champagne.

"You've set the date?" Amy demanded in delight, reaching for her glass. Her sister nodded, smiling brilliantly. "Well, terrific!" Amy exclaimed, feeling euphoric about everyone and everything. "Here's to next month's wedding!" She hoisted her glass and everyone at the table followed suit. Just as the wine hadn't tasted as good as it should have the night of the party, the champagne wasn't quite as interesting to her taste buds as it normally would have been. Still, it was drinkable, and a few minutes after the toast, Amy reached once more for the fluted glass in front of her.

Before she could close her fingers around it, Jase put out a hand and moved it aside. Amy blinked in astonishment and then smiled. "I wasn't going to spill it. I haven't dropped a thing since the night of the party."

He smiled back, amused. "I know. Nothing like pregnancy, it seems, to settle down a high-strung woman."

"Well, then," she began determinedly, reaching for the glass again.

"You've had enough," Jase told her mildly and put the glass completely out of reach.

Amy's mouth dropped open. "Jase! I've had one sip!"

"That's enough. Dr. Carson says alcohol should be avoided during pregnancy."

"Dr. Carson!"

"I got a long list of dos and don'ts from her yesterday when I talked to her," he explained easily.

"But, Jase..." Bewildered, she started to argue and then, realizing how ridiculous that was on her wedding day, she ceased at once, managing a politely aggrieved smile that brought a knowing laugh from Melissa.

"Amy isn't accustomed to having anyone look after her, Jase. And after being in charge of her own business for the past couple of years, she's used to giving the orders."

"Things will be different, now that she's married," Jase predicted complacently.

"Will they?" Amy couldn't resist taunting.

"You have a husband now," he said more seriously. "A husband is the head of the family."

"Jase, darling, things have changed a little here in the States since you've been gone," Amy began sweetly, only to be interrupted as the formally dressed waiter brought a glass of milk on a silver tray and set it in front of her.

"Drink your milk, Amy. You need the calcium."

Amy stared hard at the glass of milk. "Jase, I don't like milk."

"Dr. Carson says you're to drink it." As if that settled the issue, Jase turned to Adam and began questioning him on some of the changes in the new tax laws. Amy, telling herself the last thing she wanted to do was ruin her wedding day with an argument over a glass of milk, grimly swallowed the liquid in silence.

"So your friend Ray will be running The Serpent for you while you're here in California?" Adam was saying with interest a few minutes later.

Jase nodded. "While we're waiting for the baby, I'm going to be a full-time househusband. It should be an interesting experience. After the baby's born and the pediatrician has given the okay, we'll all be leaving for Saint Clair."

Amy's fork slipped out of her fingers as she started. It clattered loudly to her place, bringing Jase's head around in concern.

"Is there a doctor on the island?" Melissa hastened to inquire, seeing the annoyed flush on her sister's cheek.

Diverted, Jase nodded. "Dr. Kenton. He and his wife retired there a couple of years ago. Marsha Kenton is a nurse. Don't worry, Saint Clair has good, basic medical care. In extreme situations a patient can be flown to Hawaii for more sophisticated treatment. Amy, if you go for that champagne glass one more time, I'm going to lose my temper."

Amy withdrew her hand. "I think I need it, Jase," she said meaningfully. "I seem to be getting a bad case of bridal jitters." She wished he would stop talking about returning to Saint Clair. He had followed her to San Francisco and this was where they would stay! Here in civilized surroundings they could make a home.

"If you're getting the jitters," Jase said smoothly, "then

I'd better take you home. It would be too expensive to replace the dishes and all the glassware on this table."

Jase's first consultation with Dr. Carson was far from his last. He not only accompanied Amy every month for the routine visit, he always had a separate, serious discussion of his own with the rather amused but indulgent doctor. To Amy's chagrin no subject was sacred. They discussed her well-being from one end to the other while she sat on the sidelines, not knowing whether to be amused or exasperated.

"I don't think she's gaining enough weight," Jase announced on one visit, eyeing his wife with a critical look. "That book you gave me last month says she should be putting on a little more than she is."

Dr. Carson acknowledged the concern but assured him that Amy was well within normal limits.

On the next visit Jase and Dr. Carson deliberated on the matter of Amy's increasingly tender breasts, and Amy devoutly wished she'd had enough sense to keep from wincing the night before when Jase had lightly grazed her nipple with the palm of his hand during lovemaking.

"Perhaps a larger bra size would make her feel more comfortable," the doctor suggested.

"We'll go shopping for one this afternoon," Jase announced instantly.

"Have both of you forgotten that I own a lingerie store?" Amy interrupted aggressively. They both turned to look at her as if she had no business involving herself in the decision. And so it went.

While Amy spent her days at work, Jase buried himself in the San Francisco Public Library, researching the latest information on childbirth. His conversations with Dr. Carson took on an increasingly clinical tone. By her sixth month Amy began to feel as if she were in the presence of two physicians instead of one doctor and a husband.

One day during lunch with Melissa, Amy tried to explain

what was happening. "He watches me like a hawk, Mel. Every meal has to be perfectly balanced nutritionally. I haven't been allowed a potato chip for the past two months! And he's got my vitamins so carefully scheduled that, when I accidentally forgot them one morning last week, he came down to the store with the bottle and stood there amid a pile of nightgowns, making sure I swallowed the tablets! He's taking over, Mel. He's completely in charge now! It's scary."

"I think it's rather sweet," Melissa chuckled.

"The problem," declared Amy, "is that he doesn't have a job. He's devoting his whole attention to me and the baby, and when the kid's born he thinks we're all going to go happily back to Saint Clair."

"But he has got a business, Amy. The Serpent does very well, from what Adam says. Jase has spent ten years making a livelihood on Saint Clair. He's not going to walk away from that. Especially now that he's got a family to support."

"But, Mel, I wanted him to come to San Francisco so that I could make a home for him *here.* A civilized home. When he showed up on my doorstep, I thought he had decided that was what he wanted."

"He's taking his responsibilities very seriously, Amy. Just the way you always thought a man should take them," Melissa pointed out gently. "He has a very old-fashioned streak in him when it comes to this sort of thing. He wants to provide for his wife and child and he's well equipped to do that on Saint Clair."

"He could get a job here!"

"Doing what? He's been away from the States for ten years, Amy. About the only thing he could do is what he's already doing on Saint Clair."

"Running a bar?"

"Exactly. And it would take a long time to build one up to the profit level of The Serpent. Even if he wanted to try.

You know how competitive this town is when it comes to restaurants and bars.''

Amy stared out the window of the restaurant in which they sat. ''He hates the city, Mel. He tries to hide it, but the truth is, he feels out of place.''

''I know,'' her sister whispered sympathetically. ''Some men aren't meant for city living.''

''Oh, God, Mel, what's going to happen after the baby is born?'' Amy whispered, growing frightened.

''You,'' Melissa stated quietly, ''are going to have to make some serious decision.''

''I couldn't bear it now if he were to leave.'' Tears stung Amy's eyes just at the thought of such a possibility.

''Jase would never abandon his wife and child,'' Melissa said with utter conviction.

The realization that Jase didn't like the city had been forced upon Amy soon after he settled into her apartment. As far as he was concerned he was only in town so that the baby could be born in a first-class hospital under the care of a doctor Amy trusted. San Francisco was only a temporary place. The only part of it that he really seemed to enjoy was the wharf area. As the time of her delivery approached, Amy's fears became more concrete. How long would Jase stay after the baby was born? How long before he announced that they were all going to Saint Clair? What would she do when he issued the ultimatum? These days, she reminded herself, women didn't give up their careers and life-styles to follow a husband who insisted on living at the ends of the earth. The home she had envisioned creating had been a civilized setting like San Francisco.

Damon Brandon Lassiter came into the world at four in the morning, only one day before the date Dr. Carson had ordained for his arrival. For the first time since Jase and Dr. Carson had become colleagues, they were both forced to acknowledge that, after all their planning and instruction and consultation, it was Amy who finally had to do the real work. For some reason that shook Jase up more than Amy would have believed.

"Did you think you were going to be able to do this part yourself?" she teased weakly between increasingly harsh contractions. Jase was beside her, holding her hand as if he would never let go.

"Hell, sweetheart," he muttered in angry frustration, "I only wish I could. I didn't realize, I guess, that in this modern age it all still *hurt* so much."

"Give me the breathing exercises," Amy instructed briskly, aware that the only way to keep him from falling apart was to keep him working. To her relief he seized willingly on the task, remembering the role he had learned during the childbearing classes that he had made Amy attend so faithfully.

"I feel rather extraneous," Dr. Carson observed when she arrived. She smiled down at her patient. "I think my esteemed colleague, Mr. Lassiter, is quite capable of getting you through this on his own!"

Amy clutched her husband's hand more tightly as another contraction swept over her. "Yes," she panted. "He could. Jase can handle anything."

He remained by her side during the entire process, holding her hand, sponging her forehead, talking to her with gentle encouragement. At the very last, when the exhausting, painful work of giving birth had sapped most of Amy's energy and nearly all of her fortitude, she clung to the reality of her husband's sherry-rich voice, her nails biting savagely into his palm as she drew strength from him. And he was there for her.

She knew in that moment that Jase would always be there for her. It was his nature. The knowledge set her free in a way she couldn't fully describe.

When she awoke hours later, she was back in the private room that Jase had insisted on. The stark white surroundings were almost invisible behind the wall of flowers that seemed to surround the bed—huge flowers, reminiscent of the giant, lush blossoms she had seen on Saint Clair. It didn't take much effort to guess who had arranged for them.

The man responsible for the flowers was standing by the window, cradling a tiny bundle in his arms. He was staring down at his son as if he couldn't quite believe the reality of what he held. Amy watched his profile for a long moment, smiling drowsily to herself. He's going to make a fine father, she thought with absolute certainty.

Jase glanced up, the wonder and the joy gleaming in his turquoise eyes. For a long moment he stood silently, watching his wife and cradling his son. Then, very carefully, he placed the sleeping infant back in the tiny cot beside Amy's bed and came to his wife's side.

"Did we do okay?" she asked softly, made happier than she had ever been by the happiness in his gaze.

"We did just great," he breathed in hushed tones. "Oh, Amy, he's perfect. *You're* perfect. My God, I'm the happiest man alive." He hesitated and then growled forcefully. "But never again. I never want you to have to go through that again."

"I've heard it gets easier," she whispered.

"Oh, *Amy!*"

"Jase, I couldn't have made it without you."

He shook his head. "No, Amy. You could have made it without me. Women are so strong when they have to be strong. I'm the one who can't make it without you. I realize that now. You've given me so much—all of yourself and now a son into the bargain. How can I ever thank you? I love you so much, sweetheart. I know you've been worrying about going back to Saint Clair, but you can stop thinking about it. I decided while you were sleeping that we're going to stay here in San Francisco."

"But, Jase—" she started to say urgently. He shook his head firmly.

"No, this is where you're happiest. This is where your business is and this is where all your friends are. You have a busy, exciting life here. I'm going to become part of it," he stated.

"Don't be ridiculous," Amy told him fondly as she turned to look down at her sleeping son, "Damon Brandon and I will be quite content to follow the head of the family wherever he chooses to go."

"Amy, you wanted a home," Jase said softly.

"We can make a home anywhere. That was something I hadn't quite realized up until very recently. I had some preconceived notions about what constituted a 'proper' home, you see. But now I know that I'll be at home wherever you are. And so will Damon."

Jase's hand tightened around hers. "That's not a very modern attitude," he pointed out, as if obliged to do so. "Women don't make statements like that anymore."

"Probably because there aren't a lot of men around who are worth the risk. I got lucky, didn't I?" She smiled.

"But, honey, will you be content without your business to run?" he pressed anxiously.

"Who said I wasn't going to have a business to run?"

"Now what are you talking about?"

"Those letters from Ray that we get every month say that a cruise ship or two are putting Saint Clair on their ports-of-call lists, right?"

"Well, yes, but..."

"Well, let me tell you something about tourists that I thought you already knew," she drawled. "They love to take home souvenirs."

He looked astonished. "You're thinking of opening a gift shop on Saint Clair?"

"Ummm. With some really classy stuff, not a lot of cheap junk. Ray's paintings of the island should sell well to tourists, don't you think? And I'll bet there are a lot of other interesting things available. Although," she added gruffly, "I think I should make it very clear that the proprietor of The Serpent is no longer on the list of souvenirs of Saint Clair!"

Jase's turquoise eyes shone suspiciously bright. It took Amy a moment to realize that her husband had tears in his eyes. It astounded her. She'd never seen a man with tears in his eyes. "Amy," he whispered shakily, "the proprietor of The Serpent has his hands full with a family now. He doesn't have time to cater to souvenir hunters."

The modern age had given women more choices, but it hadn't provided all the answers. Amy reflected on that simple fact of life a few months later as the plane settled down on the Saint Clair runway. As long as there weren't always perfect answers, women would still take risks. And sometimes the results would be worth everything. Not all of her friends in San Francisco had understood Amy's decision to sell the boutiques, invest the money and then leave for the ends of the earth with her husband and her small son. But as Amy scanned the lush tropical atmosphere awaiting her, she decided she would never regret the risks she had taken.

The plane screeched to its customary dramatic halt on the meager runway and Jase chuckled. "I can just imagine what the pilots have to say every time they have to land on Saint Clair. The language in the cockpit probably gets extremely salty. What with the tourist trade picking up, we'll have to see about adding a few more feet to the runway."

Amy smiled and glanced out the window again. "We've got a reception committee. I can see Ray, and there's Maggie and even Fred Cowper."

"No kidding?" Jase eagerly followed her glance, and she realized that for him this was going to be a very special homecoming. He was anxious to show off his small family to his old friends.

"Here," she said, handing over his tiny gurgling son. "You take Damon and I'll bring the baby bag. I wouldn't want to get nervous and drop him in front of your friends. Very embarrassing."

Jase laughed but accepted the baby. "You know damn

well you're steady as a rock with Damon. A natural mother. I always knew you would be, you know."

The plane taxied to a complete halt in front of the old building that served as a terminal, and Jase stood aside in the aisle so that his wife could emerge from her seat. Then, looking every inch the proud patriarch, he shepherded his little family off the plane and onto the soil of their new home.

The reception committee was as enthusiastic as Amy could have wished. Ray and Maggie and Fred swarmed over the new arrivals, the welcome solid and sincere. Several of the people who worked at the terminal came out to add their greetings.

"It's about time you came back Amy. I knew you'd be returning one of these days. When Jase left to get you, I knew it was only a matter of time." Maggie released Amy from a huge hug and reached for the baby in Jase's arms. "Let me see what it was that kept you so long in San Francisco!"

With a grin he made absolutely no attempt to conceal, Jase handed over his son for inspection.

"Well, I'll be damned," Ray chuckled, examining Damon as Maggie held him. "Will you just look at those eyes!"

"I've only seen one other human being in the whole world with eyes that shade of turquoise blue," Maggie mused. She looked up at the one other person and smiled. "You have a beautiful son, Jase. He will grow up strong and healthy here on Saint Clair."

Much later that evening, Amy drifted out of the master bedroom of her new home and stood on the veranda, inhaling the scented tropical breeze. Saint Clair really was a lovely slice of Paradise, she decided. A woman could do a lot worse for herself than taking on the job of making a home in Paradise.

She turned her head to glance back over her shoulder as Jase emerged behind her, fresh from a shower. He was wearing only a towel loosely hitched around his lean waist. "I can't decide whether you're sexier pregnant or unpregnant. Either way, you drive me out of my mind," he drawled, coming up behind her and fitting his hands to her hips.

"It's the nightgown," Amy explained demurely, smoothing the folds of the fabulously expensive peach-colored silk. "The French designers can do wonders for a woman's image. I brought along a year's supply of lingerie."

"At the end of the year we'll have to fly back to San Francisco and get you another year's supply," Jase decided. "But to tell you the truth, I don't think the nightgown has anything to do with it."

"You don't think so?"

"Nope. I'll show you. Watch what happens when I remove the gown." With a sweeping movement of his palms he slipped the gown down to her hips and then over the full curves to let it fall to her feet.

"Jase!" she gasped, half laughing, half appalled. She felt absurdly vulnerable standing on the veranda with nothing on, even though she knew that no one could see her. Automatically her hands came up to cover herself.

"This is an experiment, remember? We're trying to see whether it's you or the gown I'm reacting to tonight."

"And...?" she taunted.

"And there's no question but that it's you." He pulled her firmly back against his thighs, cradling her rounded bottom into the flaring heat of his body. "Any doubts?"

"I think," Amy whispered with wry laughter, "that this is how I got into trouble the last time I came to Saint Clair."

His hands slipped around to her stomach and then stole lower as he bent his head to nuzzle the line of her throat. "Don't worry," he teased, "Dr. Carson assures me that you're no more likely to get pregnant this time than you were the last time."

"Yes, I know, but I can be so amazingly clumsy!" Amy turned in his embrace, wrapping her arms around his neck. She looked up into his gleaming eyes and smiled dreamily. "Oh, Jase, I love you so."

With a husky exclamation of passion he moved his rough leg between her soft thighs, forcing her gently against him. She felt the heavy, waiting masculinity and sighed passionately. "You are my life, Amy," Jase said. "Together we'll be able to share Damon for the years he's growing up, but we'll have each other for the rest of our lives. My God, I love you, Mrs. Lassiter. Come to bed and let me show you how much."

Amy put her hand trustingly into that of her husband's and allowed herself to be led toward the shadowy bed that awaited them. Loving Jase involved no risk at all. His love and passion carried a lifetime guarantee.

* * * * *

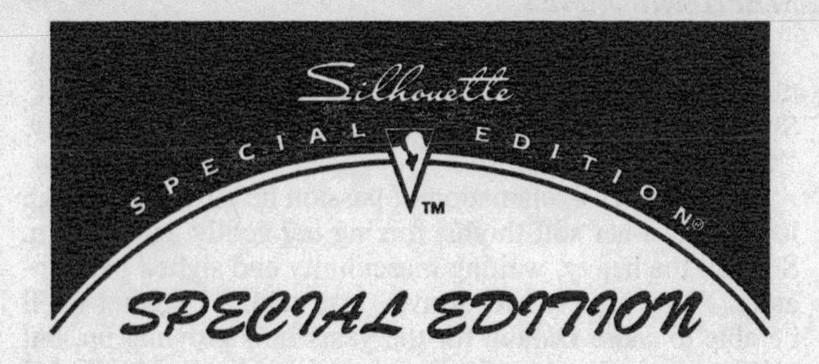


Stories of love and life, these powerful novels are tales that you can identify with—romances with "something special" added in!

Fall in love with the stories of authors such as **Nora Roberts, Diana Palmer, Ginna Gray** and many more of your special favorites—as well as wonderful new voices!

Special Edition brings you entertainment for the heart!

SSE-GEN

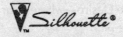

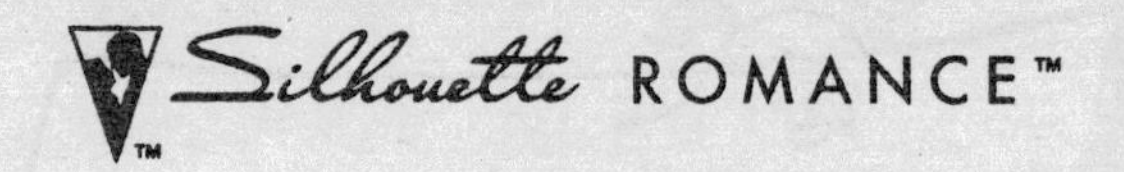


**What's a single dad to do when he needs a wife by next Thursday?**

**Who's a confirmed bachelor to call when he finds a baby on his doorstep?**

**How does a plain Jane in love with her gorgeous boss get him to notice her?**

From classic love stories to romantic comedies to emotional heart tuggers, **Silhouette Romance** offers six irresistible novels every month by some of your favorite authors! Such as...beloved bestsellers **Diana Palmer, Annette Broadrick, Suzanne Carey, Elizabeth August** and **Marie Ferrarella,** to name just a few—and some sure to become favorites!

Fabulous Fathers...Bundles of Joy...Miniseries... Months of blushing brides and convenient weddings... Holiday celebrations... You'll find all this and much more in **Silhouette Romance**—always emotional, always enjoyable, always about love!

SR-GEN

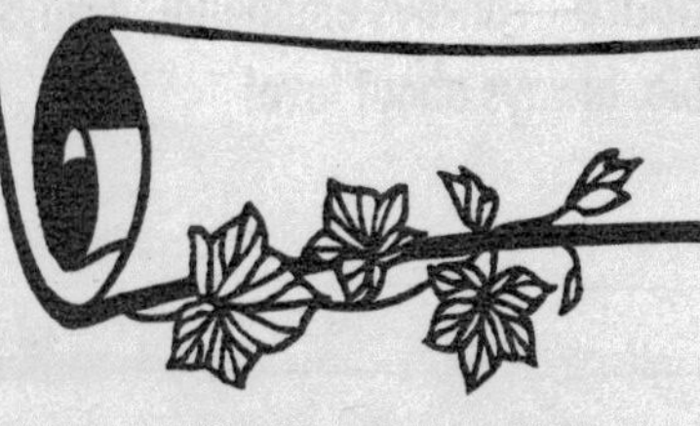